PRAISE FOR

"Parks, in her debut novel, has clearly done her research and never disappoints when it comes to crisp dialogue, characterization, or surprising twists and turns."

—*PUBLISHERS WEEKLY*

"Besides having a resourceful and likable heroine, the book also features that rarest of characters: a villain you don't see coming, but whom you hate with relish . . . *A Cry from the Dust* will keep you hoping, praying and guessing till the end."

—*BOOKPAGE*

"Renowned forensic and fine artist Parks's action-packed and compelling tale of suspense is haunting in its intensity. Well researched and written in an almost journalistic style, this emotionally charged story is recommended for fans of Ted Dekker, Mary Higgins Clark, and historical suspense."

—*LIBRARY JOURNAL*

"Parks's fast-paced and suspenseful debut novel is an entertaining addition to the inspirational genre. Her writing is polished, and the research behind the novel brings credibility to the story . . . an excellent book that is sure to put Carrie Stuart Parks on readers' radars."

—*RT BOOK REVIEWS*, 4 STARS

"A unique novel of forensics and fanaticism. A good story on timely subjects well told. For me, these are the ingredients of a successful novel today and Carrie Stuart Parks has done just that."

—CARTER CORNICK, FBI COUNTERTERRORISM
AND FORENSIC SCIENCE RESEARCH (RET.)

"Parks's real-life career as a forensic artist lends remarkable authenticity to her enthralling novel, *A Cry from the Dust*. Her work is a fresh new voice in suspense, and I became an instant fan. Highly recommended!"

—COLLEEN COBLE, *USA TODAY* BESTSELLING AUTHOR OF THE
HOPE BEACH SERIES AND *THE INN AT OCEAN'S EDGE*

"In *A Cry from the Dust*, the novel's courageous protagonist—a forensic artist recovering from cancer—finds herself facing 'blood atonement' when she investigates the death of a young woman. This superbly researched mystery, based on actual events, shows what can happen when lack of education is combined with religious fanaticism."

—BETTY WEBB, AUTHOR OF *DESERT WIVES* AND *DESERT WIND*

"Things I loved about *A Cry from the Dust*: the fascinating and painstakingly researched historical tapestry into which the story is woven, the frantic but intensely believable arc of events that makes you hold on extra tight, the compelling and flawed heroine who has absolutely no idea she's the heroine. Part *CSI*, part *Lie to Me*, and all relentlessly original, *A Cry from the Dust* blends rich characters, little-known history, and a dose of conspiracy into a very modern storytelling style. Can't wait to tear into Gwen Marcey's next adventure."

—ZACHARY BARTELS, AUTHOR OF *PLAYING SAINT* AND *42 MONTHS DRY*

"With a strong heroine and suspense that keeps the pages flipping, *A Cry from the Dust* is full of twists from the past, secret societies, and a sinister race against the clock. Highly recommend!"

—ROBIN CAROLL, AUTHOR OF THE JUSTICE SEEKERS SERIES

THE BONES
WILL SPEAK

OTHER BOOKS BY
CARRIE STUART PARKS

A Cry from the Dust

THE BONES
WILL SPEAK

A Gwen Marcey Novel

CARRIE STUART PARKS

Thomas Nelson
Since 1798

NASHVILLE   MEXICO CITY   RIO DE JANEIRO

Published in Nashville, Tennessee, by Thomas Nelson. Thomas Nelson is a registered trademark of HarperCollins Christian Publishing, Inc.

Thomas Nelson titles may be purchased in bulk for educational, business, fund-raising, or sales promotional use. For information, please e-mail SpecialMarkets@ThomasNelson.com.

Publisher's Note: This novel is a work of fiction. Names, characters, places, and incidents are either products of the author's imagination or used fictitiously. All characters are fictional, and any similarity to people living or dead is purely coincidental.

Library of Congress Cataloging-in Publication Data

Parks, Carrie Stuart.
 The bones will speak : a Gwen Marcey novel / Carrie Stuart Parks.
 pages ; cm
 ISBN 978-1-4016-9045-8 (softcover)
 I. Title.
 PS3616.A75535B66 2015
 813'.6--dc23
 2015007861

Printed in the United States of America

15 16 17 18 19 20 RRD 6 5 4 3 2 1

To Frank,
For holding on to the handlebars
—grasshopper

PROLOGUE

"THE BOMB KILLED FOUR PEOPLE." MIKE HIGGINS, rookie cop from Kellogg, Idaho, snapped his fingers. "Just like that."

Margie Sheehan, his ride-along that day, looked around the quiet street. "Oh."

"Yep, they had to scrape—"

Margie's face grew pale.

"Don't worry." He nodded toward the neat, mint-green bungalow they'd parked in front of. "Mrs. Jackson, the lady that called in the report, is a 10–96."

"What's a 10–96?"

"A mental. A nutcake. Cats. I don't just mean five or six. The woman collects them like baseball cards. She must have fifty at least."

"I like cats." Margie smiled slightly, revealing perfect teeth.

Mike tried to keep from staring at his attractive passenger. "Right. Um. So . . . she also calls dispatch at least once a week to report something. Last week she said space aliens snatched one of her cats and turned it into a sack of baby diapers. Dirty diapers." His nose wrinkled at the memory. "This week she claims the two men wanted in Spokane for the Planned Parenthood bombings are living nearby. Said the composite sketches are like portraits of them."

"But what if she's right this time? I mean, Kellogg is only about an hour from Spokane." Her cheeks flushed.

Mike's stomach gave a slight lurch. *Should I call for backup?* He could just hear his sergeant's voice on that request. "So, Higgins, you needed backup for the cat lady? What's the problem? One of her space aliens pulled a ray gun?"

He sat up straighter in his seat. "You'll need to stay here, just in case." He stepped from the patrol car, straightened his vest, and strolled toward Mrs. Jackson's front porch. Modest, blue-collar homes stretched on either side of the street in the small mining town, and newly budded maple trees shaded the trim lawns from the spring sunshine.

The front steps groaned under his weight, and a radio somewhere inside the house played a twangy country-and-western song from the local KWAL station. The covered porch stretched the width of the house, with wide, square columns at equal intervals. A black-and-white cat eyed him suspiciously from under a shrub.

The screen door let out a screech as Mike opened it. He knocked, then peeked back at his car. Margie had rolled down the window and was staring at him.

The music stopped, and Mrs. Jackson opened the front door. The odor of unattended cat-litter trays made him blink rapidly. A ginger-striped cat draped across the older woman's arm. "There you are. I called the police two days ago. I could be dead now. They're killers, you know."

"Yes, ma'am."

She turned, dropped the cat, and picked up a folded newspaper on a nearby table. "See? It's like a portrait." The front page featured two composite drawings, with the headlines blaring, "Terrorism Strikes Again!" She'd taken Wite-Out and painted part of the hair and beard on one of the drawings and inked a mustache on the other. "They're those priests. Those whatcha-call-it priests."

"Phineas Priesthood."

"That's it. Though why men of God would set bombs and kill people is beyond me." She pursed her lips as if sucking on a lemon.

He shifted his weight and glanced back at Margie. "Yes, ma'am. They're not really priests. Their religion is more like the Aryan Nations. You said you saw the—"

"They're hiding right there." She stepped onto the porch and pointed at a white house across the street.

Higgins turned to see where she pointed. A flicker of movement to his left caught his attention, a flash of red plaid shirt disappearing behind a garage.

"What—"

The front door across the street flew open.

Pop, pop!

Mrs. Jackson's window shattered.

Adrenalin surged through Mike's veins. He grabbed the startled woman and shoved her backward into the house. Spinning, he screamed at Margie, "Get down," then dropped to the porch on his stomach, scrabbling for his shoulder mic.

Pop, pop, pop! Bullets pounded into the wall above him.

He couldn't remember the 10-code. "Shots fired. They're shooting at me." He let go of the mic and fumbled for his pistol. From his prone position, he couldn't see over his patrol car.

Car doors slammed.

Taking a deep breath, he rolled left behind the porch column.

An engine revved.

He stood.

A faded-red Toyota pickup backed from the driveway and raced down the street.

Higgins holstered his pistol and sprinted for his car, shouting into his shoulder mic, "They're getting away . . . I mean, I'm in pursuit . . ." He slid into the seat, started the engine, and slammed the car into gear. Picking up the car radio, he continued, "A red Toyota pickup, two suspects . . ." He turned on his lights and siren. "Heading east on Mission . . . No, they've turned south on—"

A hand grabbed his arm.

Higgins dropped the mic. The car swerved.

Margie unfolded from an impossibly tiny position on the floor and slid into the passenger seat. She pulled the seat belt tight across her body. Her face was ashen.

Snatching up the radio, Higgins said, "They've just turned east onto I-90. I'm in pursuit. Request backup." He twisted the wheel and skated to the on-ramp.

The truck accelerated ahead.

Higgins floored the patrol car.

The pickup shot onto the highway, narrowly missed a van, and overcorrected. Dust and gravel spit from the spinning tires.

Gripping the steering wheel with both white-knuckled hands, Higgins lifted his foot from the accelerator.

The pickup spun, smashed into the guardrail, and twisted back into traffic.

The eastbound, fully loaded logging truck tried to avoid the pickup, but was too close. It slammed into the pickup's side. The smaller truck folded around it like an aluminum can.

Higgins stopped.

As if in slow motion, both vehicles left the highway and plunged into the shallow Coeur d'Alene River, running parallel to the highway.

Margie gasped.

Reaching for the radio, Higgins cleared his throat. "Dispatch, request an ambulance and tow truck . . . and I think you can tell Spokane PD they don't need to worry about their Phineas Priesthood terrorist cell anymore."

CHAPTER ONE

APRIL 15, FIVE YEARS LATER

I CHARGED FROM THE HOUSE AND RACED across the lawn, frantically waving my arms. "Stop digging! Winston, no!"

Winston, my Great Pyrenees, paused in his vigorous burial of some form of road kill and raised a muddy nose in my direction.

"I mean it!" Why hadn't I bought one of those nice, retriever-type dogs who mindlessly played fetch all day? Winston spent his time wading in the creek, digging pool-sized holes in the lawn, and—judging from the green stain—applying *eau de* cow pie around his ear. I crept toward him.

He playfully raised his tail over his back and dodged left.

"I'm warning you." I pointed a finger at him. Phthalo-blue watercolor rimmed my nail, making my gesture less threatening and more like I was growing a rare fungus.

Unfazed, he darted toward the line of flowering lilac bushes lining the driveway, temporarily passing from sight. *How could a hundred-and-sixty-pound canine move so fast?* I circled in the other direction, slipping closer, then carefully parted the branches. No dog.

This was ridiculous. I could chase my dog until I retrieved the road kill from his mouth, or scrub it off the carpet for the next week. And it was getting dark, with Prussian-blue shadows stretching between Montana's pine-covered Bitterroot Mountains.

I glanced to my left. Winston crouched, wagging his tail. I moved toward him. He snatched his prize and shook it.

Two black hollows appeared.

I couldn't move. The air rushed from my lungs and came out in a long hiss. I patted my leg, urging the dog closer.

Winston lifted the object, exposing a hole with radiating cracks.

Crouching, I extended my hand. "Come on, fellow. Good doggie, over here."

He placed his find on the ground. It came to rest on its even row of ivory teeth.

I approached gingerly, knelt on the soggy ground, and inspected the sightless eye sockets. "Oh, dear Lord."

Winston nudged the skull forward.

I yelped and sprawled on my rear. An overfed beetle plopped out of the nasal aperture and landed on my shoelace.

Heart racing like a runaway horse, I violently kicked the offending bug, skidded backward, and stood. Fumbling my cell phone from my jeans pocket, I punched in Dave's number. "Leave it to you, Winston, to find a skull full of bugs—"

"Ravalli County Sheriff's Department, Sheriff Dave Moore."

"She's dead. You've got to come now, Dave!" Winston pawed at the skull like a volleyball.

"Stop that, Winston. You're just going to make more bugs fall out." I bumped the dog away with my leg.

"What is it now, Gwen? You're calling me because Winston has bugs?"

I rubbed my face. "Of course not. Don't be silly. I already told you she's dead—"

"Question one: Are you okay?"

"Yes! Well—"

"Good, good. Now, question two: Where are you?"

"I'm home. Near home. The edge of the woods—"

"Choose one."

"Doggone it, Dave, don't patronize me." I wanted to sling the phone across the yard, then race over to the sheriff's office and kick Dave in the shin. "Stop being irritating and get over here."

"Ah, yes. That brings me to question three. Who's 'she'?"

"She's a skull. Or technically a cranium. Didn't I say that? She was murdered."

"Murdered? Are you sure she isn't a lost hiker or hunter?"

"Oh, for Pete's sake, Dave. She's got a neat bullet hole in her forehead, and a not-so-neat exit wound shattering the back." The dog reached a paw around my leg and attempted to snag his plaything. I tapped it out of reach with my shoe. I sincerely hoped no one was watching me play a macabre version of skull soccer with my dog. I already had a reputation for being eccentric.

"Are you positive it's female?"

"Just look at it!" I realized I was holding the phone over the skull and quickly put the cell back to my ear. "I'm not a forensic anthropologist, but if I had to guess, I'd say female. There's a lack of development in the supraorbital ridges, the zygomatic process is less pronounced, there's an absence of the external occipital protuberance—"

"Speak English."

"Don't interrupt. She has signs of animal activity—chewing—and is missing the lower jaw. Hence she's a cranium, not a skull, but her teeth are in good shape in the maxilla. That's the upper jaw."

"I know what that is. You're a forensic artist. Since when has a skull spooked you?"

"It's not the skull; it's the bugs."

"Yeah, yeah, you and your insect phobia. I think you're just out of practice with the real thing. You've been doing too much work on plaster castings."

"I don't even want to *think* about plaster castings." It was only eight months since my work in Utah and I still had nightmares.

"Speaking of that case, didn't you find some body parts on your property in that case too? Are you turning into Montana's version of the body farm?"

"Very funny." Leave it to Dave to know how to simultaneously calm me down and irritate me beyond belief. He treated me like a kid sister, which, in a sense, I was. His family took me in when I was fourteen.

"I will concede that I haven't reconstructed a skull from a homicide case for a while." I smoothed my paint-stained denim shirt. "But in the past, they've always arrived cleaned. In a neatly labeled evidence pouch. All the slithery things inside them boiled away."

"You're getting mighty prissy about receiving evidence."

"Ha. Do you have any missing-persons reports?" I took a

deep breath, then scratched my dog behind the ear. I stopped and looked at my hand. Fresh, cow-pie green. Great. I wiped the poo on the grass.

"One came in less than an hour ago from the Missoula Police Department. Possible abduction this morning of a fourteen-year-old girl, name of Mattie Banks."

"If she was abducted this morning, she'd hardly be down to bone by evening . . . unless someone boiled her head . . ."

"You have a sick mind."

"So you like to point out."

"I'll check missing persons, also give a call to the state guys, see how fast they can get here. We're really shorthanded. I got two officers on sick leave, but I'll be over within the hour."

I gazed at the vast Bitterroot wilderness stretching past my yard. Churning indigo clouds now blotted out the setting sun. April weather could change in a second in the mountains.

"On second thought, don't come over tonight. A storm's about to break." I thought for a moment. "Unless you want to call in half the law enforcement in Montana, the National Guard, and every Explorer Scout in the West, I need to see if I can narrow down the possible perimeter for this homicide. Pyrs can retrieve road kill or tasty dead critters from about a five-mile radius. That gives us a lot of back country to search."

"Then we'll get Winston to take us to her body."

"Ha! Forget the 'we.' If you show up, Winston will just want you to pet him. Let me see what I can do with the dog first."

Winston wagged his tail.

"You've undoubtedly compromised everything to boot, Winston."

A splash of rain struck my arm, and I glanced up. The wind

brushed through the pines, creating a sibilant murmur. "I'll get my noble hound to track tomorrow. I'll call you."

I dropped the phone into my pocket. "Come on, Winston. I'm not leaving you alone with your prize. Heel." We crossed the yard to the house. "Sit. Now, stay. I'm not handling that thing with my bare hands, even dung-covered." I stepped into the kitchen, scrubbed up, grabbed a pair of latex gloves and a large paper grocery bag, then went outside. After placing the skull in the bag, I folded the top closed and carried it to my studio. Winston trailed behind.

I set the package on my drafting table. A host of nightmarish insects were in there. What if they got out? I rubbed my arms to make the little hairs lie down, then fastened a continuous line of staples across the top and applied two-inch tape over the staples.

"Mom?"

I jumped and dropped the tape.

Aynslee, my fourteen-year-old daughter, stood at the door. "You got a phone call. Some attorney or something from Spokane. He said you're getting a subpoena on an old case."

"Did he say what case?"

"Something about a priest. When's dinner?"

"Dinner? Is it that late?" I glanced at my watch. "Turn on the oven. We'll have pizza tonight. Special treat."

"It's not special if we have it every night," Aynslee muttered as she left the room.

"We didn't have it last night," I called after her.

"Yes, we did. Pepperoni. And two nights ago we had sausage and extra cheese."

You'd think the child would be grateful I wasn't cooking.

Tuna noodle casserole with potato-chip topping was the extent of my culinary skills. A blast of rain struck the windows, pelting it like tiny marbles, and a deep rumbling shook the glass. Winston raised his head from his bed in the corner.

"Don't worry, ole boy. It's just thunder." I cupped my hands against the window to block out the room's light and watched the storm gather momentum, then turned and stared at the paper sack. "How long have you waited," I whispered, "for someone to find you?"

CHAPTER TWO

THE FIRST DROP STRUCK HER FACE.

Mattie Banks stirred and moaned. Another cold drip fell on her cheek, crept to her chin, hovered for a moment, then slithered down her neck. She shivered, opened her eyes, and blinked.

Nothing changed the absolute blackness.

Her head thumped. That rodent, Ace, must have sold her some bad coke. Again.

The thumping increased. Not just her brain. The drumming of liquid . . . or was it rain hitting metal overhead?

She tried to move. Something held her arms—her hands—together behind her. She tugged. What? The answer smacked her like a judge's gavel.

That man.

Jerking harder, stabbing agony shot up her arms, the juvenile arthritis that twisted her fingers protested her movements. Her stupid copper bracelet didn't help the pain at all. *I'm fourteen and already have old-lady hands.*

She lay still. Her heart beat in time to the patter of water.

Her head seemed full of dust, her thoughts whirling around and hard to form. She needed to hook one, pin it down. Gotta think. That man. Think about that man. Where was he? He knocked her out, but for how long? He must've hit her and thrown her . . . where?

Her stomach heaved and throat burned. Did that dirtbag poison her? Give her bad stuff? She struggled like a bird caught in a net until her bound ankles rapped sharply against something metal.

The pain all over her body made her gasp and squeeze her eyes shut, pinching out rare tears. Wheezing short puffs of air, she waited until she could catch her breath. Another drop tapped her eye, and she jerked. *Lay still! Think.* She forced her muddled brain to sort things out. Metal. Plastic. A smell she couldn't place. She was folded into a tiny area. Like a car trunk, but small. If she was in the trunk of a car, it wasn't moving.

Opening her mouth to scream for help, she froze, then clamped it shut and listened. Beyond the tapping above her head, there was a hissing sound like . . . yeah, rain on leaves. She couldn't hear any street noise. So she had to be somewhere outside of Missoula.

She took a deep breath. His trunk was dirty. Gritty sand and gravel bit into her bare arm. He'd partially covered her with a stinking tarp. Edging her feet forward, she nudged the metal again with the sole of her sandal, then used her big toe to explore the shape. Slightly curved, a point at one side . . . a shovel.

No! Her brain screeched the word as she lurched away. Another drip struck her ear, then slid in like a cold tongue.

Stupid! She'd been so stupid. Everyone said she could always spot a crazy. How'd she get sucked in by this one?

She lifted her face and the tarp slid to her shoulders, allowing a gentle, cedar-scented breeze to flutter her hair. Blinking rapidly, she tried to see around her.

This wasn't the trunk of a car, more like some kind of compartment inside a car or truck, and the top was open. Did he make a mistake? She bent her legs and tried to roll over. The tarp slipped more, letting the rain splash down her back, soaking her flimsy top. She rocked back and forth again, pushing, straining, almost, almost—*please, I gotta get up!*

"Yes," she whispered, then froze again to listen. Rain sliced through the leaves, water rushed to her left, making her want to pee, and frogs croaked in the distance.

Twisting to her knees, she scrabbled at the rope binding her ankle. It was so tight! She concentrated, exploring the knot, tugging at a different angle. It moved—a tiny bit—but it moved.

Furrowing her brow, she clawed at the knot like a starving alley cat in a Dumpster. Sharp jabs from fingernails broken to the quick added to the burn of her arthritis. The blood and rain made the rope slippery.

The drizzle fused with hot tears. *Come on, come—*

"I shouldn't have left you alone."

She jumped and banged her head. Sparklers flashed in her brain. A brilliant light blinded her, and she closed her eyes against the onslaught. "Ah, ah, ah . . ." She tried to form words.

"I'm sorry." His voice was deep and rich. "I should have told you."

She cringed from the voice. Told her? He was a crazy. He'd played her like a pro.

He cleared his throat. "Look."

Keeping her eyes shut, she shifted back farther.

"Look," the voice insisted.

She cracked open an eye. He aimed the flashlight at his hand, holding a roll of cash. A hundred-dollar bill showed on top. The hand gently swayed from side to side.

Licking her lips, she watched, mesmerized.

"I should have told you I enjoy a little fantasy." He turned the cash upward. More hundred-dollar bills.

Her tongue snaked over her uneven teeth, her gaze riveted on the money.

"I'm going to untie you now. I'll pay you very well for your, uh, discomfort."

"Yeah, you should've told me," she said, then flipped her hair off her face and gave him a let's-party smile. That was better. She'd make a bundle tonight.

Effortlessly he lifted her out and untied her hands and ankles. She swayed as the blood rushed to her feet. He gripped her upper arm and steadied her against him. Warmth seeped from his body, and it felt good. She shivered.

"You're cold." He slipped off his jacket and draped it over her shoulders. She pulled it close. It smelled of wood chips with a hint of cologne. Very male.

"Business first." She held out her hand, and he placed the thick roll in her palm, folding her bent fingers around the money and squeezing slightly. It hurt, and her grin slipped. She struggled to replace it.

He let go, and she quickly slid the money into the pocket of her skirt. "So, whatcha want?"

"Oh, I've paid for quite a lot, don't you think? So let's not rush." She could hear the smile in his voice. "How old are you . . . Sherry, is it?"

17

"Mat—uh, Cherry. My name's Cherry. I'm twenty." Just adding six years. She felt thirty.

"Twenty? Okay. If you say so." He touched her hair. "Perfect." Letting go, he nudged her toward a peeling shack, and she stumbled toward it on still-numb feet. At least they'd be out of the storm.

They passed through the doorway, the darkness ebbing from the probing flashlight revealing a blanket spread on the dirty floor. Crude for a guy with his kind of money. She stepped on the blanket and turned to him, then slowly opened the jacket. She knew he'd like the way the wet top clung to her.

"Stop!"

She jumped and snatched the jacket closed.

"I usually enjoy more . . . uh . . . outdoor sport. But it's raining, you see. That changes everything." He illuminated his hand, now holding a syringe loaded with a clear liquid. "We'll just have to have fun indoors."

"I don't do H. Not anymore." She stepped away.

"This is special. You'll love it." His gentle voice soothed and caressed. "It makes you feel like you're floating. Nothing hurts; it's all good." He offered the syringe again.

She slowly sank down, and he crouched next to her. He smelled good. She focused on his jaw. "Do I know you?"

He paused, then shook his head. "I don't think so."

"You look familiar."

He shrugged. "I look like a lot of people." Placing the flashlight next to him on the floor, he touched her hair, then pulled out rubber tubing.

She held out her arm. She'd always been able to spot a crazy, never been wrong. Never.

He shifted, knocking against the flashlight and rotating the beam toward a rotting wall, plunging her into darkness.

A handcuff clamped on one wrist, then the other. She started to scream, but a viselike grip caught her throat and squeezed.

She opened her eyes. *I must have passed out.* Her throat felt raw, her body broken. What a nightmare . . .

Blinking her eyes, she tried to focus. She was lying on her side, both hands stretched in front of her on the floor.

"Are you awake?" His voice stirred the hair by her ears.

She cringed.

"Good. Remember the number—"

"Oh—"

"Listen to me. Twenty-five, six." The light glinted off the handcuffs and a metal shape.

She'd seen a shape like that before . . .

The shape moved and rose.

She recognized it just before the hammer smashed her fingers, one by one.

CHAPTER THREE

I WOKE WITH A START. A GAPING MOUTH LINED with gleaming teeth was inches from my face. Foul, hot air blew over me. The tongue splashed burning drops of saliva on my arm.

Winston.

I rolled over in bed and watched a glint of sunlight stream through the curtains. Something made today different. Drowsy, I slid my leg under the covers to the cool side of the mattress. That side of the bed was undisturbed for over a year and a half. Since my divorce.

Winston sniffed my hair. *Winston*. Something about . . . the skull! I bounded from bed, startling the dog, and sprinted to the bathroom. I showered and dressed in record time. The stapled and taped paper sack waited on the table in my studio.

After slipping on latex gloves, I took a craft knife and sliced into the side of the bag and nudged the skull free. A long-legged spider dropped from the eye orbit.

I gagged and bolted away, then took off my shoe and anni-hilated the bug. That was probably a significant arachnid to a forensic entomologist. I debated saving the squished remains, then scooped them up with a paper towel and tossed the bundled mess in the trash. Let the entomologist find his own bugs.

Moving to the floor-to-ceiling shelves filling the west wall of the studio, I retrieved a plastic container from the bottom shelf. I opened it and selected a packet filled with modeling clay. I propped the skull on a sculpting stand, a high, three-legged wooden structure resembling a stool with a rotating top. Using the clay, I arranged the skull into a Frankfort horizontal plane, the angle used to photograph and reconstruct faces. Adding an evidence ruler, I snapped several digital photos from different angles. "Smile. You look mahvalous, dahling." *I'm talking to a skull.*

After taking measurements of the nasal spine, I lowered my face until I was level with the skull and gently rotated the top of the stand in a clockwise circle. I should've studied to be a forensic anthropologist. They could look at just the skull and be eighty- to ninety-some percent sure of gender. What little I did know still made me think the remains looked female.

I sucked in a deep breath. So, where was the rest of the body?

Aynslee, wearing pink flannel pajama bottoms and a short T-shirt, drifted into the room. Her long, ginger-colored hair tangled below her slender shoulders.

"Shouldn't you be hitting the books?" I asked. "You have an English essay due." I'd started homeschooling my daughter last fall.

"I don't know what to write."

"Your online assignment was an analytical research paper." I pulled out a sketchpad to jot some notes on the cranium. "You need to start by identifying the genre, topic, and audience. You could start with the audience. If they are like you, what are you interested in?"

"I don't know. Boys. Vampires . . ."

"I was thinking more along the lines of academic topics," I said dryly. "Literature? Politics? History?"

"Maybe crime?" Aynslee asked.

I blinked. "Crime?"

Aynslee grinned. "It's not so much that it's interesting. I figured with all the stuff you have around here, it'd be easier to write."

"Well—"

"Could I write about one of your cases?"

"It would need to be an adjudicated one." I pointed at a three-ring binder on my shelves. "You can check through the newspaper articles in there."

"'Kay." She wandered over, pulled out the binder, and placed it on my desk. After browsing through it for a few moments, she unsnapped several pages and held them up. "I've found a couple. Which one should I write about?"

"Leave them on the desk and I'll look them up."

"Also, could you look up that priest case? The one you're supposed to get a subpoena on?"

"Sure, once it arrives. Why?" I moved around the skull.

"Just wanted to read about it." Her mouth stretched into a jaw-cracking yawn. "Whatcha doing?"

"Working."

Her eyes widened when she spotted the skull. "Is that real?"

"Yes. Winston found it."

"Uck, gross. I'm never letting that dog lick me again." She came closer. "What happened to him?"

"Her." I pointed to the bullet hole. "She was shot. I was

just getting ready to have Winston show me where he discovered her."

"That's just so gross." She started to leave, then stopped. "Are you going to have to take that"—she pointed at the skull—"that thing to Missoula or anything?"

"I don't know. Why are you asking?"

"My birthday's coming up next week, and there's a movie marathon starting this weekend. I could stay with Dad."

A hot flash rocketed up my neck and across my face. I took a quick breath and waited for it to end. Robert rented an apartment in Missoula while waiting for the completion of his new home. "I'll think about it. In the meantime, did you finish your chores?"

"Almost. Don't think about the movie thing too long or the marathon will be over." Aynslee started to leave, then paused. "We've got ants."

I froze. "Are you sure it's ants? Not spiders?"

"Yeah. They're coming from over there." She pointed to the cupboard under the studio sink, then shuffled from the room.

I thought I'd fixed that. I opened the cupboard. Sure enough, the temporary plywood shelf was still there from when a leak under the sink rotted the cabinet bottom. A line of ants paraded from the crawl space under the house. If ants could get in, so could spiders. Resisting the urge to slap at my clothing, I found a can of insect spray and emptied it under and around the cabinet.

Fumes from the spray filled the room. *Time to leave and find a body.* The thought cheered me up. Dave was right; I really did have a sick mind.

Reaching through the security bars on the windows, I opened a few to let the room air out. After placing the skull in a fresh grocery bag, I folded the top closed and stapled it shut, this time adding two strips of tape to keep it closed.

Any walk in the woods required some kind of weapon. Chances were slim that an irate black bear or cougar would see me as a potential meal, but a startled moose could be in need of shooing off with a loud noise. Hopefully. As for a grizzly, well, I'd just have to pray I didn't have that problem. I debated between my SIG Sauer pistol and the .223 rifle, settling on the .223. The bullets were cheaper.

My Remington Model 700 North American Custom rifle stood in solitary glory in the ten-rifle display case by the front door. Robert, although he never fired a gun, took all the other rifles. I'd purchased this gun as a gift to myself for completing cancer treatment, then ordered it in pink camouflage. My choice of finish probably broke the heart of the gunsmith, but I was pretty much guaranteed that no self-respecting man would take it or try to steal it. Besides, I think pink's a killer color.

Slinging the rifle over my shoulder with its matching pink camo strap, I snatched the camera and stuck it in my pocket, then picked up my drawing kit. I passed Aynslee in the living room making a lackluster attempt to dust. "Don't forget to unload the dishwasher."

"Slave labor," Aynslee mumbled. "Mail came. It's on the kitchen table."

After placing a small pad and mechanical pencil from my forensic kit into my pocket, I left the rest of the supplies by the kitchen door. Winston raced out of the house in front of me. The clean morning air smelled of cedar and wet grass. I turned toward the trees, but jerked to a stop. Would Dave have planted bones to have an excuse to hire me? After the Utah case, I'd gone from reserve deputy to a paid position as forensic artist, then the bean counters told Dave to lay off all nonessential personnel, and I was shifted to being paid on an as-needed basis. The interagency forensic art position I'd applied for was on hold, and for some reason, law enforcement agencies weren't calling. Dave knew I was having trouble making ends meet.

Nah. That wasn't ethical, and Dave was by-the-book honest.

But he hadn't sounded surprised by my call last night. *No.* I really couldn't see Dave doing anything the least bit shady.

Winston stood at the edge of the lawn, dancing with impatience.

"Did Dave give you that skull?" I approached the dog. He blinked at me and wagged his tail. "Never mind. Where did you find her?" Now I was talking to a dog *and* waiting for an answer.

Winston spun toward a point where the trees and underbrush formed a dense wall and pushed through on a barely discernible game trail. I followed, plunging into an eerie twilight.

A hawk shrieked. Small branches bent and snapped like a cap gun. The strange dusk made color seem muted and gray.

Something landed in my hair and skittered across my head. I screamed and did a whooping spider-in-the-hair dance.

I shook my head, ending with a shudder, then calmed my breathing. A quick pivot assured me that no human had watched me do the insect boogie, and I trotted after Winston.

We followed the trail east for almost half a mile. Winston would trot forward, stop, sniff, then resume his quest. I recognized the route. We'd eventually end up at the old McCandless farm, less than a mile through the woods. I'd painted a watercolor of the house a few years ago. It was part of my only sold-out art show.

With all that had happened in the past two years, I'd completely forgotten about that show.

The trees thinned, then opened to an overgrown hayfield dotted with white daisies and purple lupine. On my right, pressed into the forest, the landscape slowly devoured a grayed building, the windows level with the earth sucking it down. The old farmhouse.

In the two years since I'd painted a watercolor of the site, a thick blanket of field grass obliterated the dirt driveway. A creek, khaki-colored with spring runoff, flowed from the woods, swerved toward the house, then meandered off to the county road. Dense, waist-high snowberry bushes enveloped the ground between the house and driveway.

Winston followed the creek, his white fur the only light spot in the forest, until he came to a large, moss-covered log spanning the rushing water. After bounding across the log bridge, he turned and waited for me.

The creek's flooding gouged a new channel, exposing a rib cage of tree roots bordering a level clearing. This had to be her grave.

I paused and swallowed hard.

Beneath Winston's paws, tattered plastic escaped from the disturbed ground. A bone jutted from the center of the clearing, sprouting a wisp of blackened material. The wind shifted and ruffled the plastic, as if beckoning me to come closer, just a little closer. It carried the odor of rot, dank soil, and moldering plant life.

Don't act like a rookie. First step: secure the site.

"Winston, here, come." I coaxed the dog off the grave. He drifted over and sat.

"Good boy." I scratched his ear, unslung the rifle that was digging a trench in my shoulder, and leaned it against a tree, then knelt and leaned forward. It was enough to cause a small cascade of dirt to slither off the plastic into the rushing stream. I rocked on my heels. Winston definitely compromised the scene when he retrieved the cranium. Then again, if he hadn't brought me the evidence, how long before anyone would have found this spot?

Tugging out the small pad of paper and pencil, I studied the scene. Might be some evidence on the surface. Fingerprints on the plastic? The killer attempted to conceal his victim's body instead of leaving it out in the woods. Based on the plant growth and winter snow covering this area, he'd probably dug the grave no later than the fall of last year. Shallow. In a hurry? The earth over the plastic seemed recently moved. Maybe loosened by Winston's snooping? I jotted some notes. If it hadn't been for the spring rains and my dog's discovery, no one would have found—

Winston's paw landed on my shoulder. "Winston! Stop it. Not now." I shoved the dog away and brushed off the dirt. I should've brought my camera. *Stupid mistake. Move on; keep looking.* So who's missing? Dave would've—

Again, a giant paw slammed into my back.

"Darn it, Winston!" I turned to push him away, but he dodged me, shook something blue and red, then placed it in my hand.

A cheap sandal. Smeared with blood.

Fresh blood.

CHAPTER FOUR

I DROPPED THE SHOE LIKE IT WAS A SNAKE AND scrubbed my hand on my jeans. *Fresh* blood?

The sandal fell on its side, and Winston sniffed it.

I grabbed Winston's ruff, pulled him away, then looked past the dog to the old farmhouse.

My scalp felt prickly. Was this both a dump site and a kill site? I jumped up and raced toward the house, then stopped dead. The open door yawned like a skid-row drunk, revealing the sepia interior, dimly lit from a glassless window frame.

My legs seemed rooted to the ground.

Look down. Concentrate on moving forward. One foot. Now another. I'd worked hundreds of crime scenes. *Yeah, but it's been awhile since you've had a homicide.*

Not that long. Seven months.

Pausing in the doorway, I took a deep breath. The stench of cheap lilac perfume made my nostrils burn.

I raised my head.

The interior looked more like an abandoned cow barn than a one-time residence for humans. Colorless, tattered wallpaper drooped off the drywall. The remains of a shredded piece of calico draped from a sagging wire in the corner.

I forced my gaze downward.

A body sprawled in the center of the room. Her ginger-red hair tangled in the dirt.

Aynslee.

My vision narrowed and lungs emptied. I dropped to my knees.

Please, dear Lord, not Aynslee. It can't be. I left her at home. She's home.

Winston crowded next to me in the doorway and licked my face. I put my hands over my mouth.

Can't be Aynslee. Look. Look carefully. She was tiny. And young. *Look.*

I grabbed Winston. Held on, gaining strength. My vision cleared enough to see a small tattoo on the girl's ankle. A butterfly. Aynslee didn't have a tattoo. And I'd just left her at home. This was not my daughter.

I waited until I could feel my legs again, then used Winston to stand.

"You poor thing," I whispered. *Don't get emotional. Check details.* I inspected the ground. Dirt and dried manure formed a thick gray matting, not capable of holding my footprints if I approached the body. "Good, good. I won't be leaving my shoe impressions to confuse the crime-scene technician." Hearing my voice slowed my racing heart. After checking for spiderwebs, I approached her, hunching slightly to keep from scraping the low ceiling. The young woman, girl really, lay on her back on an old

Hudson's Bay blanket. The killer must have brought the floor covering. It was too clean to have been left here by the prior occupants. He, or maybe she, had prepared well for a murder. *Organized.*

Closer yet, I studied her face. She did look a bit like my daughter. I wiped my sweaty hands on my jeans.

She'd died with her eyes mercifully closed. I hated the half-open, flat look of unknown remains. Garish pink lipstick was smeared on her lips. Had the killer done this? "Posing?" I whispered. "Some kind of ritual with the lipstick? The perfume could be hers or maybe part of his fantasy."

He'd arranged her left hand, complete with screaming fuchsia nail polish, on her chest, and hiked up her short skirt. Rape? One bare and deeply bruised leg ended with a slender foot still encased in a cheap sandal, a match to the one Winston had found. She'd ripped a toenail, and blood streaked down the other foot. She'd fought her abductor. Judging by age, she was probably the kidnapped girl from Missoula.

May. Marsha. No, Mattie.

I stepped closer and glanced at her face again.

She turned her head and looked at me.

I jerked upright and banged my head on the ceiling. It couldn't be . . .

Mattie blinked, then closed her eyes.

Oh, dear Lord!

I leaned over the girl's mouth, listening for breathing. Go through the drill. ABC . . . airway, breathing, circulation. I placed my hand on the girl's neck and felt a faint *thump, thump, thump.* Was she bleeding? The blanket showed tiny smears of blood: no puddles. I snatched my cell phone from my pocket and hit Redial. Nothing happened. I stared at the display. No reception.

Resisting the urge to throw the phone, I jammed it into my jeans pocket, then yanked off my jacket. I started to cover her but halted. Locard's exchange principle. The transference of evidence occurs . . . *Darn it, Gwen! She's alive and probably in shock! Hang Locard.*

I gently covered her. "I don't know if you can hear me, but my name is Gwen. I'm going to call the sheriff and get help." I touched Mattie's cheek. Ice cold.

Winston appeared on the other side of the prone figure, sniffed her face, and then lay beside her, instinctively knowing she needed warmth and protection. Outside, the breeze rustled the trees, sounding like cars in the distance.

"I'll be right back," I soothed, stroking her hair. "You're safe . . ."

I stiffened. Safe? How dumb could I be! The killer left her alive.

And your rifle is outside, leaning against a tree, in screaming pink camo.

My hand froze. I peered over my shoulder. The creek rushed yards from the front of the farmhouse. The sound would cover anyone approaching on foot.

Maybe the killer thought she was dead.

Ha. Want to bet on it?

I'd been so convinced that it was Aynslee, I'd barged into the house without thinking, hadn't secured the perimeter, hadn't even looked beyond the obvious. What if he was merely taking a walk? Dreaming up new tortures for the girl. *Get some backup. Now.*

"I'm leaving my dog, Winston." I started to stand. "He'll protect you—"

Mattie grasped my wrist. My heart lurched. The fingers were corpse-stiff, broken and swollen. I took the hand, shivering at the feel. "I have to leave you to get help, sweetheart. I can't call from here."

Mattie opened her eyes. Her lips moved. "Staaaay."

"I'm . . . I'm so sorry. You're Mattie, right?"

Mattie nodded slightly.

"I have to leave. Just for a few minutes. I'll be back." I looked at the girl's hand. The gaudy nail polish contrasted with the black-and-purple bruising. Yeah. Definitely into torture. Angry abrasion lines marred her wrists. Tied up. Check for rope.

"Nooooo." Mattie's word came out as escaping air. "Remember. Six. Twenty-five."

"I will, sweetheart. Don't worry about it." I bit my lip. "I've got to call Dave. He's the sheriff. No one knows I'm here, you see, so if I don't get help, you're going to—" I clamped my mouth shut. *Stop babbling.*

Her breathing barely lifted the jacket.

A car engine rumbled, growing louder.

My head jerked up. I glanced at her. Eyes closed.

Vaulting to my feet, ducking at the last minute before hitting the ceiling again, I looked toward the door. Dave must have figured out where I was heading. Sure. It was Dave—

A car door slammed.

You're kidding yourself. The killer is returning.

Winston stared out the opening.

I turned frantically, seeking a weapon, something, anything.

The fabric hanging from the wire wouldn't hide a mouse. Empty space mocked me, bare walls with rusting nails holding up crumbling plasterboard. The solitary window frame, minus its glass, faced the field, visible to anyone.

Bushes rustled. A twig snapped.

Winston stopped panting.

Heavy footsteps crunched, getting louder.

Winston's ears raised in alert.

I dove right and pressed my back to the wall next to the door. He'd have to step through to see me.

The entrance darkened.

A man, I could tell by the scent of wood chips and cologne, paused, his shadow reaching toward the still tableau of dog and girl. He chuckled.

My nails ground into the decaying surface of the plasterboard. His breathing was harsh, uneven, inches from me. A step forward and he'd see me.

Winston's lips pulled up, exposing sharp, ivory canines. A growl rumbled deep in his throat.

Please don't let the killer have a gun.

Hackles raised, Winston shot to his feet.

The man cursed, and the doorway abruptly lightened.

Winston charged, rushing past me. I lunged, grabbing a handful of fur, temporarily slowing the dog. His momentum pulled me forward and off balance. I fell, losing my grip. Winston disappeared into the bushes.

I launched after them. A car door slammed and the engine revved.

A *thump*, a sharp yelp . . . then silence.

I tore through the undergrowth.

Winston lay on his side, legs stretched out. "Ohnoohnoohno, please, God . . ." I halted, watching his torso to see if it moved.

Winston's chest rose and fell.

Winston. I couldn't lose Winston. My friend. My best friend. My eyes burned as I stumbled forward.

He raised his head and gazed at me. He struggled with a great effort to get his front legs under him before sinking back to the ground.

Kneeling beside him, I shifted his giant head into my lap. He closed his eyes. No blood marred his white coat. I ran my hand down his neck, stroked his shoulder, then gently felt his legs. He didn't budge. I skimmed across his ribs to the hip. He shifted, then stiffened.

"Easy, boy. Easy." I pulled out my phone.

Still no reception.

I stood and looked toward the house, then to where the road disappeared around a spiky tamarack. "Winston, stay."

I shoved through the brush, retrieved my rifle, and chambered a bullet.

Slowly approaching the tree, I worked spit back into my mouth. What if he just pulled out of sight? What if . . . ? Just think about Winston. And Mattie. I wound my way around the branches until I could see the overgrown lane. Empty. I raced down the driveway to the county road. No sign of his car or any vehicle.

I returned to Winston. He struggled to rise. "No, Winston, down. Stay. Stay here." Kneeling beside the dog, I gave him a hug. "Please."

Run for help on the road? Game trail? Someone could give me a lift, but if the killer returned . . .

Game trail.

Charging through the woods toward my house, I held the phone in front of me like a compass. The pine branches snagged my hair. "Stupid phone . . . Winston . . . That . . . poor girl . . ." A stitch in my side grew, my legs heavier, the air thinner. Too much time.

The reception bar appeared. Yes! One, two, three . . . call now. I hit the redial button and waited, gasping for air.

"Ra—County—dis—patch—"

"Hello!" Nothing.

I jogged again, hand holding my ribs. My feet were like concrete. A fallen log caught my shin, and I almost dropped the phone. Get . . . help . . . Get . . . help . . . Get . . . help . . .

I burst through the trees onto my lawn, scattering some wild turkeys. The cell phone sprang to life. I punched the number, sucking in air.

The voice was pure oxygen. "Ravalli County Sheriff's Office, dispatch."

"Help! Hurt . . . vic . . . Mc-uh-McCandless . . . farm . . . Dave . . ."

"Yeah, we got the call."

"Wh-What?"

"The sheriff's heading there now."

"Where?"

"The McCandless farm."

CHAPTER FIVE

SHERIFF DAVE MOORE HELD UP HIS HAND, HALT-ing his officers. Ahead of him, young, freckle-faced Deputy Ron Mackey pressed against the peeling siding of the old house. His white knuckles gleamed against the black grip of his gun.

Dave crept closer.

"They're inside," Ron whispered. "The dog that attacked her is there. It's huge. I think I can shoot it without hitting the girl."

"Where are the rest of the deputies?" Dave asked.

"Said they missed the turnoff. They're on their way."

Dave advanced and pressed against the other side of the doorway. "Are you sure it's a dog, not a wolf?"

Ron nodded. "It's white with long fur. Big head. Yeah, I'm sure."

Dave clenched his teeth, then made an effort to relax his jaw. "I'm going to take a look. If the dog moves, shoot it." He nodded at the EMTs waiting in the parked ambulance, signaled the rest of his deputies to draw their weapons, pulled out his own, then peered around the corner.

The corpse sprawled on her back. The canine lying between Dave and the body raised its head and stared at him.

Dave lowered his gun and stepped through the door. "Winston?"

"Move left, Dave. I haven't got a clear shot!" Ron said.

"Put your gun away." Dave approached the dog. Winston didn't stand to greet him. Dave paused midstep and stared at Winston's stretched-out rear legs, then turned and looked through the door. He could see a trail of broken and bent grass. He squatted down beside the dog and stroked his head. "Easy, Winston, easy. I need to help her."

"Dave, the dog's a killer!"

"Winston didn't hurt anyone," Dave said. "He's guarding the body." Winston nudged Dave's hand. Dave moved past him and knelt. The girl's face was ashen, eyes closed. She wasn't much older than a child. He touched her throat, feeling for a pulse he knew wouldn't be there.

He jerked his hand away.

"She's alive! Get the EMTs in here right now." He stood. "Dre," he called to Deputy Andre Arceneaux, waiting outside the door. "Secure this place. Ron, get Gwen Marcey on the phone. This is her dog and her coat on the girl. Get someone to call this in to dispatch, now, only medical staff. Move!"

The emergency medical team burst into the room, but froze at the sight of the dog.

Dave bent over Winston. "It's okay, big fella, they're here to help." Straightening, he waved the medical staff over. "Go ahead. Don't mind the dog."

The team swarmed over the girl. Dave moved out of their way and stepped outside.

Their rescue efforts hopefully wouldn't compromise the crime scene too much.

Several deputies trotted up and gathered around Dave. "Sorry we're late," one said.

"You stay with the girl." Dave pointed as he spoke. "You"—finger jab—"get out to the county road and keep anyone out who isn't supposed to be here. You"—another jab—"call the vet and let them know about Winston."

"No phone reception here," Ron said. "But dispatch was able to get through to Gwen. I mean her daughter. She said her mom left to look for a body, came back, screamed at her to lock all the doors, tore through the house looking for something, then took off in the car. Does that make sense?"

"For Gwen, yeah." Dave raised his head at the sound of yet another vehicle. A clean but battered white 2001 Audi A4 emerged from the snowberry bushes, careened into the field, and slid to a stop between a patrol car and ambulance.

Gwen jumped out and raced over to Dave. "You found her . . . I thought it was Aynslee . . . And Winston . . . and I ran . . . Dispatch said . . . He returned . . . Couldn't find my car keys . . ."

Dave took her arm and led her away from the gawking Ron. He dropped his hand. "Take your time."

Gwen looked into his eyes. "The girl . . . ?"

Dave nodded. "They're working on her now."

"I thought it was Aynslee." She shook her head.

Dave jerked his head back. He replayed his first vision of the girl in his mind. "Maybe the hair?"

She nodded. "I thought . . ." She tried to go on, then held up her hand and walked a few paces away. After a few minutes, she blew her nose, wiped her face, and returned. "I left Winston..."

"We found him guarding the girl."

"He's—"

"Fine."

"That . . . that . . . I can't think of bad enough words to describe the man who did that to that child." Gwen waved her arms. "Then he hit my dog! I need to get him to the vet."

She started to walk toward the building, but Dave restrained her. "I'll get one of my men to take care of it. I need you to tell me what happened."

Gwen turned her back to him and stood motionless for a moment. Her hair had grown since the last time he'd seen her. She absently ran her hand through the short blond waves, pausing when she met a chunk of tree bark and plucked it out. Pyrenees fur dusted her muddy jeans.

She turned. Smeared mascara under her eyes made her look like a homeless waif. He looked away quickly, remembering the day he'd met her. His dad had caught her stealing apples from a neighbor's orchard. It turned out she'd been living in their barn for who knows how long. Dad brought her home for a real meal. She'd stayed with them for the next five years. She'd never spoken of her life before that day. At least not to him.

"Okay," Gwen said.

Dave pulled out a notepad and pen, then nodded to her.

"Winston found the cranium yesterday, as you know. When I encouraged him to take me to his treasure trove, he brought me here, then he brought me the girl's sandal. That's what made me look in the house."

"Was the girl conscious when you found her?"

"Briefly."

"Did she say anything?" He waited, pen hovering above his notebook.

"Uh. Just a couple of words. 'Stay. No, remember six twenty-five.'"

"I wonder what that means."

"No clue. She nodded when I asked if her name was Mattie."

"So, we've found the missing Mattie Banks."

"The girl abducted yesterday from Missoula. Looks like she's experienced a pretty rough life. She was probably hooking, which made her a high risk."

"An easy target."

"Are you going to interrupt me? I thought you wanted—"

"Sorry." He knew better than to smile.

"Are you going to look for her folks?"

Dave couldn't read her expression. "We'll try."

Gwen folded her arms. "She's young, very young. She looks about Aynslee's age."

"I figured a runaway or throwaway." Dave watched her face carefully. Gwen might have a knee-jerk response to throwaways, children forgotten by society who ended up on the streets. Or dead. Gwen had been lucky; she could have ended up like Mattie.

A muscle tightened in Gwen's jaw, and she glanced away. "Yeah, well . . ."

Dave waited for her to continue, but she just stared off into the distance. "Gwen?"

"Sorry. Got to thinking about something else. I didn't notice track marks on her arms, but she may be into prescription drugs." Gwen's voice was husky. "I haven't looked at mug photos for a while, so I didn't recognize her." She pulled a pencil from her pocket and tucked it behind her ear. "The unknown suspect—"

"Unknown suspect? You're talking FBI-eze. You've been gone too long."

"You're interrupting again. Okay, the slimeball used control, of course, and demonstrated organized behavior, tying her up with rope or cuffs that he brought with him. Her wrists and ankles are abraded. Maybe he even used some drug to further subdue her."

Dave grinned. His dad had trained her well.

"He returned." She checked her watch. "At 0917. Winston chased him off, but the suspect hit him with his car . . ." She swallowed.

"You saw his car?"

"No, I fell trying to keep Winston from getting hurt. Fat lot of good that did." She kicked a pinecone. "The bushes over there and the way the road dips kept his car out of sight, but I heard it. It sounded like a gas engine, not electric or diesel. Unfortunately, we all drove over the same route, but maybe you'll get lucky with tire tracks. About Winston—"

"We'll get him to the vet. Is this where Winston found the skull?"

She nodded. "There's a buried body, or body parts, next to the house."

Dave opened a fresh page in his notebook. "Speculation?"

"I think my dog has a broken or dislocated hip—"

"I mean, speculation on this crime."

"Yeah, so, uh, he used the house as a kill site, with that grave indicating at least one dump site . . . You know I'm not a profiler?"

Dave looked up. "I know."

"So why are you asking me?"

"Two reasons." He held up his index finger. "Number one, you have good insight. Number two, we don't have a profiler. We're lucky to have Dre."

"Is that the guy with all the tattoos?"

"Yeah. Andre Arceneaux. A lateral transfer from Spokane, but originally from West Monroe, Louisiana. Don't let his tattoos and piercings throw you. He was an undercover agent for Ouachita Parish."

Gwen opened her mouth, but Dave was on a roll.

"We're lucky he took a couple of forensic classes last year. That's all people think about anymore. They watch TV, all those crime shows, and they think it's really like that. Case solved in an hour minus commercials, using the latest scientific gadgets. A CSI team waiting for our call, trained and ready. When my dad was sheriff, no one questioned him about forensic science."

"But your dad—"

"Not three days ago, Mrs. Post called. Stray dogs killed a bunch of chickens. She wanted me to do DNA tests on the blood." Dave violently swatted a deerfly buzzing near his head. "DNA. Chicken blood. This is Copper Creek, Montana!"

Gwen cocked her head and narrowed one eye. "So did you do it?"

"Do what?"

"The DNA on the blood?"

He folded his arms. "You. Are. So . . . Just finish giving me your thoughts about this case."

Gwen slowly turned in a circle. Dave followed her movements and tried to view the scene through her eyes. Patrol cars lined the field next to the house. One officer unrolled cadmium-yellow tape, boldly announcing Police Line—Do Not Cross in block print, from tree to tree. Methodically, he created a path to the grave before circling the house. The pine-covered mountains crowded in on three sides. The driveway dropped to the county road to their left. A faint dirt track, or logging skid trail, continued past the house toward the mountains. Rusty barbed wire, looped between gray posts, enclosed a sloping upper field. Most of the fence lay snarled in the tall grasses. The crackle of radios and the rushing stream provided the only sounds.

"If you don't think about why we're here, it's actually a pretty spot," Gwen said, still looking around. "I painted it once, put it into an exhibit with a couple of other old homesteads."

"I remember the show. You sold every piece."

"Don't be too impressed. There were only five paintings." She shrugged. "Anyway, back to here. The house was well chosen. This guy knows the area. This is a difficult location to find, especially the road leading in here. It's overgrown and has a weird turn as you drive up."

"Yeah. Some of the deputies were late getting here. They couldn't find the entrance."

"Okay. So, the killer could have a connection with a government agency like Fish, Wildlife, and Parks—or Forest Service. Possibly even law enforcement. Someone who might patrol the roads and would blend in. That's probably a key, someone not out of place where locals inspect the drivers of every truck or car. That would also include hunters."

Dave looked up quickly.

"Animal hunter. Elk, deer, bear," Gwen amended. "A hunter might stumble onto this location."

"Possible, but I think he knows the locale pretty well. An

outside hunter would need maps, and this place isn't on any hunting maps. It's private land and it's posted."

Gwen took a swift intake of breath.

"What?" he asked.

"Something . . . a thought." She waved her hand in front of her face as if swatting a fly. "Gone before I could nail it down."

Dave stared at the overgrown road. "*Somebody* knew about this place. Maybe we should look at the landowner. This could be a convenient—"

"I know where you're going, but, if you pardon the expression, that's a dead end. When I painted this place, I got permission from the owner. Ida Mae McCandless."

"Wasn't she the secretary at the Congregational church?"

"Yeah. Retired now, in her seventies, a widow, and hardly a serial killer."

"Okay, then . . ." He looked up at the distant sound of an airplane. The jet was a tiny speck in the sky.

"It's an ideal spot for his work . . ." Gwen's gaze drifted toward the structure. "Ideal." She moved closer to the house.

"What?" Dave asked.

"Think about it, Dave. He abducted Mattie yesterday morning, kept her restrained and alive for almost twenty-four hours, then left. Why? He returned, but again the question is why."

"Maybe he thought she was dead and was going to bury her. He could have needed something, like a shovel."

"But he brought a blanket. He was prepared. No, no." She chewed her lip. "This place is totally hidden. No one would disturb him, yet he stopped short of killing her and left." She looked up, then squinted. "We might just have an x factor."

"Like the television show? Aliens?"

"That's *X Files*. An x factor is an unplanned . . . *something* that screws up the killer's fantasy." She stared at the farmhouse. "Not a weapon . . . His car worked just fine . . . The girl did something . . . No, I showed up after he left, so no witnesses interrupted him . . . no one. That could be it! It wasn't a person that made him stop, it was time. Daylight."

"Go on."

"What if . . . what if he took a break, or noticed suddenly that the sun was coming up."

"'The light disturbs the wicked and stops the arm that is raised in violence.'"

"Isaiah?" Gwen asked.

"Job. Just musing."

"I'm going to make a guess." She bent over and pulled a blade of grass, then absently wrapped it around her finger. "He's playing out his ritual . . . the lipstick . . . spraying her with perfume . . . whatever else." Gwen snapped the grass in two and tossed it on the ground. "He suddenly noticed he could see her without his flashlight or lantern. He got up and walked to the door. Looked at his watch. Thought, *Criminy, look at the time!*"

"Criminy?"

"You get my drift. Anyway, the girl was almost dead. She's certainly not going anywhere. Then he noticed the exposed bones. They'd be hard to miss in daylight. But he can't kill and bury the girl and rebury the bones right away because he has a job, someplace he has to be. Maybe he even starts to dig, but realizes he needs to show up at work. He doesn't want to arouse suspicion."

Dave nodded. "He checks in, or punches in—"

"Or even has to leave to call in. Remember, there's no cell reception."

"Sunrise would be around six thirty."

"But this is a north-south valley, so the sunrise would be somewhat later," Gwen said. "Assuming he'd have to go home and shower, he might have to check in or be at work before eight."

"Well." Dave shifted his weight. "That's a lot of speculation and not a lot of elimination of suspects."

"Hey, you're the one who asked me for input. I'm not done. The proximity of the kill site to the dump site could mean he's not particularly strong as it's hard to move a body any distance, even a small one. He might also want to be near his former victims. *Hmm.* This reminds me of that serial killer over in Spokane about four or five years ago. He used both physical and psychological torture and liked young, slender victims." She shook her head. "But I believe the victims were boys, and they caught him. I think."

"Maybe he's loose again. Bundy got away and killed several more women. I can find out if the Spokane killer was ever caught or is incarcerated." Dave jotted a note.

"So. Okay. Bundy. Yeah." Gwen stared off into the distance.

"Hello? Earth to Gwen. What's going on in that brain of yours?"

"Sorry." She pulled out a scrap of paper and wrote something.

"I assume that if your thought is meaningful, you'll let me know. What else did you notice?"

"He's between five foot ten and six foot, is around wood chips—"

"I thought you said you didn't see him."

"You're doing it again, Dave. Bad interviewing technique. Never interrupt the witness."

"Don't correct me! You're not on your lecture circuit—"

"And you're not your dad!"

Dave's gaze locked on Gwen. Heat rose from his chest, to his neck, then his cheeks. The silence stretched between them.

"Excuse me?" Ron approached from the house, his face pale and his hand shook as he held up a paper sack. "Is this yours?" he asked Gwen.

She looked inside. "Yes, that's my jacket. I suppose it's evidence now." She turned to Dave. "My car keys are in the pocket."

Dave snatched the bag, yanked out the keys, tossed them to Gwen, then shoved the sack into the startled Ron's hands. "Get Dre to seal it."

"Sorry." Gwen looked pale. "I don't know what got into me."

"You're rusty," Dave said.

"I deserved that." Gwen turned to Ron. "First case like this?"

Ron blushed. "First case period. I never . . ." He cleared his throat.

She gently touched his arm. "Is Mattie going to be all right?"

"She's unconscious and, like, really messed up. The EMTs are getting ready to put her in the ambulance right now."

A white van with a Missoula television logo painted on the side pulled up next to Gwen's car. A cameraman hopped out of the passenger seat and began filming while a determined-looking reporter headed their direction.

Dave groaned. "Great. Ron, have someone follow the ambulance. I want to know the minute she's awake and talking." He moved toward the reporter, still speaking. "Get some help loading Winston into your cruiser and have someone drive him to the vet." Dave stopped and turned to Gwen. "Winston will be in good hands."

"I'll take him." Gwen started toward the house.

Dave grabbed her arm. "I need you here. We have a crime scene."

Gwen yanked her arm away. "My dog's hurt. I need to take care of him. And don't forget, I'm no longer on salary."

"I'll rearrange the budget and squeeze the money out somehow." Dave folded shut his notebook and started walking toward the reporter. Two burly deputies carried Winston from the house, his limp body like a giant polar-bear rug. They placed him in the rear seat of a patrol car and shut the door. Winston stared out the window, panting.

Dave reached the reporter, then turned and watched Gwen. She slipped in the car beside the dog, hugged him, then stepped out and closed the door.

Four EMTs carrying a stretcher negotiated through the narrow doorway of the house, then slid the gurney into the ambulance and drove away, lights flashing. A deputy followed in his cruiser, then the patrol car with Winston.

Dave turned to the reporter. "How did you hear about this so fast?"

The reporter stuck a microphone into his face. "I can't reveal our sources. We were already in the area doing a story on the wolf attacks. Do you have a comment?"

"Yeah. Stay behind the police line and don't get in our way."

The reporter jerked her head toward Dave's left. "That's Gwen Marcey."

"Yeah. So?"

"I did a feature on her two years ago. Didn't know she went to crime scenes. Thought she just worked out of her studio."

Dave gave a frustrated sigh. "You didn't do a very good

interview, then. Gwen's more than a composite artist. She's . . . You know, I'm too busy to talk to you now."

Someone tapped him on the back. He spun around. Gwen.

"I'll get my kit," she said. "We can start at the grave."

Dave nodded and jerked his head. They moved away from the probing microphone. "There's something else you need to know," he said quietly. "This guy's twisted—"

"That's obvious."

Dave held up his hand. "I think *he* called in the 911 report. He said a vicious dog attacked the girl. If I hadn't recognized Winston, we would've shot him."

Gwen's face drained of color. Without a word, she headed for her car.

Dre approached and set down his duffel bag. "Is that the Gwen Marcey you're always talking about?"

"Yeah."

"Is she well enough to work the scene? I heard—"

"You heard wrong. She's fine." Dave nodded after the retreating Gwen. "More than fine. This guy tortured a young girl and hit Gwen's dog. He's got no idea who he's just tangled with."

CHAPTER SIX

I COULDN'T SHAKE THE HEART-POUNDING MOMENT when I thought I was looking at Aynslee's dead body. The drive from my place to here was just five minutes. Five minutes from my daughter. Maybe I should go home, pick her up, and bring her here. I could keep an eye on her, make sure she was safe.

No. Bringing her to a crime scene would be a big mistake. The press usually showed up and she could inadvertently be photographed. To keep her out of sight, she'd have to sit in the car, doors locked, windows up. That would last about two minutes before she'd ignore everything I would tell her and start roaming all over. She was safer at home.

I shook my head to clear it, then joined Dre. He was pulling on white protective coveralls over his lanky frame. "Hi. I'm Gwen." I put out my hand.

"Hey, Gwen. Andre Arceneaux, but call me Dre." He took my hand and gave it a quick shake. "How are you feeling?"

"Great." Dave must have told him I was in remission from cancer. *How are you feeling?* was the first question everybody asked me. Maybe I should make a cardboard sign and wear it around my neck, tied with a shoelace. *I feel fine today. Thanks for your concern.*

"Do you need to borrow some coveralls to keep clean?" he asked.

"Nope, I'm set. I couldn't get much messier. Besides, they make my butt look big."

He raised his eyebrows, then leaned back to study my rear end. "Looks right as rain to me."

"Never mind. The building first?"

"I'll start there. You can measure and sketch the gravesite, then work your way over toward the house." His soft, Southern drawl deepened. "Scene's contaminated from tryin' to save the girl, but if she pulls through, we've got a witness. We'll catch 'em." He grinned. "Dave said departments haven't been sending you work, but this here's the case to put ya back on top. I heard Wes Bailor's been doing all the work over in Missoula and with the state crime lab."

"Wes Bailor?" I clamped my jaw tight. No wonder I wasn't getting calls. Wes moved to Copper Creek two years earlier and immediately caused all the single women to have heart palpitations with his flawless olive skin, black wavy hair, and Paul Gauguin mustache.

"But I've seen your sketches," Dre said. "Compared to you, I didn't think he was good enough to draw his own conclusions."

I smiled. "Thanks for the attaboy. Wes is a decent artist."

"If you like that kind of art."

"The Thomas Kinkade–like oils are popular." I smiled over

clenched teeth. Wes had asked me a lot of questions about forensic art, then offered his services to the local agencies.

Dre gave me a wide, boyish grin. "You're in Ravalli County, Dave's jurisdiction, so no Wes to horn in here. If the girl survives, you could develop a composite. You can reconstruct that skull your dog found. Dave said you have a motto."

"I have a pencil, and I'm not afraid to use it." I touched Dre on the arm. "We have to find this guy."

"Yeah. He's definitely a snake in the grass. But Dave says you're the best. You're needed here."

Needed. I nodded, placed my kit down, and crouched next to it. Needed, wanted, desired. Turn the clock back and make the past two years go away. Before cancer and divorce. Before someone almost killed me. A burning in my throat made speech impossible. Some days it was just plain irritating to be a woman with all these hormonal emotions, not to mention my early menopausal problems thanks to the anticancer drugs. *Enough of the pity party.* I tugged out a clipboard loaded with a sketchpad and pencil, then rummaged for a sharpener.

"Ron, get over here and help Gwen." Dave's voice stopped my search. He pointed at the remaining deputies. "You four will do a grid search of the area. There's a metal detector in Dre's van. All set?"

Dre slipped a digital camera around his neck, picked up his forensic container, and moved to the house.

I placed a compass in my pocket, added an evidence scale, slung a camera over my shoulder, and tucked a clipboard under my arm.

Ron loped over, shoving his red hair off his forehead. A smear of dirt outlined his nose.

I sighed. Was it just me, or in the past year did they start hiring teenagers for the department? I stood and shoved a tape measure and a bag of stand-up evidence markers into his hands.

"What's this for?" Ron stared at the tape measure. "Don't you just take photos?"

I glanced at my camera. "I could take measurements off a picture if I had to, but, just for the record, all crime scenes are measured. It's not glamorous work, so it doesn't make it on the cop shows."

Ron blushed. "I knew that."

"Sure you did."

"What about lasers? You know, I saw something on television—"

"There's a reason we call it the CSI effect. Tape measure"—I held it up—"$15.99. Ace Hardware. Laser scanning station, $200,000 plus."

"Oh."

I followed the yellow tape until we reached the grave, a natural clearing surrounded by cedars and bracken fern, between the creek and the farmhouse. I nodded to the old house. "I did a *plein air* painting here once."

"Plane air?" Ron asked.

"*P-l-e-i-n*. It means outdoor or on location. It's a beautiful . . . ugh." The breeze shifted and I revised my opinion. Downstream, a patch of reeking skunk cabbage made my nose twitch.

Ron gazed at the other deputies, then nodded toward Dre. "Isn't Andre Arceneaux the crime-scene guy for Ravalli County? I mean, uh, shouldn't I be helping him? Aren't you just the artist? Don't you just sketch stuff?"

I snapped some photographs, then studied the young man. "I don't think he wants you to call him Andre. It's Dre. This is small-town Montana's version of CSI. We're a lot closer to the *Andy Griffith Show* than *Forensic Files*."

Ron wrinkled his forehead. "Andy who?"

"Never mind. If we lived in, say, San Francisco, I'd just draw composites and maybe dead people. Here, I record the scenes, prepare them for court, take the photographs—whatever's needed." *When they could afford me.* I quickly drew a rough map.

"What about computers?"

"Useful, but programs are obsolete almost before an agency can buy them, and the best computer programs still need someone with an understanding of forensic art." I took the tape measure from Ron and handed him the stupid end. I got a reading from the compass and aimed him toward a cedar. Moving south, I let out the tape until I reached a second tree, this time a Douglas fir. I sketched the location and direction of the two trees. After taking a small hammer out of my case, I nailed a bottle cap into the base of the pine. I ambled over to Ron and did the same to the cedar.

"What are you doing?" he asked.

"Watch and learn. We don't have any fire hydrants, sidewalks, or streets to use as reference points. No GPS reception. I need to establish a north-south line, and I can't just say it was a cedar or Doug fir. There are lots of trees around here."

"Why not use plastic ribbon like they do when they survey roads?"

"'Cause it's easy for someone to remove the tape. But bottle caps are hard to pry out, and difficult to find if you don't know where to look." After taking a second tape measure from my pocket, I measured the distance to the edge of the grave and wrote the number on the rough sketch. Strange. The killer wasted a lot of time digging a wide grave. He should've spent it excavating a deep hole if he didn't want anyone to discover the body.

"So where did you learn that?" Ron shifted his weight.

"What?" He looked like a little kid with a full bladder.

"About the bottle caps."

"It's an old trick I learned from Ned." I moved the tape measure over and recorded the number.

"Ned?"

"Dave's dad. I'm surprised you haven't heard the story. He was murdered on duty. Dave left college to help out. Ended up with his dad's job." And probably all before Ron's birth. He really was a child wearing a uniform and a Glock. Should I tell him about emptying a bladder before showing up at a crime scene? Maybe just point to a thick patch of bushes?

"Ned must've been smart." He shuffled from foot to foot, then glanced toward the woods.

"Yeah, he was one of the big reasons I went into forensic art. He also taught me to ride a green broke horse, or at least stay on for the first few bucks. He collected things. Strays."

"Stray what?"

"Dogs, cats . . . kids." I swallowed hard. "He was quite a guy." *The closest I'd ever had to a dad. And Dave the closest to a big brother.* I nodded left. "Do you want to check out that thicket of snowberries?"

He scampered off, moving faster as he approached the bushes.

The killer dug the grave a short distance from the creek,

but heavy runoff from melting snow flooded the stream, under-cutting and collapsing the bank. The spring rains rinsed loose dirt from the slick plastic and into the rushing water.

"He didn't bury the body very deep," Ron said.

I jumped. "Yeah. I was just pondering that. If Winston hadn't retrieved the skull, we wouldn't have found it. The coyotes, maybe a bear or two, or even those wolves we've been hearing so much about, would've finished carting off the bones in another month or two." And Mattie would have joined the other body.

"Do you think there are wolves here? I mean, like, right now?" His hand touched the butt of his gun as he glanced around.

"No."

"I heard about an attack last night, though, and this morn-ing. Someone's poodle was torn to bits. I think the ranchers are going to lynch the Forest Service for reintroducing wolves into the wilderness."

"Fish, Wildlife, and Parks."

"What?"

"If there's going to be a lynching, they need to hang the right government agency. In Montana, it's Fish, Wildlife, and Parks."

A high, warbling howl echoed off the mountains. Ron spun toward the sound, grabbing his firearm again. "So what's that?"

"A coyote. Where are you from, anyway?" Carefully circling the disturbed earth, I snapped several digitals. What looked like a femur lay partially covered at the edge of the grave.

"Jacksonville, Florida. That can't be a coyote. They don't come out in daylight."

"They can and they do. Bring me those markers," I said. No reply. "Ron?"

Ron slowly released the grip on his pistol. He handed me the stack of fluorescent numbered tags. I placed one beside the bone. After taking a picture, I knelt and examined it. Interesting. I slipped a magnifying glass from my pocket and lay on my stomach to scrutinize. Pine needles, fresh earth, and old bone filled my nose. A rock jabbed into my rib. I shifted and squinted through the glass. That's weird. I knew I should've taken that class in college on forensic anthropology. It looked like something chewed the victim's leg while she was still alive, or started feeding on the body immediately after death. The edges of the bite marks on the bone were curling somewhat, rather than jagged and sharp.

The brush next to me moved and a branch snapped.

I dropped the glass.

Ron moved closer, stepping on another limb. "What else should I be doing?"

"You scared me to death! Why don't you go help Dre for a bit."

He trotted off before I could finish speaking.

I changed the camera lens to a macro and photographed several more angles, then stood and worked my way into the forest to my right, following a thin game trail. The branches drooped behind me like a net curtain, veiling the grave and house. A good thinking spot.

Sitting cross-legged facing the clearing, I cleaned up my rough sketch, making sure all the measurements were complete, then attached a blank piece of paper to the clipboard. Drawing a line from top to bottom, I divided the paper. On the left side I wrote *known* and *unknown* on the right. Tapping my lip, I stared blankly at the ground before writing my thoughts.

I closed my eyes, then opened them. In front of me, an odd

pattern emerged from the ground cover. After tucking a pencil behind my ear, I reached forward and brushed aside some pine needles. Two rounded pebble shapes surfaced. I snapped a quick photo, then pulled on some latex gloves and carefully scratched away the dirt. A human mandible appeared, teeth intact, with several fillings.

"Yeesss," I whispered as I continued to free the jaw. Once removed from the earth, I photographed it next to an evidence scale, a small white ruler with inches marked out on one side and metric on the other. I placed a marker beside the jaw and extended the tape measure through the brush to the grave. Snapping off the gloves, I flipped the paper over and recorded the location and measurements on my rough drawing before returning to the list of knowns and unknowns. I removed the pencil from behind my ear and added *animal activity scattering the bones* under *known*, then doodled a wolf head, teeth stretched into a snarl, eyes narrowed.

The rumble of an approaching vehicle rose above the rush of the stream. I peered through the tree branches as a tan Crown Vic pulled in next to Dave's truck. Following close behind was a settling-pond-green Forest Service pickup. I recognized the wiry shape of Detective Jeannie Thompson from the Missoula Police Department as the driver of the Crown Vic. The driver of the pickup had a familiar appearance. I squinted. Him! He'd shaved his mustache, but I knew that expression. Wes Bailor.

My face burned as my pencil gouged a trough through the paper. What was he doing here? Bottom-feeder.

Dave strolled to the pair standing outside of the taped-off perimeter. "Long way from the metropolis." His voice carried clearly.

Jeannie put out her hand, and Dave shook it. "Hey there, Dave."

"Well, now, what brings you city cops all the way out here?"

"We heard about the excitement. Seems your attempted homicide is our kidnap case. Mattie Banks, but calls herself Cherry on the streets. We're here following up." Jeannie produced a small photo from her purse and handed it to Dave. "She's fourteen. Already has a record for robbery and hooking. Wears a copper bracelet for juvenile arthritis."

Dave glanced at the picture, then handed it back. "It's her, but no bracelet. Maybe he took it as a trophy. That could be important."

"We're hoping to work with you on this."

"Sure." Dave jerked his thumb at Wes. "But we won't need him. We have our own artist."

I grinned. *That's telling them.* I wrote Wes's name under the wolf sketch.

Wes flushed slightly. "Of course. Gwen Marcey's the best. Everything I learned in forensic art came from her."

I snapped the point off the pencil. In a pig's eye I'll teach him anything else. I jumped to my feet, startling a chipmunk that chattered his anger. I reached for the branches, but stopped and smoothed my hair. My jeans were beyond straightening, but I rolled Pyrenees fur off my shirt, bit my lips to bring some color to them, then pushed through the trees. "Hi, Jeannie." Wes had disappeared by the time I emerged from the forest, so I didn't need to think of something nice to say.

"Gwen! I can't believe it!" Jeannie waved. "How are you feeling? We heard you were—"

"Dead?" I forced my smile to stay in place. "No. I'm doing

great. Working, as you can see. And ready to work any cases you have for me."

Dre stepped from the house and handed Ron a bag sealed with red evidence tape. "Put this in my van. We might get something off that blanket. Working this crime scene is like trying to poke a cat from under a porch with a rope. Half the stray cattle in the county must've taken shelter in there. Hi, Jeannie."

Wes joined us. He'd taken the time to put on blue nitrile gloves. "Hi, Gwen. I haven't seen you since your one-woman show. Still cranking out those landscapes?" His gaze drifted to my chest.

I contemplated stabbing him with a dull pencil, but that would be a waste of a perfectly good drawing tool. I turned to Dave. "I'm done with my measurements, so if you'd like to do some digging?"

"Good. Jeannie will need a copy of any reports, so remember to insert a carbon between the pages," Dave said to Dre, winked, then turned to Jeannie. "We've got another body." He nodded at the grave.

Jeannie's eyes widened as she turned in the direction he'd indicated. "A dump site?"

"Could be."

Yellow crime-scene tape fluttered in the slight wind, oddly resembling the cheerful streamers at a carnival. A thickset deputy holding a clipboard wrote the names of officers and the times they entered or left.

With Dre leading, we tramped single file to the grave where Dre shifted the loose soil to uncover more of the plastic tarp. No one spoke. The breeze chilled the air, the rushing of the icy stream providing the only sound until the soft clicking of my camera joined in.

Ron and Dre exposed the plastic and then peeled it open, revealing the contents.

Not *a* body.

Two. In different stages of decomposition.

I felt light-headed and tried to breathe through my mouth.

Dave's face paled, his lips pressed in a thin line as he tapped his finger on his bushy mustache. "So, we have a serial killer."

The bodies jumbled in the ground like carelessly tossed dolls. Both appeared to be women, if hair and clothing were any indication. The one nearest the stream lay facedown, the red hair sloughed in a tangle from the skull. Little flesh remained on the arm raised above the head. The top corpse was the most recent, minus the skull.

"What happened to that one?" Wes asked.

"That's what brought me here," I said. "The cranium's in my car. Her mandible, or the probable mandible, is over there." I slowly circled the grave, photographing it from all angles.

"I'm going to need the state crime lab on this," Dave said, "and what's-his-name, the forensic pathologist. We can't afford to miss something because we damaged the bones. Dre, you get that portable tent in case it rains again. Gwen, finish your notes and diagrams and get them to me. Bring me that skull your dog found. Jeannie, I appreciate your help—"

A shout came from the nearby trees.

I flinched. More bodies?

A deputy loped over waving an evidence container. It held a cell phone.

"I found it over there," the deputy said. "Where the snowberry bushes stop and the driveway starts. And, yes, I did photograph and measure first, Gwen, before you jump all over me."

"Sweet," I said. "A sloppy serial killer."

Dave examined the phone through the clear plastic before carefully handing it to the deputy. He swiftly walked to his truck, looked inside, then returned. "That's my cell phone."

I rolled my eyes. "You were giving me a hard time about acting like a rookie. Anything else you want to confess to? Did you smoke a few cigarettes and drop the butts? Perhaps ran your fingerprints over a few cans? Toss your business card on top of tire marks?"

"I guess I didn't make myself clear." Dave's voice was grim. "I was never near those bushes. I didn't drop it."

CHAPTER SEVEN

THE WORLD WAS BLINDING, WITH MOVING ROUND globes. Mattie squinted, then closed her eyes until she could barely see through her eyelashes. The globes—no, faces—came close, then drifted away. Echoing words made no sense.

"She . . ."

"X-ray . . . soon . . . Do you . . ."

"Kit . . . not now . . . Call the . . ."

Her brain seemed filled with gauze. Vomit rose in her throat, then receded. The smell of disinfectant and alcohol made her think of the free clinic she used to visit. Cool air swirled around her, but a warm blanket covered her and kept away the buzzing voices. Was that her mom's hand stroking her face?

No! He is back!

The nausea surged, filling her mouth with caustic bile. She swung her fist at his head, missed, swung again. Connection.

"Uff! She hit me! Grab her arm. She'll pull out the IV!"

He held her arms down, and she tried to bite him. More hands clutched her legs. He was everywhere!

"She needs restraints. Get a doctor in here."

She arched her back, struggling. Something clamped her wrists and ankles.

"Mattie. Mattie, stop. You're safe. Do you hear me?"

The face took shape: eyes, nose, mouth. A stranger. Not *him*.

"Mattie," the lips moved. "Mattie, I'm a nurse. You're protected here. You're in a hospital. Do you hear me? Do you understand what I'm saying?"

Mattie blinked, and the nurse's image bounced, then drifted out of focus. Mattie's thoughts floated again. The world retreated.

She opened her eyes. She was alone. Something *click-click-click*ed above her head. Her hands felt odd, muffled somehow, stiff. Partially raising one hand, she saw a white mitten. Not a mitten, a splint holding her hand and fingers immobile, with an IV threaded into her wrist. Restraints held her bound to the bed. She felt exposed and helpless.

The room was dim and painted pale blue, with cream-colored blinds partially drawn across the window to her left. A curtain hanging from the ceiling on a metal track was closed on her right, but the clattering of gurney wheels and chattering of voices in the hallway carried clearly.

"You'll let me know when she's awake? We'd like to get a composite sketch out as soon as possible." The male voice spoke with authority. It sounded like *him*.

"So you've told us about a hundred times, detective," the female voice snapped.

A surge of relief flooded her. It was a deputy. *He* wasn't here, and she was safe. "Thank You, Jesus." *Where did that come from?* She didn't believe in Jesus. Or God. Or anybody. Not for a long, long time.

Her mind drifted, enjoying the freedom from pain. The bed was soft and clean. A woman's face, like an angel, emerged from her musing. *My guardian angel?* Wavy, short hair. Blue eyes. Gentle hands. The lady at the house.

The house.

Adrenalin shot through her veins. Her eyes flew open. Where was *he?*

No. She was safe, at the hospital. She'd get out of here and go . . . where? Missoula was out. He'd found her in Missoula. She could go to Seattle. Or Portland. Maybe farther away. San Francisco? She'd never been to California. But she wouldn't turn tricks anymore. Maybe she could make a living drawing things. She could draw pretty well. When she had a chance. She could set up an easel on the street. Or better yet, on the beach. She'd heard they had nice beaches. She wiggled her shoulders into the mattress, feeling warm sand under her. She could hitchhike, catch a ride with a long-haul trucker.

Her stomach hurt. She was hungry. Didn't they ever feed people in a hospital? What was she supposed to do, just hang out? Boring. A television attached to the wall looked promising, but the restraints held her to the bed. Someone would come and unfasten them soon. *It's not as if I'm gonna hurt someone.* Voices in the hall and the squeaking of rubber soles grew louder, then softer as they passed her door.

"Is there any coffee around here?" The man was right outside her room.

A female voice responded, "Just down the hall, Detective. I heard Gwen Marcey found her and might do a sketch. Is Gwen . . . ?"

"Don't know her personally. I'm just supposed to let the

sheriff know when Mattie's awake enough to interview." The detective's words faded as he moved away.

Gwen Marcey. The lady that saved her had a name. A nice name. Sunlight caressed the Venetian blinds, forming golden horizontal bars across her bed. She relaxed. *Yeah.* She should go to California. Someplace like that. Lots of sunshine. No dark . . . houses.

More voices, a creaky gurney, then the whiff of food. Finally! It smelled like soup: tomato soup. Her mouth watered. Tomato soup with a grilled cheese sandwich was her favorite.

How would she eat? They'd have to untie her. That'd be good, then what? She bit her lip and stared at her hands. *Useless.* Using her elbows, she partially propped herself up. The walls twisted and whirled around her, making her want to puke. She slid down, concentrating on the ceiling and counting the tiles until the sickness passed. The side rails on either side of her head felt like jail bars. Nudging the pillows, she managed to block the view. *Better.*

When was the last time she ate?

The curtain glided on its track.

"That smells good." Mattie continued to stare at the ceiling. "I was starting to think I'd starve to death. That would be funny, wouldn't it? Croak in a hospital."

Silence. *Figures. No sense of humor.* Footsteps shuffled to her bed. A *click* as the nurse placed something beside her on the table.

"You're gonna have to untie me. And I don't know if I can sit up," Mattie said. "I need a remote for the TV." Strange. It didn't smell like lunch. It smelled like flowers, sweet lilacs, and choco- late. She loved chocolate, especially the kind with caramel in the center.

Tilting her head back, she sniffed again. It smelled like . . . wood chips.

She couldn't move. *No!*

"They tell me your real name is Mattie."

His voice. Soft, caressing her, so gentle, so deadly.

"I know you can hear me."

She was rigid, unable to move. Black edges encircled her vision.

"Despite your disgusting flaws, you did exactly right and everything went as planned." The whisper of fabric, his voice now closer. "I could kill you now. But I'm not done."

Her bladder released. The acrid smell of urine flooded the room. She tugged the restraints. If she could just reach the Call button. *Get help. Move away. Do something.*

"I have one more task for you. I know you'll do it, but just to be sure you remember how easily I can reach you, I'm leaving a gift." His voice was inches from her ear, his breath stirring her hair.

The blackness grew, filling her mind.

"Remember."

The blackness won.

CHAPTER EIGHT

I RESTED MY CASE ON THE GROUND AND FOLDED my arms. This looked ugly.

Dave's face paled, his umber-brown mustache standing out in stark contrast and his brows knit together. "My cell was on the front seat of my truck. Someone deliberately removed it and threw it into those bushes."

"Are you saying"—Jeannie flushed and her lips compressed as she moved closer—"you think one of my people—"

"Somebody did. And I'm going to find out who." Dave glared at each officer individually. "And when I do, someone's going to walk." He finally looked back to Jeannie. "We can't afford to compromise this case. I'm not going to let a greasy defense attorney throw the whole thing out on a technicality. I've already called in the state guys. I'm turning jurisdiction over to you *for now*."

Jeannie nodded, stepped away, and crossed her arms.

The deputies closed rank around Dave. I pulled out my pad of paper and wrote each person's name on a clean sheet of paper. I'd find the skunk that tried to frame Dave. I could do statement analysis on each one, determining through their written language who was lying. No one was going to smear my friend.

A skiff of wind passed over the grave and rammed the odor of rotting flesh against my nose. I held my breath. I'd forgotten to throw something in my kit for smell. The breeze drifted past the officers. Two of Dave's deputies turned away and gagged. Jeannie covered her nose.

Dave frowned. "Keep me informed." He turned and stomped to his truck, slamming the door so hard, I thought the window would break.

Jeannie strolled to her car and pulled out the handset of her radio. "Yeah, this is a 10–36 . . ."

Dave backed up, then drove off. Two patrol cars followed. The meadow seemed suddenly empty.

Wes sauntered over to me.

"Well, that was awkward," I said.

"Yeah."

"Uh . . ." I plucked some Pyrenees fur off my jeans. "So . . . where'd you get the Forest Service pickup?"

"They auction them off up in Missoula."

I didn't want to tell him that the hue reminded me of his favorite palette: abnormal colors not found in nature. More importantly, a Forest Service truck would pass unnoticed by the locals. "So they're pretty easy to buy?"

"Sure. Why?"

"Just wondering."

"Yeah, well, I'm sorry about all this. Tough break."

"Dave will figure out how his phone got there. And I wouldn't want to be the person responsible."

"I meant a tough break for you."

"Me?"

"Sure. I'm the forensic artist for Missoula. I have a contract with them to do all the work. Full-time. Paid."

My mouth opened and closed, but no words came out. Contract! I'd never thought to ask for a contract. My hands formed fists, nails digging into my palms. *No wonder I wasn't getting any work or referrals.*

"You could save me some time by giving me your notes." He held out his hand.

I stared at it, then at his face. The corner of his mouth twitched.

I wanted to spit at him, claw that smirk off his face. He took my work to get even with me. He didn't need the job. His insipid art sold like half-priced Tupperware.

Bending down, I bit back the words I wanted to fling at him. I grabbed my notes from the kit and held them out.

He took them, smearing my writing with his thumb, glanced down, then stuffed them into his back pocket. "Thanks." He swaggered away.

I blindly looked for my case, found it, then jogged to my car and fumbled for the key. Okay, then, no big deal. Let Wes have Missoula. It was one department. There were many agencies that didn't know I was working again. FBI. ATF. I had some connections with an arson investigation group in Helena. I'd do a promotional tour. Demo all my skills: crime-scene sketching, surveillance clarification, facial reconstructions, unknown remains, image modification. The turnover could be pretty high in law enforcement, and people didn't know—or had forgotten —what I could do for them.

But Missoula gave me the most cases.

No whining. Look on the upside. Wes could get too busy.

Yeah, right. And I could pick up his crumbs. He'd let me have the stop-and-robs, purse snatchings, and indecent exposures. Even with Robert's reluctant child-support checks, I needed a job.

Or I'd have to move. Leave the only place I'd felt safe from my past.

Wes wasn't motivated. He didn't have a killer in his back-yard, and Mattie Banks didn't look like *his* daughter.

Dre appeared, took the key, and opened the car door for me. "No worries, the cow ain't ate the cabbage yet." He winked and patted the roof.

The drive home was a blur. I should fight this. Wes couldn't reconstruct a skull. How many cases had he even worked? It wasn't fair. It wasn't right.

I parked beside my log house and rested my face on the steering wheel for a moment. Just give up. Maybe God was telling me I needed to find a new career. *Everything happens for a reason.*

A tan cruiser pulled behind me and Jeannie stepped out.

That was fast. I'd bet Wes admitted he didn't know how to work a crime scene, nor work on a skull. They needed me after all. I got out of my car.

"I think you have something for me." Jeannie's eyes flashed.

"What? You mean, but I-I gave my notes to Wes—"

"Not your notes. You have evidence in your car."

"What?"

"The skull."

I slowly shook my head, then ducked my face as a hot flash ripped up my neck. "I'm losing it." Reaching into the car, I lifted out the sack and handed it to Jeannie. "I . . . I'm sorry."

Jeannie's face softened. "Maybe it's too soon to be working. Weren't you almost killed less than a year ago? Anyway, call me if you come to town sometime." She took the bag from me, placed it in the trunk, and drove off.

Too soon to be working? I kicked the car door shut, then marched to the house. The breeze brought me the distinct odor of something very dead.

That can't be from the McCandless farm. I followed my nose around the house to the front door.

A very dead cat sprawled next to the step.

"Winston! Doggone it. You just won't stop bringing home road kill." I moved closer. The cat wasn't hit by a car. It had been mauled to death.

Coyotes? Wolves? But why didn't they eat it? I strolled to the outside kennel, picked up the pooper-scooper, and used the rake to shove the cat into the shovel part. Underneath was a piece of paper with something inked on it, but the cat's blood and fluids had smeared it.

I spun around and checked the yard, then the trees lining the lawn. *Come on, Gwen, it's just a dead cat. Hardly the first "gift" Winston's brought home.*

But what about the paper? A message?

Or just that, a piece of paper.

Leaving the cat, I pulled out my keys and reached for the front door.

It was unlocked.

A chill ripped through me. The killer could have driven over here after leaving the McCandless farm. He could have walked right into my house. Used my phone to call Dave.

Killed my daughter.

72

Racing to the car, I yanked my rifle from the trunk, then returned to the house.

The living room was empty, but I could hear clattering from the kitchen. I crept down the hall and peeked into the room.

Aynslee turned and spotted me. "You got a bunch of phone calls. Did that detective guy get ahold of you?" She stacked the last dish from the dishwasher on the shelf.

"Was someone here? Did you hear anything?"

"No. Why?"

"Someone may have left a dead cat by the door."

She shrugged. "It was probably Winston. You know how he is."

I slung the rifle around my shoulder. "And you left the door unlocked."

"It's always that way. None of the locks work." She eyed the rifle.

"The outside doors lock just fine if you push hard. I told you to lock it after me. From now on, you're not to let anyone in this house except me. Do you understand?"

"What? Are you grounding me? What did I do wrong?" She picked up a dish towel and threw it into the sink.

"I—" How much to tell her? I'd tried to keep the more sordid part of my work out of her young life. The last case changed that. She had been front and center when I was shot.

"Please sit down." I pointed to a chair, then walked to the entry and put my rifle in the display case. When I returned to the kitchen, Aynslee was seated at the kitchen table playing with her hair.

"You remember what happened to me just a few months ago?" I sat beside her.

"How can I forget? But Winston . . ." She sat up and stopped twirling her hair. She stared at me, then stood and looked out the window. "Where's Winston?"

"That's what I'm trying to tell you. Winston's at the vet."

She spun. "What do you mean? Is he okay?"

"Yes. A detective drove him over to be treated. I think he has a dislocated hip."

She bit her lip. "What happened?"

I told her about finding the grave, Mattie, and Winston. I withheld the phone call about a "killer dog" that could have gotten Winston shot by Dave. Aynslee slowly walked back to the chair and sat. "So that's why I need you to listen to me," I finished.

"It's not fair that I have to be locked up just because there's a sicko loose."

"Humor me on this one."

"When can we pick up Winston? I'm safe with a dog. Nobody messes with a Pyrenees."

"Soon."

"Okay, then." Aynslee leaned forward. "I did all my chores. We need to pick up Winston and you need to decide if I can go to the show."

"Give me a few minutes, then we'll drive over." I stared at her hair and thought about Mattie. "About your movie marathon . . . you absolutely cannot go alone. And what kind of movies are we talking about?"

"Like, romance kinda stuff."

"Romance kinda?"

"You know, special love, like that."

"Sweetheart, in my world, Ed Gein is special-love-romance kinda stuff."

Aynslee puckered her lips. "Who's Ed Gein?"

"The inspiration for *Psycho*'s Norman Bates."

"No, Mom. Like vampires and zombies. That kinda stuff."

"Ah, yes. Well, that's reassuring." I gave her a wry smile. "That's a no to vampires. And zombies. Anyway, I'm not going to Missoula after all. Isn't there something running in town?"

"It isn't the same. Missoula's a big city. Copper Creek is . . ." She waved her hands in the air. "Backward. They're showing a Disney flick." She stood and moved to the sink.

"Backward, huh? Well"—I combed my fingers through my hair—"maybe your dad will pick you up and take you . . . to the Disney, not the vampire show."

"I tried calling him already." She kicked the dishwasher door shut with a well-aimed blow. "He's not answering."

"Call again."

"I could hitch a ride to Missoula. I'm almost fifteen."

"Not in this or any other lifetime." Heading down the hall to my studio, I paused at the open door of Robert's office. Divots in the oatmeal-colored carpet, his battered desk, and a folding chair bore the only remaining evidence of his presence. I closed my eyes and pictured him bent over the computer keyboard, his lips pursed in concentration. The desk lamp backlit his profile with an exquisite chiaroscuro. His flannel shirt draped over his broad shoulders, sleeves rolled from his lean wrists. He had beautiful hands, musician's hands.

Hands that hadn't touched me since the doctor said, "You have breast cancer."

I'd been trying to turn Robert's office into my own, with mat board stacked against the wall and case boxes stacked in the closet and next to the desk, but somehow his presence was still imprinted on the room. Taking a deep breath, I silently closed the door and continued down the hall to the studio. After blowing my nose, I moved to the mirror above the sink. Today was the granddaddy of bad days, but then again, what did I expect? I'd been unable to work on any forensic cases for almost a year because of my cancer, then picked up the project in Utah. That made me both out of state and out of mind for law enforcement. Of course Missoula would find a replacement.

I was damaged goods to Robert. I'd endured the surgeries; the lumpectomy, then the double mastectomy, the port inserted just below my collarbone, the months of chemo and radiation, and the premature onset of menopause; just as long as I defeated cancer.

But cancer claimed our marriage. Robert served the divorce papers before the doctors performed my first surgery.

Robert was a successful author, hailed as the next Hemingway. After our marriage and the birth of our daughter, his creative well dried up, which, of course, he blamed on me. Once divorced, he found his voice by writing an e-book, fictionalizing my life and cancer battle. It's been on Amazon's top ten e-books for almost a year now.

Moving closer to the mirror, I studied my face. Did it show? Maybe around the eyes? The hair, definitely. My supershort bangs looked like twenties retro. Or Mamie Eisenhower, if you were old enough to remember. My best friend, Beth Noble, said they were the height of fashion. I tugged at my bangs until they straightened to my eyebrows, then let go. They curled up at the top of my forehead. *Stupid hair. Chemo hair.*

The Scripture verse posted on the wall reproached me. ". . . run with endurance the race that is set before us." Beth brought me a biblical quote once a week. I leaned closer to the mirror. At least I wasn't bald anymore. Even if I were, I still had a closet full of hats and wigs people gave me.

Don't knock baldness. I saved a bundle on hair-care products. Not to mention the justification in buying a killer pink camo rifle. *Ha-ha.* Stand-up comedy at the cancer support group at church. They loved me. I washed my face, then applied mascara and lip gloss.

Aynslee stomped into the room. "Still no answer from Dad. Where do you think he is?"

"Did you check his schedule? Maybe he has a book signing."

"He's supposed to be free this weekend."

"We'll call again later." I grabbed a sweater, a garbage bag, and a paper sack. "Give me a minute." Aynslee nodded. Opening the front door, I dumped the dead cat in the garbage bag and tied the top. I'd have the vet dispose of it. Burying it in the yard or woods would just keep Winston happy digging it up sometime in the future. The piece of paper might yield something once it dried. *Assuming the cat and paper were some kind of message.* I scooped it into the paper sack, then placed both into the trunk of the car.

Returning to the house, I yelled at Aynslee, "Let's go." The county paved the road for the first four miles out of town, leaving the rest as a washboard gravel lane meandering between the mountains, following the path of Copper Creek. Our home was two miles beyond the paved section. I deliberately turned my head when I came to the almost invisible McCandless turnoff, then continued slowly until I reached the asphalt. We soon reached the edge of town.

The veterinary hospital was a single-story building on a

wooded lot with a barn in the rear and high, frosted windows facing the parking lot. I entered and stepped to the counter.

The technician spoke into a phone tucked under her chin. ". . . yeah, really; I heard it's, like, a serial killer and they've found, like, a dozen bodies! No, I'm not kidding. Listen, I gotta go. Call me later." She hung up, then wiggled her fingers at my daughter. "Hi, Aynslee."

"Hi, Shelley," Aynslee answered.

"Where did you hear about the serial killer?" I asked.

"Everybody knows about it! My brother Ron was actually there. He said there were bodies everywhere. I called all my friends and told them to lock their houses up tight." She gave a theatrical shiver.

"Uh. Okay. I'm here about Winston."

Shelley frowned. "What about Winston?"

"Didn't the sheriff's department bring him here? I think he has a dislocated hip."

"No."

The hot flash ripped up my face as I tugged out my phone and dialed.

"Ravalli County Sheriff. Dispatch."

"Hi, this is Gwen Marcey. One of your deputies supposedly took my dog to the vet. He's not here."

"Just a minute, Ms. Marcey. Uh . . . yeah . . . here. They took him to Mountain View Veterinary. That's over on—"

"I know where it is." I nodded at the woman, then returned to my car. Mountain View was a new practice on the south end of town. I'd heard it was the most expensive animal hospital in Montana. And I was dead broke and out of a job.

CHAPTER NINE

THE IMPOSING BRICK BUILDING FEATURED A two-story arched entrance, custom matching windows, landscaped grounds, and a huge boulder in the front with the name of the practice etched deeply in the rock. A sprinkling of new Mercedes SUVs and beamers gleamed in the asphalt parking lot. The door opened automatically at our approach and ushered us into an atrium-style lobby with a curved, wood-paneled reception desk. A young technician in starched scrubs looked up as we entered. "How may I help you?" she asked, then spotted my daughter. "Hi, Aynslee."

"Hi, Megan."

"I believe some deputies brought my Great Pyrenees, Winston, here," I said.

"Oh, sure." Megan lifted the phone, pushed a button, and murmured a few words.

I glanced around the room, then shoved my tattered purse out of sight and avoided checking my shirt for dirt stains.

"Please have a seat." Megan pointed toward beige chairs at

the side of the room. "You're very lucky. Dr. Hawkins personally will handle your case."

Aynslee and I moved to the chairs. I didn't want to admit to her that I'd never heard of Dr. Hawkins, personally or otherwise. Fortunately, a glossy, full-color brochure on the end table enlightened me.

ABOUT OUR STAFF

Tim Hawkins, DVM, graduated with honors from Cornell University and worked at several practices before joining the staff here. The author of numerous articles published in *Modern Veterinary News*, Dr. Hawkins also contributed to *Secrets to the Successful Veterinary Practice* and *Winning Veterinary Strategies*.

Dr. Hawkins also operates a mobile clinic where he donates his time to caring for the pets of the elderly, people without transportation, those with reduced incomes, and others who need his help.

A photo included in the brochure showed a man about my age with deep-set hazel eyes beneath bushy brows. He had even features and sandy-blond hair.

"Ms. Marcey." A male technician, dressed in carelessly pressed scrubs with a name tag *Danny*, waved us toward a door. "Your dog is in the back. I'm supposed to take you to him, then Dr. Hawkins will see you. Okay?"

I nodded. We followed him into the treatment room, past gleaming counters and stainless steel sinks, to a door on the far side. A window next to the door overlooked an outside series of runs. I paused. "Do you board dogs and cats here?"

"As of last year when we completed this section. But we board and treat dogs only. The cat practice is next door."

"I sometimes need to leave Winston when I go out of town. This is a lot closer than driving him to Missoula. Do you have room for giant breeds?"

He tapped the window. The kennel area erupted in barking as a German shepherd, Lab, Bernese mountain dog, and two huge mastiff-types responded. "Yup."

"How much do you charge?"

"Sixty-five dollars a day."

Aynslee poked me in the back. I ignored her and tried to keep my face bland. I'd stayed in motel rooms for less.

A buzzer went off.

Danny sprinted across the room. A second technician joined him. They grabbed a gurney, slammed a door open, and disappeared outside. Two more technicians and a man I recognized as Dr. Hawkins raced into the room. The vet sent the technicians scurrying to gather up various items.

"What's going on?" Aynslee asked.

"Looks like an animal emergency," I said.

Danny reappeared shoving the gurney. On it was a large collie-shepherd mix, followed by a man in Levi's and a plaid shirt. They maneuvered the gurney next to a stainless steel treatment table and Danny and the vet shifted the dog. For a moment, Aynslee and I got a clear look at the shepherd mix. Aynslee turned away and covered her face. I grew faint.

No dog could recover from those fearsome injuries.

The vet raised his hand and everyone froze, waiting. He bent over the dog, listening for a heartbeat through his stethoscope.

The rancher stood away from the table, shifting his weight from foot to foot. "Found him like that, next to a dead llama," he said to no one in particular. "Musta happened early this morning."

Dr. Hawkins put down the stethoscope, walked over to the rancher, and murmured something. The rancher put a hand over his eyes. His shoulders shook.

Danny suddenly noticed Aynslee and me standing by the wall. He hurried over. "Sorry, I'll take you to your dog."

"What happened to . . . ?" Aynslee pointed to the still form on the table.

"Wolves," Danny said quietly.

"Oh." I put my arm around Aynslee. "Speaking of wolves, I have a dead cat in the trunk of my car. It may have been killed by wolves. Or coyotes. Do you dispose of dead animals?"

"Sure. Is it in a plastic bag?"

"Yes."

"Put it by the side door. I'll take care of it."

I nodded. We entered an inside kennel area with chain-link runs on both sides, high windows, and an exit on the opposite wall. He pointed to the last kennel. "Your dog's over there. He's been sedated."

A few quick strides and both Aynslee and I were at the gate. Winston lay sprawled on a blanket, but raised his head slightly at my voice. My daughter dove on him and covered his muzzle with kisses. I stepped inside, crouched next to him, and stroked his head. "Good boy. You're my good boy. You get better, okay?"

Winston seemed in a twilight stupor, bloodshot eyes sagging.

I cleared my throat and waited a moment before standing. "How much is it going to cost to fix his hip?" I stepped from the run. Aynslee gave him one last hug and reluctantly left his side.

Danny closed the door and looked at the dog. "It depends. I'll get Dr. Hawkins for you. He can give you an estimate if you'd like."

"Yes, please."

He led us toward the front of the building, through a spacious room where a young blond staff member was hosing down a large, stainless steel tub. The smell of cleaner and wet dog floated in the air. Pointing right, we moved into an office that opened into the lobby. One wall was book-lined and surrounded a fieldstone fireplace. The cherry wood desk was spotless. Windows overlooked the landscaped parking lot. Two chairs upholstered in western scenes faced the desk.

"I'll get the doc for ya." Danny bobbed his head.

The watercolor painting above the fireplace caught my attention. I moved closer.

"I enjoy watercolors."

I jumped. I hadn't heard Dr. Hawkins enter.

"Gwen Marcey?" The man extended his hand. "I'm Tim Hawkins. Nice to finally meet you. I've admired your watercolors ever since I attended one of your shows. What did you call that exhibit?" Doc Hawkins was slightly taller than me and wore starched, verdant-colored surgical scrubs. He smiled easily.

"*The Last Best Places*. I only had time to research and paint five watercolors in the series."

"They were great." He turned to Aynslee and held out his hand. "I don't believe we've met."

"Hi." Aynslee gave him a limp handshake.

"This is my daughter, Aynslee."

"Nice to meet you, Aynslee." He turned to me. "If you decide to paint a few more landscapes like you did, let me know. I'd like to see them before you put them on display."

"Sure."

"But be sure to watch out for the wolves."

"So it was a wolf that killed that dog?"

"Yes. And their pet llama. The owners are really nice people. I'd just been out there on a farm call yesterday. And now . . ." He frowned.

"How did you know it was wolves, not coyotes?" I asked.

"Wolves don't care if the animals are dead before they start eating. There's always lots of blood, drag marks, signs of a prolonged struggle."

"An animal crime scene. I'd never thought of it."

"You're a forensic artist. The next time I go out on a large animal call involving wolves, would you like to come?"

"Sure." Go figure. I was dumped off a human case the same day I have a chance to check out an animal killing. Maybe that was my new career: forensic critter artist. "About my dog?"

"He's beautiful," he said. "Obviously well-bred."

"Thank you. I used to show him. He's a champion. Is he . . . ?"

"He's fine. We went ahead and x-rayed him. He has a dislocated hip. We'd like to try to get the femur into the socket by manipulation. If we can't, we'll need to do surgery."

I sank to a chair. "What's all that going to cost?"

He pulled a piece of cream linen paper from a drawer and scrawled on it with a Montblanc pen. Holding it out, he said, "This is just a rough estimate."

I stared at the total.

Air escaped my lungs as if punched. So much! I took a deep breath and let it out. "You mentioned you liked watercolors."

"I do."

"Would you . . . would you consider bartering Winston's treatment for a painting? I could do another *Last Best Place*."

Dr. Hawkins frowned. "I don't know. I don't own this practice, so I'd have to run it by the partners. They're . . . pretty tight."

A hot flash bathed my face, and I looked down so Dr. Hawkins wouldn't see my flushed cheeks. When the heat subsided, I looked at him. "What . . . what would happen if I . . . didn't treat him?"

"Mom!" Aynslee's eyes were open in shock.

"Well." Dr. Hawkins stared first at my daughter, then me. "This is awkward. Without treatment, your dog will be crippled. You'll at least need to pay for the treatment so far. We do accept credit cards."

"I . . . I don't have a credit card." Taking a deep breath, I picked up my tattered purse. "Go ahead and take care of him. I'll find the money somehow. Call me when we can pick him up."

Pouring rain greeted us as we left the vet hospital, fat drops sliding down our backs. I swiftly removed the cat and left it by the side door. Once in the car, I stared out the window as the rain drummed on the roof, increasing to car-wash intensity.

"Mom, do you think I could get a weekend job? Like at a vet hospital? All my classmates have jobs like that. And we need the money."

"I'll think about it." Now all I had to do was keep my daughter safe from a serial killer, find a remote house or barn to paint, sell the art to get enough money to pay the vet bill, and avoid marauding wolves.

CHAPTER TEN

DAVE SLUMPED IN HIS OFFICE CHAIR AND pinched between his eyes to ward off the headache he felt coming on. A stack of papers sat in front of him. Statements from all his officers. Gwen would go over their words to check for anyone lying about his cell phone. She'd look for unnecessary words, their choice of pronouns, changes in nouns, and incorrect verbs. She was spot-on in ferreting out the liars.

Not that he expected any deception from his own officers. He still needed to hear from Jeannie, Wes, and a few of the Missoula officers.

He glanced up as Ron entered.

"Did you get the last of the statements?"

"That female detective just looked at me. Here's two more from the Missoula police. The artist guy—"

"Wes."

"Yeah. He said he'd get to it when he had time."

"Keep after him. Who's over at the hospital watching the girl?"

"Missoula took over."

"Did you hear if Mattie was talking yet?"

"No." Ron strolled from the room, quietly closing the door behind him.

Dave looked at the stack of papers again and clenched his teeth. He'd bet it was someone from Missoula. At least there would be a bright side. The bulk of the cost of the investigation would come from their budget, not his.

Dave strolled to the bookshelves and pulled out a textbook on crime-scene techniques. The book his dad had written. Big Ned Moore, his hero and Gwen's savior. At times like this, he missed talking to him.

The book fell open to a highlighted passage:

Evidence found at the scene is a building block to a case, but forms only one part of the investigation. The investigative process itself is ancient, found in the Bible, the book of Deuteronomy, in chapter 13:

"Then shalt thou enquire, and make search, and ask diligently; and, behold, if it be truth, and the thing certain . . ."

This is a process for investigating that trained detectives follow today.

Ned used the Bible for everything, even crime scenes. *I wish he'd marked a passage on how to stretch a law enforcement budget.*

Someone behind him softly cleared her throat.

"Yes, Louise?" he asked without turning.

His matronly secretary, Louise, waved a handful of papers. "More problems. Another dog's dead, torn up by the wolves, along with a llama. The Stansbury brothers set out some wolf traps and caught a prize bluetick coonhound. Someone spray-painted *wolves: shoot, shovel, and shut up* on the side of the Fish, Wildlife, and Parks headquarters, and they've called three times about it." She sniffed. "I think that particular agency needs to do a little target practice themselves on those wolves. They started this whole mess—"

"What else do you have?"

"Well." She pulled out a stapled set of papers. "The Citizens for Nature—that's what they call themselves, a bunch of tree-hugging, leftover hippies, if you ask me—signed a petition to prevent wolf hunting."

"Of course."

She held up another sheet of paper. "But here's the piece of resistance."

"Don't you mean *pièce de résistance*?"

"That's what I said. The city council approved this permission for a torchlight parade."

"Who's sponsoring it?"

She raised her eyebrows. "The American Christian Covenant Church."

Dave chewed his lip for a moment. "Is there some Christian holiday I'm missing?"

"Not exactly. They want to have the parade on the nineteenth of this month."

"And what's so special about the nineteenth?"

"It's the day before the twentieth." She gave him a smug look.

Getting information out of Louise was like catching a fish with a closed safety pin. "Louise—"

"Okay, Mr. Grumpy Pants. April 20 was Hitler's birthday. This parade is in memory of the torchlight parade Hitler had for himself in 1939. He made his birthday a national holiday."

"So this American Covenant—"

"American Christian Covenant. Yep, one of those neo-Nazi-type churches. New group. Still advocating making the northwest into a white homeland. Reminds me of the troubles we had here when your dad was sheriff, with the Militia of Montana and the Freemen of Montana. Anyway, they stuck a bunch of fliers under car windows at the Safeway. I put a copy in your in-box."

Dave rubbed his eyes. Where was he supposed to come up with enough officers to cover an event like that? And the money to pay them?

"Spokane PD returned your call on that serial killer," Louise continued. "They said they haven't caught him and if you have something for them, they're interested. They faxed some case information over, and I've put it in your in-box as well. Oh, and speaking of Spokane—or at least Washington—they sent over a subpoena for you to serve on Gwen Marcey. Said they already told her it was coming."

"It must be for an old case."

"I looked it up. It was some composite drawings she did on a domestic terrorists bombing a few years ago."

"Give it to—"

"I already did. Craig Harnisch called in sick." She placed the papers on his desk. "Everyone's got the flu. My daughter—"

"Thank you, Louise."

"I'll bring you a nice cup of tea." She turned to leave. "You're probably bound up. Makes people grumpy."

"I'm not—"

She shut the door.

"—bound up." He rubbed his chin. "And I hate tea."

The phone rang, and he grabbed the receiver. "Ravalli County Sheriff's Department, Sheriff Dave Moore."

"Dave, it's Jeannie."

He leaned back. "Yeah. How can I help you?"

"It's a zoo out here. Hey!" Her shout blasted his ear. "Get those people out of there!"

He winced and yanked the phone away, then cautiously put it closer.

"Half your town's parked outside the entrance to the farm." Her voice returned to a normal volume. "The state crime lab people are having trouble getting through. I need you to send over some deputies to clear the road."

"Traffic control?"

"Thanks. Hey, you there, get—"

Silence, then the dial tone.

CHAPTER ELEVEN

THE RAIN LET UP AS WE PULLED NEXT TO THE house.

"That's twice," Aynslee said. "Twice in one day you said you'd think about something. That's just another way of saying no, isn't it? I never get to do anything anymore." She barely waited for me to put the car in park before bolting to the kitchen door. It was locked, so she crossed her arms and glared at me until I could unlock it.

Once inside, I started a pot of coffee to warm up.

Loud music blared from Aynslee's room.

The rain tapered off to a fine mist. Taking my cup with me, I strolled to the studio and booted up my computer. The crunch of gravel in the driveway drew me to the window. My best friend, Beth, parked, slipped from her silver SUV, tugged two recyclable grocery bags and a lavender case from the backseat, then strolled to the door. I flung it open and gave her a quick hug. "Hey there, girl."

"Greetings." Beth placed the bags on the counter, then draped her coat over a chair. She gathered her damp hair into a neat bun and anchored it with a clip. She looked like a young Katharine Hepburn in *The African Queen*, with her black turtleneck, tweed skirt, and brown leather boots. Her porcelain complexion bore only a hint of makeup.

I self-consciously gave my short bangs a tug. "You look nice today."

"Thanks. You look . . . Uh, do you have any coffee?"

I poured her a cup. The rich aroma of freshly brewed beans filled the room. I nodded toward the bags. "Isn't today your plant day, or ladies group, or book club, or something? It looks like you're planning on moving in."

"It's not plant day; it's Garden Club. Not ladies' group, Big Sisters, and I'm not in a book club. You have an emergency. We have work to do. And I brought sustenance for a proper repast."

I should keep a dictionary handy when Beth comes around. "I can fix us lunch, if that's what you mean."

Beth started unpacking the bags. "Pizza is not acceptable."

I opened my mouth to comment, but she held up an index finger. "Nor is that inedible concoction—"

"Tuna noodle casserole?"

She shuddered. "I brought spinach salad with chèvre and roasted shallots, chicken bisque soup, and a fresh baguette."

Aynslee entered. "Oh boy! Real food." She snatched the bread, tore off a hunk, and stuffed it in her mouth. "Hi, Beth," she mumbled around the food.

Beth pushed her away. "Off with you, child."

Aynslee grinned and skipped from the room, humming.

I glared at her back. *Traitor.*

Reaching into her purse, Beth pulled out a laminated card with only a chapter name and verse printed on it. She presented it to me. "I spotted this at the Christian bookstore and thought of you. It has a magnet on the back."

"Thanks." I attached the card to the refrigerator. Colossians 3:13. "What does the verse say?"

Beth paused from rummaging in my cupboards. "Ah, you're going to have to look it up. And you'd better do it soon. You're teaching the women's Bible study next week."

"Do you think I'm ready?"

"Oh yeah. More than ready."

"So the topic and verse must be about everything happening for a reason—"

"No. But the subject should motivate you." She wagged a finger at me. "But speaking of motives—"

"I knew it wouldn't take you long to bring up the murders."

"It's all over the news, and that's why I'm here. Together we'll solve the crime. So tell me, what's the modus operandi of the killer?"

Aynslee entered the kitchen again. "Movie oper—?"

"You have movies on the brain," I said. "Beth was asking about modus operandi. Method of operation. Discovering clues that can lead to the thinking of the killer."

"Oh." Aynslee snuck another piece of bread. "So when's lunch?"

"Soon," Beth said. "You'll ruin your appetite."

"Nope. I'm always hungry." Aynslee made a show of placing the loaf in a wicker basket before grabbing another slice and racing from the room.

"Maybe you need another hobby besides me," I said.

Beth paused in her food preparation. "You're not my hobby. Your work makes a real difference."

I shrugged. "Yeah, well."

Beth pointed a pepper mill at me. "I sell geraniums to raise money for young women to go to college. I raise dahlias to bring some beauty into the world. Nothing I do challenges my mind, or is as . . . important as helping you. And I do help you, don't I?"

"Yes, your research is stellar. But what about your former job? Don't they ever call you?"

"Yes, but I left Microsoft with plenty of their stock options that I can use to indulge in my passions. I only do research for you now. And you're changing the subject. We were talking about the killer's mind."

"He's a sociopath."

"What's that?" Aynslee asked as she reentered the room.

"I don't know a formal definition off the top of my head. Someone who knows he's doing wrong, but doesn't care. No conscience."

Beth blinked at me, then opened the cupboard. A set of brightly colored, plastic bowls crashed to the floor. "Well. I found them." Picking up the set, she retrieved the largest and returned the rest to the shelf. "By the way, don't plan on going anywhere quickly. Traffic was horrible in front of the body farm."

"What did you just say?"

"Horrible?"

"No. Body farm."

"That's the name given by the press to the McCandless property," Beth said. "This morning on television I saw two deputies transferring Winston from an old building to a patrol car. I tried calling, but you didn't answer. Was he injured?"

I rubbed my forehead. "Dislocated hip, but he'll be fine."

"The media anointed your dog a hero, said he saved a girl's life. They mentioned your name as well, so ergo, here I am."

"Huh?"

Beth's face flushed with excitement. "Not just to bring you food and inspiration. I'm your confederate, collaborator, aide. Watson to your Sherlock, Koko and Yum Yum to your Qwilleran—"

"Those are cats."

"How about Robin to your Batman?"

"You're not thinking of wearing spandex." I bit my lip to keep from smiling.

"No. Together we can decipher the clues—"

"Ah, I get it. Just one problem. Missoula police is running the case."

"Then you'll just have to work for them. Bigger city—"

"And they have their own forensic artist. Wes Bailor."

"The abecedarian." She opened a series of matching Rubbermaid food storage containers and emptied the contents into the bowl. "Good. I've wanted to use that word for a week."

"Uh, I thought you already had a word for the week."

"It's a carryover. Waaait a minute." She paused, then waved a red plastic lid. "Isn't he the artist that painted six fingers on a portrait?"

My giggle came out a snort. "It wasn't six fingers. It was a phthalo-blue nose. Maybe he was making an artistic statement."

"Ha. If he was such an illustrious artist, what's he doing in Copper Creek, Montana?"

Stealing my job? "That's a really good question. I heard he was an established artist in Seattle or San Francisco or someplace like that." I frowned at her. "Anyway, what it comes down to is I don't need a sidekick if I don't have anything to do."

Beth's shoulders slumped. "Oh."

I cleaned off the kitchen table, shuffling quickly through the mail that Aynslee had stacked earlier. Three bills, a supermarket flier, and a pamphlet, *The* Brüder Schweigen *Declaration of War*. I reached over to toss it into the garbage, but Beth stopped me. "Someone put one of these under my windshield wiper at the store."

Before I could move, someone knocked at the front door. Beth strolled across the kitchen and peeked out the window. "It's a police car. Maybe they've changed their minds about you working on the case." She raced down the hall to the living room and opened the door.

"Oh, sorry, wrong house." Dre, the tattooed deputy, turned to leave, then spotted me. "Oh, good. Dave sent me over with—" His eyes widened at something. I turned. Aynslee was standing behind me.

"With?" I prompted.

"What?" he asked.

"You'd better come in. We're letting in all the mosquitoes." I opened the door farther. The man entered, gaze still riveted on Aynslee.

I glanced back and forth between the man and Aynslee. My stomach tightened. "Dre, this is my daughter, Aynslee, and my friend, Beth Noble."

"Ma'am." Dre stared at Aynslee. "Wow. She looks plumb close to the girl you found." He finally looked at me. "Here are the statements so far. And you got a subpoena."

I reached for them. "Thanks."

"So, you got one of those too." He nodded at the pamphlet in my other hand.

"Someone put it under my windshield wiper at the grocery store," Beth said.

"They're all over town. Lots of complaints. And they're planning a torchlight parade."

"Parade?" I asked.

"Yeah. Look on the back of the pamphlet. It's a church . . . well, they call themselves a church. Neo-Nazi kind of stuff. The parade is the night before Hitler's birthday."

"Just what Copper Creek needs. We can become the capitol of the Fourth Reich," Beth said.

He stared at Aynslee one last time. "Amazing." He turned to leave, then paused. "Oh, by the way, I smell something dead out here."

"A dead cat. I found it this morning."

He shook his head and left.

I handed the papers to Aynslee. "Tape the subpoena to the fridge, then take the statements and put them on my desk in the studio."

Beth waited until Aynslee was out of earshot. "Um, dead cat? A Winston find?"

"Maybe. There was a piece of paper under it. I forgot about it until just now. Let me get it from the trunk of my car."

"I hate to ask, but why is it in your trunk?"

"I didn't want it stinking up the house, and leaving it outside would attract critters. My trunk is a fast way to dry it out."

I trotted outside to my car, retrieved the sack with the piece of paper, and returned to the house. Beth followed me to my studio. After slipping on some rubber gloves, I pulled out the paper and quickly transported it to a clear ziplock bag, then placed it on the deep window ledge. Even though I worked rapidly, the smell of dead cat enveloped the room and I opened the window.

"Phew," Beth said. "Why didn't you put it in a clear plastic bag in the first place, like they do on television?"

"The plastic won't let the paper dry out and affects the evidence." I set the pamphlet on the ledge next to the paper.

"What are you doing?"

"I don't know, maybe a wild hunch. See the church's logo? A cross with a Z through it, a bit like a swastika?"

"Yes."

"I was trying to see if the paper under the dead cat had the same logo." I pointed. "There is part of a line like a cross, but the smeared part seems more rounded. Like the letter P maybe."

"What would it mean if it *was* the same?"

"Someone in this church is warning me."

"I don't get it. I thought folks like this didn't like Jews. You're not Jewish."

I handed her the pamphlet, then strolled to the kitchen. Beth followed. "They don't like people of color, Jews, mixed marriages, or homosexuals. Since I'm none of those things, and the logo doesn't match, I'm just letting my imagination run wild. Dead cats tend to do that to me." A prickly feeling of unease still tapped the back of my neck.

Beth nodded at the subpoena on the fridge as she placed lunch on the table. "Well, even though you don't get to work on the body farm, you *do* have a case."

"Ancient history. I assume it's for the priest case they called about."

"What do you mean?"

I tapped the paper. "Read what it says? *The State of Washington v. . . .* ah . . . *Jerome William Daly.* I have no idea who Jerome Daly is or what he did. The subpoena is probably for a composite I did several years ago. I don't really remember doing a priest case."

"But you should remember."

"I'll recall details about the case once I get more information. A composite sketch doesn't come with a name; it's a tool to help identify someone. I'll have to call the prosecuting attorney's office and find out which case is going to court, then look it up in my files. I may have to give a deposition as well. Fortunately they'll pay me as an expert witness." I pulled up a chair and Aynslee joined us.

"You live in a strange world."

"Ha. You're the one interested in weird declarations of war by some . . . church-going German group."

Beth bowed her head in prayer, and we followed suit. "Lord, thank You for this meal and bless our time together. Amen."

"Amen," Aynslee and I repeated.

"Mom"—Aynslee spoke around a mouthful of salad—"I'll keep trying to get ahold of Dad, but if I can't, could I go to the movies with Megan?"

I frowned at her table manners. "Chew your food first. Are you talking about the girl from the vet hospital?"

"Yeah."

"Are her parents going?"

"No. Danny's driving."

"Danny. The young technician?"

Aynslee frowned. "He's not so young. He's eighteen!"

"No—"

Aynslee threw down her napkin, shoved back from the table, and rocketed from the room. The slam of her bedroom door followed.

"Oh my," Beth said.

I stood. "I'm sure she'd love to lock her door as well, but none of the latches work."

"Why's that?"

"Log houses never stop settling. She'll get over her hissy fit pretty quickly, but we need to work on her attitude, so if you'll excuse me—"

The phone rang. I reached over and picked it up. "Forensic Art Studios."

"Is this Gwen Marcey?" the male voice asked.

"Yes." I opened the drawer, selected a pencil and pad of paper, and placed them on the counter.

"I'm Dan Swanson, reporter for the *Missoula Times*. I'm writing about the bodies your dog found at the old, let's see, yeah, McCandless farm. Sources say both you and the sheriff were thrown off the case, and that the Missoula Police Department is going to handle it. Do you wish to comment?"

I slammed the receiver down. Beth spun and opened her mouth to comment.

The phone rang again.

I snatched it up. "Get your facts straight, and don't call me again."

"Mrs. Marcey?" A different voice, muffled and distant.

"Oh, I'm sorry. I thought you were the press."

"Do you mind if I call you Gwen? Mrs. Marcey is so formal."

"Who is this?"

"You can say I'm an admirer of you and your dog. That was your dog, the big white one on television?" His voice was glassy-smooth, hypnotic.

I stayed silent and started doodling a sketch of Winston. Crank call? Crime brought out the lunatics.

"I'm delighted it was you." He sighed deeply.

"Delighted it was me *what*?" Definitely a nut case. I jotted the time. Underneath I wrote in shorthand: *male caller, educated, follows news broadcasts.*

"Finding it. It's been awhile, but I always say the best things in life are worth the wait."

Television would've given him enough information to "confess." Strange, though, they usually confess to the police. Maybe the lines were busy, and he found me in the phone book or the web.

"Thanks for calling. If you give me your number, I'll have the police contact you." I doodled a halo over Winston's head.

"Oh, that's very funny. And I know you found my blanket."

My head came up with a jerk. The blanket wouldn't have been mentioned in the news. "What are you talking about? What blanket?"

"The Hudson's Bay blanket. The cream one with the stripes."

I held my breath. *Ohmigosh. Him!*

"And, by the way, I'm sorry I hit him. Your dog, I mean. That part was an accident."

CHAPTER TWELVE

"HE CALLED."

"Gwen." Dave straightened in his chair. "When?"

"About three minutes ago. I've locked the doors and pulled the blinds."

"How do you know it was him?"

"He talked about the blanket. No one knows about that except those working the scene and the killer."

"Did he say anything else?" Dave picked up a pen and jotted some notes.

"He didn't mean to hit Winston. 'That part was an accident.' What did he mean by that?"

"I don't know. You said you didn't get a look at him. How'd he know who you were? Do you think he saw you?"

"No. Only Winston, but Beth said everyone saw my dog on television and they mentioned my name."

"Strange. Didn't you tell me that there hasn't been any record of retaliation on a forensic artist?"

"Yes. You're right. Why would he target *me*?"

"You might want to think about that. In the meantime"—he checked his watch—"I can beef up the patrol in your area. Or better yet, is it possible for you to go someplace for a few days? Maybe with Beth?"

Gwen didn't answer for a few moments.

"Gwen? Are you there?"

"Yeah. I'm thinking." Her voice was replaced by a tapping sound.

"Stop drumming your pencil," Dave said. "What are you thinking?"

"Right now he has the advantage. He knows who I am, but not for long. I'm going to find out who *he* is." *Click.*

Dave stared at the buzzing handset. It may not be his case anymore, but his job just got a whole lot more complicated.

After hanging up on Dave, I waited until the hot flash passed, silently trying to convince my body that the room had not changed temperature. My hot flashes were courtesy of post-cancer hormone treatments. They seemed to come every time I stressed, in addition to the usual inconvenient moments, especially whenever I wanted to appear sophisticated.

I'd given my notes to Wes, but I still remembered the list. I strolled to my studio and picked up a yellow legal pad, then drew a line down the middle and wrote *Known* on one side, *Unknown* on the other. On the *Known* side, I wrote down every word the man on the phone had said, then my original notes as well as Mattie's comment about six and twenty-five. The scrap of paper from my conversation with Dave was still in my pocket. I removed it and wrote *Bundy signature?* on the *Unknown* side.

"What on earth is going on?" Beth asked from the doorway.

I jumped. I'd forgotten she was here. "It looks like you're getting your wish." I gently set down my pencil. "We have to catch a sociopath. And he already knows who I am."

A fog swirled around a dark forest and the trees had grotesque faces, but the doorway promised escape. The wavering light ahead beckoning Mattie to run faster. Behind her was the pulsating evil . . . thing. She reached forward, grasping toward freedom, but the ground sucked her feet, reaching after each step with muddy fingers. Her steps grew slower as she sank farther into the muck. It gained on her, the hot panting growing closer, the clicking of its feet growing louder. It shrieked.

She gasped and shot upward, swinging her arm.

It shrieked again, a persistent ringing.

The phone.

Mattie wiped her splinted hand across her face, shoving her hair off a drenched forehead. The phone rang again, but she ignored it and concentrated on calming her breathing. It rang a third time, then stopped.

The nurse had removed her restraints earlier. Weak morning light sifted through the blinds, and the window ledge held various stuffed animals someone had delivered while she was asleep. The clattering of the breakfast cart drifted through the door.

Swallowing, she looked toward the door, searching for some water to wet her parched mouth. The glass sat on the table next to her, beside a vase of flowers, a box of chocolates, and a teddy bear. *He'd* brought them. As a reminder that he was still around. If she stretched, she'd be able to knock them to the floor.

The phone shrilled.

Heart pounding, she reached for it, then paused. Her hands were on a rigid framework and encased in gauze. She rolled over and grasped the receiver with both hands, bringing it to her ear.

"Do you want to live?"

She froze.

"Answer me. Do you want to live?"

Her mouth moved, but no sound emerged. *Nononononononono.*

"One last chance. Mattie, do you want to live?"

"Uhhhhhhhh." She couldn't form words.

"Good. Now, you must do exactly as I tell you." His voice droned on.

She nodded. When he finished speaking, she returned the phone to its cradle, then stared at the ceiling. Useless tears burned down her face.

"Ohmigosh, ohmigosh." Beth flipped her hands in the air as if drying them. "He *called* you? He called *you*! You're back on the case. You have to work it now. And I can help."

I nodded. "As Sherlock would say, 'The game is afoot.'"

"Actually, Shakespeare said it first in *Henry IV* . . .'"

I put down the paper I'd been studying and stared at her.

"Er, well, give me a moment." She left. The kitchen door squeaked, followed by the slam of a car door. She returned a minute later with a stack of books. "I stopped by the library on my way over. These were all they had on the subject."

"What subject?"

"Criminal profiling. I marked a few—"

"Beth."

"—passages with my initial research—"

"Beth!"

She stared at me.

A hot flash charged up my neck and onto my face. I waited until it passed. "Just one problem: I'm not a profiler. I'm a forensic artist. I draw. Crime scenes. Unknown remains. Composites. Courtroom proceedings. I work with victims and witnesses of crime. Not the slimebags—"

"Don't you call them perpetrators?"

"Ah, no. Sometimes I call them scumbags. Tweekers—"

"What's that?"

"A meth-maggot."

"Oh. How about a bottom-feeder?"

"That's Wes Bailor."

Beth looked at me a moment, then slid into a chair and carefully typed the definitions into my computer. "I've heard Sheriff Moore ask your opinion on cases. Specifically, profile-type opinions." She stroked the top library book with a manicured finger.

"Yeah, well. Probably because I give them for free," I muttered. "I'm not trained in profiling. I use my own techniques."

"So how will you identify the perpetra—uh, slimebag?"

"I'll begin with the question: why did he call me? We'll start with his exact words on the phone." I saw her puzzled expression as I handed her my notes. "This isn't profiling. It's statement analysis. I do know how to do that."

She swiftly typed them into a Word document. I leaned over her shoulder and pointed to the yellow pad. "Start here. He said, 'You can say I'm an admirer of you and your dog.' *You can say* modifies the sentence, as in *you could say this*, or *I can only say*. He's concealing information. He also isn't really an admirer of me."

"That proves he has no taste."

"You're sweet, Beth. The next thing he said was, 'I'm delighted it was you.'"

"I don't understand."

"I didn't either, so I said, 'Me what?' He said, 'Finding it.' 'It' must refer to Mattie, which confirms my calling him a sociopath."

Beth shuddered. "How disgusting."

"That's why we need to identify him." We looked at each other for a moment before Beth leaned into the computer screen. "You wrote, 'It's been awhile, but I always say the best things in life are worth the wait.' So he'd been waiting for something."

"Or someone." I picked up a pencil and twirled it through my fingers. "Maybe, maybe, maybe . . ."

"You're driving me insane. Maybe what?"

"I told Dave that I thought he left Mattie alive because he was interrupted. An x factor. But what if . . . what if he left her alive deliberately?"

"Why would he do that?"

"To deliver a message."

CHAPTER THIRTEEN

MATTIE CLOSED HER EYES AND THOUGHT ABOUT her next move. Someone opened the hospital door. She couldn't see who with the curtain partially blocking her side of the room.

Her pulse thumped hard, but she lay still and sniffed the air. The stench of the flowers beside her bed made it difficult. Footsteps approached and she concentrated. Soap, medicinal. A nurse. She pretended to be asleep. A warm hand checked her pulse, the rustle of starched fabric moved away from the bed, a pause before a pen scratched on paper, then the door clicked.

Mattie jerked at the tiny sound. She counted to four slowly, then opened her eyes a slit. The room was empty. *Hurry.* The nurse would return in an hour. Rolling onto her side, she swung her legs over the edge of the bed and sat upright. The world spun for a moment, then steadied. The IV line in her wrist would be a problem. She hooked her arm around the IV pole and wheeled it to the window. Her room was on the ground floor. Perfect.

"Why would you think the girl was delivering a message?" Beth asked.

"Maybe she *was* a message or *had* a message. But he had to make sure I'd get it. *Hmm.* Thinking back, when Winston headed toward the McCandless place, every little bit he'd stop and sniff."

"So he was tracking. I taught him that." Beth smiled at the memory.

"Ah, yeah, that might be it. But what if . . . Let's go for a walk."

Beth jumped to her feet. "Is it safe? I mean, the killer just called you."

"That means he's pretty far away. Only one spot here gets cell service." I nodded toward my lawn. "So that means either a landline in town or cell, also from town. And I'm going to be prepared." I swung by my bedroom and strapped on my holstered SIG Sauer, then tapped on Aynslee's door. "We're going for a walk. Did you want to get outside for a bit?" I didn't wait for a response. She joined us in the kitchen.

"Where are we going?" she asked.

"Part way to the McCandless farm. Keep your eyes open."

"What are we looking for?" Beth pulled on her jacket.

"I'm not sure." I found a sweatshirt in the pantry. "Dog treats? Meat? Something to lure Winston in a particular direction." Both of them looked startled but trooped after me.

The sun peeked through the clouds, adding a bit of warmth to the spring day. Flowering shrubs perfumed the air, and black-capped chickadees called to each other with their distinctive *fee-bee-bee, fee-bee-bee.* Once we entered the forest, chipmunks scolded us for our intrusion.

Aynslee spotted the evidence shortly before the McCandless farm came into sight. A cube of meat, now swarming with flies, lay along the game trail. We gathered around it like it was an ancient artifact. "Why didn't Winston eat this last piece of meat?" Aynslee asked.

"I suspect we're close enough to the grave, and Winston's find, that he focused on that goal," I said.

"Can you get fingerprints off that?" Beth asked.

"No." I suddenly felt exposed, as if a hundred eyes were on me. "Let's get back to the house." My hurried walk turned into a trot, then a run. Both Beth and Aynslee were in better shape than I was, even though I'd been working out to regain my strength, so I was the one gasping for air when we finally slammed the kitchen door.

"So," Beth said.

"Yeah." I yanked off my sweatshirt, now bathed in sweat. "Aynslee, if you want to go anywhere, you'd better get your schoolwork done."

"Right," she said. "In other words, warden, exercise period is over. Back to your cell." She strolled from the room.

"I'm telling you, Beth, when my hair turns gray, I'll have earned every strand."

"*Mmm.*" Beth plucked some dog hair off her sleeve. "I could leave, maybe return those books to the library . . ."

"Stay. That is, if your sweet husband can spare you?"

"It's income tax time and his clients are keeping him busy. I don't think he even knows I'm gone during the day."

"Good. We have things to do. For some reason, there's a very personal aspect to this killer's actions. And apparently something bigger he's planning. Let's see what else isn't a coincidence."

A half an hour later, I sat back at my drafting table. "That's all I can remember. Read what we have so far."

"Under 'Known' are the exact words he said, then: 'male, knows the area, at least two other bodies, control, restraint, leaves little evidence, educated, prepared, drives a car, returned to the scene, knows you or about you, mentioned Hudson's Bay blanket, baited Winston to go to the farm, said hitting your dog was an accident, about five foot ten to six feet tall, around wood chips.'" Beth looked up. "That's a lot."

"But not enough. Read on."

"Under 'Unknown' is: 'Mattie message, leaving bait for Winston to find? Or grave? Why returned to site? The numbers six and twenty-five. Does not like/admire you? Waited for something or someone? May be thin or weak (bodies near kill site).' What's the six and twenty-five mean?"

"Mattie said it. Maybe she was victim twenty-five, or it's a time, 6:25. A date, June 25?"

Beth bent over my computer's keyboard. After a few minutes she glanced up. "I'll need more in the way of parameters to run down these numbers."

"And she could have reversed them, so twenty-five and six. I don't even know if it's connected. We'll come back to it. What else do we have?"

"On your yellow tablet you wrote 'Bundy signature.' Elaborate."

"It has to do with victimology."

"But isn't signature the same as MO?" She reached for a library book.

"No. People don't just wake up one morning and say, 'Today I'm going to become a serial killer.' It's a process. They learn what works and what doesn't work, and what best satisfies their desires. That's two different things."

"Go on."

"So the modus operandi are the methods used to commit the crime. Like the location, restraints, weapons, how they left the scene, that kind of thing. That can change, evolve as the killer learns his craft. The signature is *why* he does it. It's a message from the offender, meant to be seen and understood, that fulfills their need or fantasy."

She looked up from a page she was reading. "Ah. It says here a signature is like tying a special knot."

"Sure. Or he could leave notes, engage in necrophilia, and so on."

"You wrote 'Bundy.'"

"Ted Bundy chose his victims based on how they looked. Another signature."

"Didn't Bundy experience a traumatizing incident from a girlfriend and subsequently select and murder women based on their conformity to her appearance?"

"Possibly, or Bundy was just attracted to certain women." I tapped my pencil on the desk for a moment.

"What aren't you saying?"

"Huh?"

"Tapping your pencil. That usually means you're contemplating something." Beth looked at the list, then back at me. "Bundy?"

"It's probably nothing, but I just keep seeing that poor girl and how I thought it was Aynslee."

"So what does Mattie Banks look like?"

I stood and pulled a pad of Bristol paper from my taboret,

then sat at my drawing table. I reached for a pencil, choosing the sharpest one from the lineup.

"You do know you have two pencils behind your ear?"

I touched them. "Backup." I closed my eyes for a moment and pictured Mattie's face, then opened them and began to draw. Her image emerged under my rapidly moving pencil. As I continued to shade, Beth stood and wandered over.

"Finished?" she asked.

"Yup." I turned the drawing in her direction.

"Extraordinary. Eyes, nose, mouth, hair . . ."

"There's a difference in her face shape." I taped the sketch to the window next to my drafting table, then pulled a photo of Aynslee out of the taboret drawer and attached it next to the drawing. "But you can see why I was so shocked."

She nodded.

"It wasn't just the idea of Ted Bundy. I worked on a case a couple of years ago where one signature was the appearance of the victims. Come to think of it—"

The phone rang.

I jumped.

Beth picked it up. "Forensic Art Studios, Beth Noble speaking." She listened for a moment, then held out the receiver. Her cheeks held a faint flush.

I stood and moved toward the desk. *Who is it?* I silently asked her.

Robert, she mouthed back.

My stomach bunched into a knot. I jerked to a stop.

Beth impatiently wiggled the receiver.

The room seemed Africa-hot and sweat broke out on my forehead. I took the phone from her. "Yes?"

"Gwen?" Robert said.

"Yes."

Silence.

"What do you want, Robert?" I finally asked.

"I . . . I'd like to see you."

I clamped the phone harder to my ear. "Your daughter's been trying to call you. She wants to go to the movies. She left you messages—"

"I got them. That's one reason I want to talk to you."

"Why?" Another hot flash seared my face and neck.

"Look. Not over the phone. Can I please come and see you? Alone."

My hand ached and I loosened my grip. "When?"

"Tomorrow."

"Where?"

"There. At our house."

"I guess so." Slowly hanging up the phone, I looked at Beth. "Well, that had to be the strangest phone call I've gotten in a while. Robert wants to come here."

"Rather odd, I agree."

"The weird part is he said 'our house.' When someone uses the pronoun *our*, it means he's unconsciously thinking of togetherness."

Beth straightened in her chair. "Someday you'll need to instruct me on statement analysis. I'd love to interpret people's real thoughts." She glanced at the stack of statements Dave sent over for me to look at. "Like those. What are you going to look for?"

"I'll give you a quick glimpse if you'll do me a huge favor."

"Agreed."

Picking up the stack, I ruffled through them. "Statement analysis takes time and concentration, neither of which I have an abundance of right now." I pulled out one sheet. "Dave told each person to write what happened, in ink, on the front side only of a piece of paper. This is Ron's statement, and I'll use him because I was with him and knew what he did. I'm cheating, but this is fast." I walked over to where Beth was sitting. "Notice how he goes through the events with great detail."

Dispatch told me to go to the McCandless farm, located at 16517 Copper Creek Road, at 1000 hours, and investigate a possible dog or wolf attack. I was the first to arrive . . .

"Okay."
"Now look here." I pointed.

. . . Gwen nailed a bottle cap into a tree to mark the north-south line. Later I held the tape measure . . .

"So?"
"He used the word *later*. There's a gap in his story between the bottle cap and the tape measure. He left out something. His statement jumped forward at that point."
"Ron threw Dave's phone into the bushes! Just like that." She snapped her fingers. "You solved the mystery—"
"Maybe, but more likely he left out having to go to the bathroom in a patch of bushes. Not a lie, just a simple omission to cover a rather embarrassing event. I can pick out more than lies from these." I fanned the papers. "Now, for that huge favor . . ."

"I want to know more."

"All in good time. For now—"

"Do you want me to research something? Interview suspects? Go undercover—"

"Would you take Aynslee into town for a movie tomorrow?"

Beth stared at me, speechless.

"Pretty please? I don't know what Robert wants, but he asked to see me alone. With a killer out there . . ."

"What's the movie?"

"A Disney something." I picked up a pencil.

"I don't know. I still get all teary eyed just thinking about *Old Yeller*."

"That was a long time ago." I doodled a dog's head. "I'm sure this is a recent release."

"So was *Eight Below*. Those poor huskies. I cried for hours. And did you ever see *Hachiko*?"

"I'm sure there're no dogs in it!" Too late. Beth dove for a box of tissue.

Dave stared at the teapot. "Louise, how many times—"

"It's one of my special blends." The older woman beamed at him. "It will have you regular in no time. Chamomile, fennel, cardamom, and with my secret ingredients, it will work wonders on digestion—"

The phone rang. Dave snatched it up like a lifeline. "Sheriff Moore." He gently slid the teapot to the other side of the desk.

"Sheriff? This is Dr. Hawkins, the vet. I'm on a farm call. It's wolves. You need to get out here."

Dave let out a deep sigh. "We don't exactly investigate wolf attacks—"

"You'll want to investigate this one."

"Why?"

"Because I found a woman's body."

CHAPTER FOURTEEN

THE EARLY-AFTERNOON SUN STREAMED
through the security bars outside and horizontal blinds within,
forming a checkerboard on my studio's white tile flooring. I
gazed at the pattern while Dave outlined what he wanted me to
do. "Right. Okay. I'll be there," I said.

Beth leaned forward in her chair.

I slowly hung up the phone. "That was Dave. He said they
just found another body. Looks like you'll get your wish to work
with me on a real case."

"Oh my! Was she like the other? Will I have an assignment?
Should I bring anything? How did she die?"

"I don't know. Yes. Notepaper and pencil. Uh . . . maybe
wolves."

Beth froze in her gathering of materials. "Wolves?"

"That's what Dave said. He told me the veterinarian was
on a farm call checking out a sick calf. He found the girl's body
nearby. Wolves killed the calf, and the girl was . . . torn up like
the calf."

"But that's implausible. Wolf attacks on humans are extremely rare."

"Not anymore."

I hesitated to leave Aynslee alone, but taking her to a crime scene with a dead body wouldn't exactly get me a nomination for mother of the year. Under threat of severe child abuse and promise of a movie with Beth, Aynslee agreed to stay in the house with the doors locked. "Remember," I had said to her, "only let someone in if they have the password of . . ."

"How about *Winston*?"

"*Winston* it is."

Holding a piece of paper with the directions, Beth pointed out each turn. We passed from paved county roads to graveled Forest Service lanes to a tooth-rattling, dirt driveway. The spring rains had damped down the clouds of dust our passage would kick up in another month. The driveway opened up to a series of fields enclosed by barbed wire strung between uneven cedar posts. We had no trouble spotting the wolf crime scene. Numerous police vehicles huddled together at the end of the last field. We parked behind a marked SUV. "You know, Beth, I think I've been here before."

"Really?"

"Remember that series of watercolor landscape paintings I did two years ago? *Last Best Places*?"

"Sure. The show was at the library and, uh . . ."

"City Council." I pointed. "If there's a pole barn behind that row of pines, it's the one I painted. Small world." I gulped in some air and gave Beth a nod. "On to the scene. Stay close to me. Don't touch anything. Look interested but slightly bored so they think you've been at crime scenes before. And try not to puke. Okay?"

Beth nodded, eyes shining.

I pulled my drawing kit out of the back of the car and headed toward Dave with Beth following. We passed through a gate made of wire looped around two poles and into a closely cropped field dotted with cow pies. A row of flowering forsythia and lilac bushes, their scent perfuming the air, separated the field from an ivory-colored farmhouse with peeling paint and fire-blackened streaks above the windows.

Dave waved me over. Both Dre and Dr. Hawkins wore khaki, short-sleeved coveralls and faced a gray-haired man in stained jeans on the side of the pasture near the bushes. Dr. Hawkins nodded a greeting.

"Hey, Doctor," I said. "How did it go with Winston?"

"So far, so good." He smiled. "We were able to do a closed reduction—"

"What's that?" Dave asked.

"We were able to manipulate Winston's dislocation back into place without surgery. 'Reduction' means the correction of a dislocation or fracture." Hawkins looked at me. "He has an Ehmer sling now, but I'd like to keep him another day to make sure his leg doesn't swell and that all is going well. You can pick him up Sunday. We're open from four thirty until six."

"I'll be there." I'd have to ask Robert for the money. That wouldn't go over well at all.

Dre's gaze drifted past me toward my car. "Where's your daughter?"

"Home." I folded my arms. "Why?"

"Just wondering.".

I chewed my lip and stared at him.

He shrugged. "You okay with leaving her alone and all?"

"She knows not to open the door to strangers. And that's better than dragging her where there's a dead body."

He nodded. "Makes sense."

The farmer bobbed his head at us. "So, I was saying, when the house caught fire four years ago"—the man jerked his chin in the direction of the structure—"the wife and I moved closer to town. Seemed like a good idea, us getting older and all. Sold off a few cows too. Simplify, that's what we agreed on."

"And you returned?" Dave prompted.

"Oh, yeah. So, this morning I drove out here. Would have been here sooner, but the wife was sick, so I didn't get out here for a couple of days to check on the calves." He shook his head. "Doc was already here. Couldn't believe it when he told me about the calf." He kept his gaze averted from the dead animal at his feet. "And I saw the carcass. Beefalo. Paid a pretty penny to inseminate my herd." He kicked a dirt clod. "Anyway, while we were lookin' at the calf, we heard the buzzin'."

"Buzzing?" Dave asked.

"Flies," Dre said. "The girl's been dead for a spell."

Beth's face paled a bit, but she gamely followed us as we strolled away from the road and toward the far edge of the field. The small herd of Herefords, many with chunky beefalo offspring, paused in their grazing to watch.

"Stay in single file," Dave said.

We passed the remains of a shredded plaid coat. Ahead, cottonwoods and alders outlined a small stream, while a steeply pitched hillside, covered with dense pines, formed a backdrop.

The light wind shifted.

I flinched and pinched my nose. Beth spun, bent double, and vomited. "Sorry," she said, still bent over.

My stomach lurched. Fortunately we were at the end of the line and no one turned or noticed. I stepped over to where Beth stood. "Are you going to be okay?" I whispered. "Do you want to wait by the car?"

"How can you endure that stench?" Beth croaked and wiped her mouth.

"I usually don't work on stink cases. I tell the law enforcement agencies to send photographs. Anyway, we'll move upwind and you should take a couple of deep breaths."

Face pea green, Beth did as I suggested, gagging a bit on the first few breaths.

The sound of a car came above the soft murmuring of the wind through the pines. Wes Bailor's pickup pulled up next to my vehicle.

I kicked a clod of dirt. "What's he doing here?"

"The Forest Service?"

"That's Wes Bailor's truck."

"Ah. The bottom-feeder."

"Come on." I turned my back on Wes, pretending I didn't see him wave at me. Soon, too soon, we caught up with the men now standing in a semicircle. The girl's body sprawled in the center. After the wolves were through, the inevitable decay of a body left unburied had made her almost unrecognizable.

Except for her long, ginger-colored hair.

I felt as if someone punched me in the stomach. She'd been young and tiny, like Mattie. And Aynslee.

Coincidence. This girl wasn't a victim of a serial killer.

Are you sure?

I checked her hands, looking for the same signs of torture as Mattie had experienced. Her fingers appeared unbroken on her left hand, but under her right was a hint of white. "Dre, there's something under her hand."

Dre joined me. "I see it." He pulled on exam gloves, then using tweezers, he picked up a torn piece of paper and placed it in a clear, plastic evidence bag.

"Can I see that?" I asked.

He handed me the bag.

I stared at the paper. "Beth, do you have the map I drew to get us here?"

"Sure." She rummaged in her purse for a moment. "Here."

I took the map, then held up both so Dave could see them.

Dave rubbed his mustache, then cleared his throat. "So what's a dead woman in a cow pasture doing with something you drew?"

"You remember the one-woman art show I had two years ago? I called it *Last Best Places*. I had an artist's statement—"

"That's very nice, Gwen," Dave said. "But—"

"Don't interrupt," I said. "I'm getting there. Anyway, I wrote about the paintings and drew maps showing the location of each site. This"—I raised the evidence bag—"is a copy of that map."

Dave snapped his fingers. "Then you would have also drawn a map of the McCandless farm."

I nodded.

"What does all this mean?" Beth asked.

"I don't know yet." I lay the bag on the ground and quickly snapped a photo before handing it to Dre. Something was different from the original map I drew, but I couldn't think of what. "I painted both the McCandless place and the pole barn over there. We've found dead women now in both locations, so there's a connection. And we found raw meat leading to the McCandless place."

"Raw—" Dre said.

"Yeah," I said. "As if someone was luring my dog to find Mattie."

"I see," Dave said. "Did you recover the meat?"

"It was covered in flies," Beth said. "Quite disgusting."

"Plus, I found a dead cat on my doorstep this morning, laying on a piece of paper with a symbol."

"Okay." Dave smoothed his mustache. "There seems to be personal and directed actions against you, Gwen. Can you build me a scenario?"

I stared at the burned-out house. "She got away from him and—"

"She? Him?" Dave asked. "What are you talking about?"

"She." I pointed to the body. "Him. The killer. Look at her wrist. Don't you see a slight ligature mark? And she looks like Mattie."

"I don't understand," Dr. Hawkins said. "Who's Mattie? Meat? Killer? Dead Cat? And what's with the map? This girl was killed by a wolf. Look at all the blood. And the ripped—"

"Yeah, we see." Dave nodded toward Beth, who'd turned even paler. "Gwen, start over. I think you're going down the wrong path on this one."

"I think it's a perfect place to start. The killer goes to my opening, or just stops by and picks up the handouts. Now he has a handy guide to remote locations. His choice of victims is similar. This girl resembles Mattie, the hair, the build. She's near an abandoned house and has marks like she might have been restrained. What if she was tied up in the house, managed to get away from her abductor, and was running for her life. She interrupted the wolves and . . . well . . ."

The farmer cleared his throat. "She wasn't in my house. Couldn't be. Floor's gone, burned clean through. Least on the first floor."

"And she has no sign of charcoal on her," Dre said. "If she got near that place, she'd have black soot all over."

"It can't be a coincidence," I said.

"Before we run off with a bunch of theories, let's see what we've got here," Dave said.

"Well," Dre said. "No identification on her body or that coat. No sign of a purse. Is there enough left of her face that you could draw her?"

"Yes." I placed my drawing case on the ground. The more I studied the body, the more my conviction grew. She was a victim of the serial killer. She looked like Mattie. A possible signature. "Dave, Dre, is there a chance that she was murdered and the wolves simply . . . uh, chewed on her body?"

"The medical examiner will be able to tell for sure." Dave folded his arms and stared at me. "You seem to be pretty obsessed with linking her with the serial killer."

Unless I could prove my theory, Dave wouldn't believe me.

Before I could frame an answer, Dre spoke. "There's a whole lotta blood here." He crouched by her leg. "Dead folks don't usually bleed."

No one spoke for a few minutes, the silence filled by the chuckling creek and cheeping ground squirrels.

"She's not a hiker." Dre finally spoke again. "Look at her clothes and shoes."

Her turquoise sandals were missing the heels. Though now covered in flies, I could see matching turquoise polish on her toenails. High-cut shorts exposed what at one time had been shapely legs. The tattered remains of a black leather camisole encircled her chest.

"What was she doing way out here?" Dre's voice interrupted us.

We gazed at the surrounding mountains. The only answer we heard was the call of a pair of ravens riding a current overhead.

"She *must* have interrupted the wolves attacking the calf," Dr. Hawkins said. "Wolves are very territorial about their kills."

"Okay, Gwen," Dave finally said to me. "She couldn't have been in the house, and she isn't a hiker. Build another scenario."

"Well," I said slowly. "She might have been on the road, hence the map. But if that's the case, where's her car?"

"Maybe someone dropped her off," Dre said.

"Hardly a main highway out here, but let's assume she was walking on the road. If she saw the wolves chewing on that calf, she'd run for the farmhouse. If they caught up to her, her body would have been over there." I indicated the direction.

Beth pulled out a lavender-colored notebook and started writing.

"If, on the other hand, she was coming from the woods," I continued, "with the wolves pursuing her, that structure would look safe. You can't tell there was a fire from this side. Wires are still attached to power poles, like people live there. And she's facing that direction."

They all nodded.

"What's over there?" I asked the farmer, pointing at the steep hillside in front of us.

"Nothin' much. You're looking north. The other side of that ridge is the Copper Creek drainage. I know that a few years ago they did some logging, so I'd expect you'd maybe find some overgrown logging roads, skid trails, that kind of thing."

I slid the sketchbook into my case and moved toward the stream, examining the ground before placing my foot.

"Don't believe we have any snakes out here," the farmer said.

"I'm not watching for snakes. I'm making sure I don't disturb any clues." Reaching the creek, I squatted and stared at the ground. The churned-up mud showed numerous recent cow tracks. "If she ran through here, the cattle stomped the evidence into oblivion." I turned and looked at Hawkins and the farmer. "I would guess that both of you have been tromping around this field as well."

Hawkins shrugged and the farmer gave a sheepish grin.

Returning to the men by the same route, I tugged my camera out of my bag. "Her coat is about halfway toward the calf, as if they were dragging it, and the calf is partially eaten."

The farmer glanced at the calf, then down at his shoes.

I jerked my chin at the fence. "Assuming she's running from the woods, she had to slow down to crawl through that barbed wire. Simple enough if it's daylight, but if it were night, she'd run right into it. That would slow her down quite a bit. I'd suggest someone walk the fence line. Look for fabric or hair caught in the barbs."

"Without identification, how do you find out who she is?" Beth asked.

"You start with who's missing, then how she's dressed, until my sketch is done. The 'who's missing' works if someone reported her. As for how she's dressed, as Dre said, we should start with her shoes and clothing."

"Oh, sure," Beth said.

"You know . . . ?" I asked with a suggestive nod toward the body.

Hawkins and the farmer apparently didn't have a clue.

"Okay, what I'm trying to say is her choice of clothing might make her a prostitute." Dave and Dre nodded.

"But that's another reason I think it's the same predator who tortured Mattie Banks. I think he picked her up and drove her up one of those logging roads. I think she escaped and was running for freedom."

Dave carefully closed his notebook. "Then indirectly, she was killed by a different type of predator."

CHAPTER FIFTEEN

I LIFTED MY CAMERA AND STARTED PHOTO-graphing the girl.

Wes sauntered up wearing pressed jeans, a maroon plaid shirt, and tan oxfords. This time he hadn't bothered to slip on blue nitrile gloves. I didn't know if that irritated me more or less.

"What are you doing here?" Dave frowned at the man.

Wes moved to where he could clearly see the woman. "Investigating." I waited for him to blanch and vomit, but he seemed frozen, staring at the body. *Interesting.* I was pretty sure this was his first ripe-smelling death scene beyond the bodies in the grave, which had only been bones.

"Investigating?" I asked him.

He didn't respond. A sheen of sweat appeared on his forehead, and he shuffled closer to the corpse.

"Wes?"

He blinked as if waking up. "Huh?"

"I'm curious," I said. "Investigating isn't usually the role of a forensic artist."

"Missoula police and the state crime lab see me in a larger role."

I winced. Why didn't I ask for a contract to do their forensic art when I had the chance?

Dave caught my reaction. "I think the Mattie Banks case has given you a serious dose of Superman Syndrome."

The old farmer's forehead crinkled. "What's that?"

Beth answered, "A contumelious appellation epitomizing a forensic artist overstepping their function. Wow. I didn't think I'd get three words of the week into one sentence."

"Huh?" The old man took off his John Deere baseball hat and scratched his head.

"Nice, Beth. Translation: it's not a good thing." I looked at Wes, who'd been ignoring the whole exchange. "In other words, Wes, you are out of your jurisdiction and as far as I'm concerned, out of your league." I concentrated on photographing the body.

"Oh, I'm not here on this case," Wes said, seemingly unaffected by my sarcasm. "I'm still working the Banks case. I was trying to get ahold of you, but you're not getting cell reception here."

"You could have used the police radio," I said.

Wes rubbed his nose and cleared his throat, "You're wondering why I didn't use the police radio?"

"Don't bother to answer." I shook my head. "You're going to lie."

"No, no, no. I wanted to ask you a question. The vic is awake, but unresponsive to my attempts to draw a composite. She refuses to see anyone."

"Vic?" Beth asked.

"Victim." I turned to Wes. "You are referring to Mattie Banks, I assume. Are you asking me to do the sketch?"

Wes's eyes opened wide and his head jerked back. "No! I mean, no. I just wondered if you had a technique that worked on noncooperative vics."

"Yes, I do, and it starts by thinking of them as people with names, not labels."

Beth gave me a startled look.

"Wes, there's a chance," I said, "a really good chance, that Mattie will not talk to you. You're male. You represent what another man did to her. Why don't you just let me do the composite?" *And save me from having to sneak in to do it.*

"Sorry. My case." Wes pulled out his phone and snapped a photo of the girl.

I grabbed for his cell and missed. "Well, this is *my* case, and you're not part of it. Stop taking photos and leave."

Wes shrugged and wandered toward the dead calf.

I was struck by a thought. "Dave, did anyone find fingerprints on your cell phone?"

"Just mine. What made you ask?"

I thought about Wes and the blue nitrile gloves. Was he enough of a snake to grab Dave's phone and toss it into the bushes to get us thrown off the case? "Did you get statements from everyone regarding your cell phone? I'd like to work some more on the statement analysis."

"Pretty much," Dave said.

"What about the press? That reporter lady."

"I forgot about that. I'll give her a call. Otherwise, I've heard from everyone but Wes over there," Dave said.

"Why doesn't that surprise me?" I muttered.

A cloud blocked the sun and the temperature dropped. Dave tugged his jacket tighter and stared at the body. "Jezebel." He didn't realize he'd spoken aloud until he felt everyone's gaze.

"Harsh, Dave," Gwen said.

Beth shook her head. "Not nice at all."

"Oh, no." Dave's face burned. "I wasn't referring to her profession. The biblical Jezebel's body was eaten by dogs. The narrative always stuck in my mind." He waved his hand at the girl. "Unfortunately, now I have a vivid picture to go with the story."

Another sheriff's vehicle pulled into what now looked like a used car lot, followed by a black, first-call minivan with *Duncan's Funeral Services* stenciled in white letters on the side.

Dave looked at each person in turn. "I'm going to have the deputy coroner transport her body to the medical examiner in Missoula for an autopsy. Dre, until we have some kind of final word on cause of death, I want you to cordon off the area and process the scene as if it's a homicide. Check out that fence line like Gwen said. Also, didn't you tell me you were doing some logging on the weekends?"

Dre nodded. "Mostly just working with small cuts, making firewood from slash piles, that kind of thing."

"Good," Dave said. "See what you can find out about any logging or Forest Service roads north of here. Gwen, can you sketch the woman's face here?"

"I could, but it's far more accurate to work off a tracing of the face. For example, the lips are missing . . ."

Beth's face was turning a strange shade of green.

"I'll get you the drawing the second I'm done," I quickly finished.

Dave shook hands with the farmer and Dr. Hawkins.

Dre started tying yellow crime-scene tape to the nearest fence. Dave hiked over to the calf carcass. Wes stood near the head and was scrawling notes on a small, spiral pad of paper.

"See something interesting?" Dave asked.

"Maybe." The man didn't look up.

Dave thought about Gwen's comments. When Wes arrived, he had walked past Dave's sedan at the McCandless place. The cell was lying in plain sight on the seat and the windows were down. A quick grab and toss and, presto, Dave and Gwen would have to surrender the case to Missoula. Time to put a bit of pressure on the Missoula police.

Gwen, Dr. Hawkins, and Beth joined them.

"Poor creature," Beth said. "Wolves are such vicious predators."

Wes cleared his throat. "Not really. Wolves are nature's balance."

"That doesn't look too balanced to me." Gwen nodded at the calf.

"Wolves prevent overpopulation of wildlife," Wes continued. "They often kill the weak and sickly."

Dr. Hawkins nodded. "You're saying survival of the fittest? That would apply to this calf. I had been treating it for a bad case of scours. I got worried when I didn't hear from the owner, decided to swing by. Was a seemingly well-bred calf but obviously the immune system wasn't functioning like it should. And as for that." He jerked his thumb at the carcass. "Wolves don't kill and eat. They eat. See the gouge marks on the ground from the calf's hoofs? This calf was eaten alive."

Beth turned and vomited again.

"Are you okay?" Dave asked.

"You promised not to puke," Gwen said to her. Beth shook her head.

Gwen looked at Dr. Hawkins. "How long do you think this wolf pack—"

"I don't think it's a wolf pack," Dr. Hawkins said. "I think it's a single wolf doing all the killing. Possibly two at the most."

Dave patted Beth on the back and continued to his car. If he had wolves killing people, he had a nightmare on his hands. But if this were somehow connected to Mattie Banks and the bodies they'd found at the McCandless farm . . . the nightmare was just starting.

CHAPTER SIXTEEN

IT WAS IMPOSSIBLE TO TURN AROUND WITH ALL the vehicles parked next to the field, so I drove past the burned-out farmhouse to where the road widened. A barn nestled against the hillside, its wood siding weathered to a deep umber.

"That's the barn you painted, isn't it?" Beth asked.

"Yeah." The wind had blown a few more cedar shakes off the roof, and old hay formed a brown rug in front of the door. "Did you know Wes said he was at my show? I bet he was trying to steal compositions. He's never had an original idea."

My friend looked at me strangely. "Did you know that your expression changed just now? You didn't even look like yourself."

I tried to laugh it off. "So what did I look like?"

Beth was silent for a moment. "I don't know. Not very attractive."

I gripped the steering wheel harder. "I earned the right to be angry. Wes stole my job." I explained about the gloves and my theory on Wes's involvement.

"But that's criminal. He should be arrested," Beth said.

"No proof. Yet. But I told Dave. And I think Dave agrees with me."

"So what are you going to do about it?"

"Me? Nothing. I leave heads-on-a-platter to Dave. I just need to get him my analysis. More importantly, I need to help identify this killer before he can murder someone else."

I turned the car around. As we drove past, neither of us looked toward the body in the field.

"I'm not sure when Robert's arriving tomorrow," I said.

"Don't worry. How about I keep your offspring overnight after the movie? That will give you plenty of time with your husband." She gave me a sideways glance.

"Ex-husband. Forget it, Beth. There's no way I'm getting back together with Robert."

"I was thinking more along the lines of forgiveness."

"Ha! That's a laugh. There's no way I'll ever forgive Robert. Not after all he's done to me."

"Forgiveness isn't for Robert's sake," Beth said quietly. "It's for yours."

The hot flash left me breathless for a moment. "That's easy for you to say, Beth. You've never been betrayed by your best friend. You've never sat in your living room, unable to get out of the chair, seeing your life in tatters. We were supposed to grow old together. I poured out my life to him . . . told him every-thing . . . my whole past." I made an effort to relax my death grip on the steering wheel. "I didn't mean to say all that. Sorry."

Neither of us spoke for a while. Finally Beth turned to me. "I'm sorry too. Maybe someday you'll share your past with me."

"Someday. When I know it's safe."

She looked at me strangely.

"Forget I said that. So, do you mind a quick detour?"

"Where to?"

"Two of the locations I painted for the show have turned up bodies. Why don't we take a quick peek at the remaining three?"

The first location was an old farmhouse and pole barn next to the county road. "I doubt our killer would want to be so close to traffic. He'd want privacy." We parked the car anyway, stepped over a chain barrier, and checked out both structures. A number of cars and trucks passed by, and all slowed to see what we were doing.

Finding nothing but dust, sagging timbers, and knee-high weeds, we moved on to the second site, a rustic log cabin in the woods.

The cabin was gone. In its place stood a brand-new home with labels still on all the windows and a roughed-in deck. The ground was churned-up mud from the bulldozer leveling the earth.

"I suspect if any bodies were around here, they would have shown up by now," Beth said.

"Um. Two down, one to go."

The final place looked promising. The road showed evidence of recent use, and the green metal gate was open. We pulled off the county road to the driveway that should have led to a tumbled-down structure next to a small stream.

The structure was still there, but a skid trail to the left ended with a landing of logs waiting to be transported to the mill.

"This won't work either," I said. "Loggers have been working here every day. Way too much traffic for a killer. So that leaves just the McCandless place and maybe the burned-out house as murder sites. I want to let that simmer in my brain for a bit."

"Let me know what you cook up. Cook up. Get it?" Beth grinned.

I rolled my eyes at her and headed home. As we entered the kitchen, a freshly showered Aynslee was sitting at the table, surrounded by crumpled paper from a notepad, her homeschool books, and her laptop. "Some guy called while you were away."

Beth and I looked at each other. "Did he leave a message?" I asked.

"No. Just said he wanted to talk to you. I finished my math."

I pulled up a chair next to her and caught a whiff of lilac perfume. The vision of the slaughtered calf lying next to the lilac bushes tainted the moment.

Beth, heading for the coffee pot, must have made the same connection. Her face paled. "Would you—"

"Yes. Aynslee, sweetheart, would you try to wash off the perfume you just put on?"

"I thought you liked it."

"Usually, but right now it reminds me of the case we just went out on," I said.

She shrugged and left the room.

"I read that odors trigger the strongest episodic memory," Beth said.

"Yes. I usually ask about scent in the course of a composite interview."

Aynslee returned, now smelling of soap, and sat down. "You said you'd look up the stuff on that priest case." She nodded at the subpoena.

Pulling the subpoena down, I moved to the counter and dialed the listed number.

"Prosecutor's office, how may I direct your call?"

"Hi. This is Gwen Marcey. I have a subpoena on a Jerome William Daly, case number—"

"Oh yeah. I know *that* one."

"Could you fill me in?" I pulled a small sketchbook and black Sharpie from the junk drawer at the end of the counter.

"You're the forensic artist, right?"

"Yes." I doodled a woman's face.

"It's a bombing and armed robbery in June, five years ago. You drew three of the suspects."

"My daughter kept calling it a priest case, but I remember the one you're referring to. I thought you caught someone pretty quickly, though." I added a blindfold to the sketch.

"Sort of. We caught Jerome Daly pretty quickly. Two others got in a shootout in Kellogg, then crashed while trying to escape. Double fatality. Some people believe there may have been a fourth, but we've never been able to confirm it."

"Why so long—"

"This has been a real roller coaster to bring to trial. The prosecutor quit and moved away. We had to have a continuance, then the lead investigator's son was murdered by a serial killer. Continuance. Then *he* committed suicide. Yet another continuance."

"Good grief. Has Jerome been in jail all this time?"

"No. He's been out on bail."

"Really?"

"He's not much of a threat," the clerk said. "Has all kinds

of medical problems. Can't even get out of bed. Anyway, we've scheduled the trial for the first week of June. Are you available?"

"Sure. Can I arrange to talk with the prosecutor or will there be a deposition?"

"I'll get back to you on that."

I gave her my phone number and hung up, then looked at my daughter. "It sounds like this could be interesting, so let me pull the file."

The three of us trooped into Robert's office where I opened the closet door. White storage boxes were stacked shoulder high.

"This is your filing system?" Beth asked.

"It works. One box per year." The box I needed was on the bottom. We rearranged everything, and I placed the container on the desk. My filing system was simple: first the year, then month, then numeric order. According to the clerk, I was looking for June of that year. I quickly found the thick, manila envelope and handed it to Aynslee, then returned the box to the closet. "Let me know if you have any questions."

Beth and I traipsed back to the studio. "I don't think we need these." I randomly opened the top book from Beth's library collection on profiling. "Active signature behaviors are methodical actions, such as repeated victim choices or specific injuries that represent a strong message meant to be understood by others."

I slammed the book shut. "Injuries. Why didn't I see that before?" Sitting at my computer, I soon found the selection of photographs I needed.

"What did you just think of?" Beth asked.

"I was so obsessed with Mattie's appearance that I overlooked the injuries to her hands. These are the photos of the bodies in the grave."

Beth leaned over my shoulder. "Ugh."

"I could see the hands of one of the bodies. It's . . . yeah, here." After enlarging the image, I examined it carefully. "Nothing." I leaned back in my chair. "It would have been helpful to have another signature."

"One that didn't involve a resemblance to your daughter."

I gave Beth a wry smile. "Yeah."

"What's that?" Beth pointed to a corner of the screen at something gray-white.

I enlarged the detail. It was rounded and partially hidden by a fold of moldering fabric. "A watch maybe?"

"Rotate it."

I gently manipulated the shape. "It's a compass." I printed out the image.

"What does it mean?" Beth asked.

"I don't know yet. I'll put it with the rest of the materials, then I think I'll get the drawing done of the girl in the cow pasture. I should have time to finish it today."

"Time!" Beth checked her watch. "Oh, I have to run. Date night with Norm. I'll call." She raced to the kitchen. After grabbing up her coat, emptied food containers, and lavender case, she gave me a quick hug and trotted to her SUV.

I locked the door after her, trying not to think about date nights, ex-husbands, and dead redheaded girls.

Shadows filled the house as a late-afternoon storm moved in. I turned lights on in the living room as I passed through on my way to the studio. *If this storm knocks out the power* . . . Before booting up my computer, I grabbed candles from under the studio sink and checked for another infestation of ants. Or worst yet, spiders. The temporary plywood bottom on the cabinet still reeked of insecticide from spraying it earlier. Good. I jotted *caulk* on a lime-green Post-it Note and stuck it to the wall above the sink.

After downloading the dead girl's photo onto my computer, I selected the best angle and printed out an eight-by-ten with her face scaled to a six-by-four-inch format. On a hunch I printed the photo of the ripped part of my map found in her hand. I placed the photo of her face on a light box, taped it down, and laid a clean sheet of Bristol board over the top. When I clicked on the light, I could clearly see the girl's torn and battered image.

I carefully traced as much of the undamaged image as possible, adjusting to account for her injuries and decomposition. I could see her eyes were not deep set or bulging. The shape of the eyelids would need to remain average and her eyes were closed. The tip of her nose was pointed and the width somewhat narrow. I guessed at the shape of her lips but could place them accurately using her teeth.

Two hours later I'd finished her drawing. I taped it to the window next to the photo of Aynslee and the sketch of Mattie.

A tremor raced up my spine. The three images could have been sisters.

"Mom?" Aynslee called from down the hall.

Hastily I pulled the drawings and photo down. "Yes?"

"What's for dinner?"

I glanced outside. The inky darkness reflected back my own image. A gust of wind sprayed raindrops against the window. I hoped Dre finished mopping up any evidence at the cow pasture.

Turning the drawings facedown on my drafting table, I flipped off the studio lights and strolled to the kitchen.

Aynslee was inspecting the contents of the refrigerator. "Bread. Eggs. Jelly. Mountain Dew."

"No milk?"

"Nope. Guess that rules out tuna noodle casserole." She walked into the pantry and opened the chest freezer. "Pizza or chicken pot pie?"

"Chicken pot pie. You start the oven." I sat on the floor and opened the cupboard. "Canned green beans, corn, peas, or . . . quartered artichoke hearts?"

"Huh?"

"I think this was from when Beth was trying to teach me to cook. How about corn?"

"Yeah."

I stood and found a saucepan. "How goes the research paper?"

"Good. It wasn't a priest case like I told you."

"I thought not."

"I mean, that was only part of the name. It was the Phineas Priesthood."

CHAPTER SEVENTEEN

OVER DINNER, AYNSLEE CAUGHT ME UP ON HER homework. "The newspapers said that the guys you drew were part of a Phineas Priesthood group. They robbed banks and did other stuff. I looked up the Phineas Priesthood, and guess what?"

"I give up."

"They're like Nazis and Hitler and stuff."

"What?"

"Yeah. They even celebrate Hitler's birthday, April 20. There was some stuff about the 'Fourteen Words,' but I didn't get that part."

I jumped up from the table and snatched up the phone. Beth answered on the second ring. "That pamphlet I gave you. From the church."

"It's right here. I haven't had time to read it yet. We just walked in the door. The . . . ah . . . American Christian Covenant Church. What about it?"

"Where are they located?"

"South of Missoula. About ten miles away from us."

"Do they list service times?"

"Yes. Sundays at eleven."

"I'm going to have Aynslee send you some information. I need you to put that ole research brain of yours to work."

"Let me guess." I could hear the grin in her voice. "We're all going to church on Sunday. But not our usual one."

"Not quite. We're all going to church, but not the same one."

"Not fair, Gwen. I thought I was your partner."

"You are. That's why you're keeping Aynslee safe and away from the Bible-and-swastika crowd."

"Speaking of Bibles and research, don't forget to prepare your Bible study for this next week. Given who's coming to visit tomorrow . . ."

"What—"

Beth hung up.

As if I didn't have enough on my mind. I looked at Aynslee. "Would you e-mail your research to Beth?"

"Sure. It took me forever to read it. I wish I could be a speed-reader like Beth."

"That's a learnable skill. Why don't you look into it?"

"Okay. I already printed out some of the stuff I thought you'd like to look at. It's on your desk." Aynslee stood and grabbed her dirty dishes. "Mom?"

"What, sweetheart?"

"These people." She took her dishes to the sink, rinsed them, then put them in the dishwasher. "Is there a chance, I mean, would they hurt you? Like last time?" She turned and faced me. "The stuff I read. They seem to hate a lot of people."

"Oh." I quickly joined her and put an arm around her. "Don't

146

worry." I gave her a quick hug. "They think differently than we do, that's all."

"But one of the articles said that hate groups have gotten bigger by over fifty percent."

I hugged her again, this time a bit harder. "Did the article say why?"

"The economy, and immigration, and stuff like that. They're afraid of the government."

"*Hmm*. That's not so—"

"They call it the 'Zion Occupied Government,' and say that the white race is being overrun and diluted by nonwhites."

"Okay, that's different. You'll have a lot to write about in your paper." Dinner solidified into a lump in my stomach. "I'll clean up. You go ahead and work on your homework."

"Deal." She moved toward her room. "What are we doing tomorrow?"

"I have some work to do." I finished cleaning the table, placing my dishes with hers in the dishwasher. "Beth will be by to pick you up for the movie in Copper Creek, and she's invited you to spend the night."

"Really? That'll be fun."

She skipped from the room. I tried to remember the last time I'd gone to a movie with a friend. And the last time I'd skipped from a room.

The earlier downpour slowed, then stopped. I started the dishwasher and headed down the hall, pausing outside of Aynslee's bedroom door. All was silent. I peeked in. She was sitting on the bed, earbuds on, and typing on her laptop.

I picked up my Bible, notepad, and pencil from the end table by my bed, then returned to the kitchen. Pulling down the Scripture verse magnet, I said a quick prayer. "Lord, inspire me, show me what is Your will in presenting this topic to the women's group." I looked up Colossians 3:13.

"'Make allowance for each other's faults, and forgive anyone who offends you. Remember, the Lord forgave you, so you must forgive others.'"

"You're kidding me, Beth. I'm supposed to talk about forgiveness?" Jumping up, I slammed my Bible shut. "You'll have to find another presenter."

I stalked down the hall, entered Robert's office, and turned on the lights. My gaze roamed around the masculine, green-plaid walls and stark window treatment. I squeezed my hands into fists. *This is not Robert's office. He's gone. Never coming back. Now it's my room. My space.* Walking to the center of the room, I slowly turned around. I could set this up like a task-force room. With visuals and case files. The first chance I got, I'd paint it pink.

When Robert comes tomorrow, he'll see no sign he'd ever lived here.

After shoving the desk away from the windows and to the right side of the room, I took the folding chair into my studio and returned with the leather desk chair.

From the supply closet in my studio, I yanked an uncut piece of white, thirty-by-forty-inch foam core, the material I used for the backing when I framed artwork. I took it into my office. Returning to the studio, I picked up tape, the drawings, and a portable easel.

After taping the drawings and notes to the board, I found a county map in the kitchen junk drawer and added it to the display. Three brightly colored pushpins marked where we'd found bodies and Mattie. The list of known and unknowns completed the display. The space was looking like a regular investigation room. *Better.*

Dave's question was a good one. Using a black Sharpie, I wrote *Why me?* on the board.

Returning to my studio for notepaper, I found Aynslee's research on my desk. The top sheet was a printout of the front page of the Spokane newspaper, dated five years earlier.

I gasped.

Dave leaned back in his chair and closed his eyes. It was late, and silence replaced the normal hum of voices. With budget cuts, officers out sick, and now these new cases, he was scrambling to have the county covered. At least the state crime lab completed their work on the McCandless farm and released the scene, so the officer directing traffic could be reassigned.

Once Gwen brought him the sketch of the Jane Doe in the pasture, he'd get Craig to check out missing persons and maybe release the drawing to the press.

He glanced at the program on his computer screen. Dre would be putting in for overtime, Gwen needed to be paid, and he'd need to bring in everyone to work on that torchlight parade, so his budget was already in the toilet, and it was only mid-April.

He could have an open hunting season if the autopsy proved wolves killed that girl. He already had a serial killer preying on women. It could be coincidence, but Dave didn't really believe in coincidences.

Pinching away the looming headache, he reached for his

pen. A delicate, rose-decorated cup of cooling tea rested beside his elbow. He shoved it away.

Gwen thought Wes was the culprit in throwing his cell phone into the bushes so he could take over the forensic work on the McCandless farm murders. He wrote *Call Jeannie and reporter* on the yellow legal pad in front of him.

The phone rang.

"Dre here. Just finished up with the body in the field. Gwen was right about her smacking into the barbed-wire fence. We found some torn material down a bit from the body."

Dave jotted a note. "I'll call Search and Rescue first thing in the morning to see if they can get a hound to track her route."

"Good luck on that. We just had a real frogwash of a rain."

"We'll at least give it a try. Go on home and get some sleep."

"You too."

P̶

The symbol seemed to leap from the paper. A capital letter *P* with a line through it.

The headlines above screamed "Terrorist Suspects Identified." I read the article as I slowly walked to the office.

The FBI revealed today the identity of two men who died last week in a traffic accident in Kellogg, Idaho, while fleeing from the scene of a shootout with police.

Kenneth Allen Weeks and Peter Lowell Evans opened fire on patrol officer Mike Higgins, then attempted to flee. They were struck by a logging truck driven by Harold Patton of

St. Maries at the I-90 Division Street on-ramp. Patton was treated and released. Weeks and Evans were pronounced dead at the scene.

After the two men rented a house on Mission Street, one neighbor noticed a "striking resemblance" between the men and sketches released in the search for suspects in the fatal bombing of a Planned Parenthood site.

The composites, drawn by well-known Montana forensic artist Gwen Marcey, have been circulated by area police asking for the public's help in identifying the suspects. The neighbor called police, and when Officer Higgins showed up, the men opened fire.

Wincing at the mention of my name, I skipped down and resumed reading.

Weeks and Evans were part of Spokane's Phineas Priesthood cell, part of the Christian Identity movement.

I knew that symbol. The piece of paper under the dead cat, still in the plastic bag resting on the window ledge, contained the smeared Phineas Priesthood mark.

But I was missing something. I'd seen that symbol, or a part of it, one other time.

Picking up a pencil, I twirled it in my fingers as I walked around the room, pausing by the downloaded images from the body in the cow pasture. Of course. The scrap of map in the girl's hand. In the far corner was a hand-drawn shape. A portion of the Priesthood symbol.

Taking the article, newspaper, and photo of the map with

me, I trotted down the hall to the office. After taping everything to the foam core, I stepped back.

Why would an old Phineas Priesthood bombing case in Washington be connected to a serial killer in Montana? I drew the composites on the Priesthood case, but I'd basically been thrown off the local serial killings. And Dave's question still remained. *Why me?* I shook my head, then pulled my sweater closer. Robert's—no, *my* new office felt cold and smelled musty. Tomorrow I'd air out the room.

Sitting at the desk, I stared at the display, but nothing connected. Absently I tried the desk drawers one by one. A lined notepad, an empty tissue box, a broken stapler, a crumpled piece of paper, and a writer's magazine featuring Robert on the cover. I stacked everything on top of the desk, then propped Robert's face against the box. Smoothing out the paper, I recognized a list I'd thrown in Robert's face during our last, epic fight. I'd written down every terrible thing he'd ever said or done to me.

The bottom drawer yielded a pistol. I pulled it out and placed it in front of me. I remembered Robert buying it on a whim.

Memories flooded my brain, whirling around, making me clench my teeth. When will I stop thinking about him? When will he no longer have the power to hurt me?

"I really want to hurt you," I said to Robert's image on the magazine cover.

I took a deep breath, held it, then let it out slowly. A massive yoke seemed to settle on my shoulders. I crossed my arms on the desk, rested my forehead on them, and closed my eyes.

A soft hand touched me.

I jerked upright.

Aynslee stood in the doorway, face pale. Beth was standing beside me. Early-morning sun streamed through the window.

"Musta fallen asleep." My brain was as muddied as a gouache painting. I ran my tongue over my teeth, wondering if someone had left a dirty sock in my mouth.

"Did you hear me?" Beth asked quietly. "Gwen. It can't be that bad."

"What?"

"Please, just give me the gun." She slowly reached for the pistol I still had in my hand.

"You mean this?" I aimed the pistol at Robert's image and pulled the trigger.

CHAPTER EIGHTEEN

BETH SCREAMED.

A stream of water splashed across his printed face.

"Aahhh!" Beth danced away. "You're crazy, you know that? You scared me to death!"

Aynslee giggled. "You should have seen the look on your face, Beth."

"You imp." Beth pointed at my daughter. "You *knew* it was a squirt gun."

Aynslee stopped giggling and slowly turned around. "Hey. You moved Dad's desk. And you put a lot of stuff in here."

I stood and gently placed the water pistol on the desk. "It's now my office. I . . . uh, I'm going to move my computer in here." I checked Aynslee's expression, then Beth's. "And I'm going to paint it pink."

Aynslee chewed her lower lip as she completed her inspection of the room. A glance at me, then she wordlessly left.

I raised my eyebrows at Beth.

"Well, *I* like the idea. And it's about time. Plus, I have a friend I've wanted you to meet—"

"Oh no. I'm not ready for the dating scene. It's taken me almost two years to get this far."

"Okay, okay, just saying."

"Give me a minute to take a shower and get dressed, then I need to show you something."

"And I need to show *you* something," Beth said.

"Mattie, I'm Dr. Haller."

Mattie focused on his face, but the morphine shot made her eyes bounce every time she blinked.

"You're going to be fine," the doctor said. "We x-rayed your hands and have immobilized your fractures with a splint for now. We want you to see a specialist, though, because of your arthritis. We'll be transferring you to Missoula soon. Do you understand what I'm saying?"

Mattie nodded.

The doctor smiled, then quietly closed the door, leaving Mattie in semidarkness. She bit her lip and tried to concentrate. She'd have to leave, escape from the hospital. But how? A policeman was right outside the door. He was supposed to be guarding her, but *he'd* found a way in. She'd just have to wait for her chance.

Once showered and dressed in jeans, a white cotton tee, and a denim shirt, I followed my nose to the kitchen. Beth, wearing a merino wool turtleneck and matching royal blue trousers, bent over the stove stirring something deliciously fragrant.

Aynslee hovered over the toaster. "She's making eggs Benedict."

"I could get used to this." I poured a cup of freshly brewed coffee and moved to the window to check the weather. Sunshine poked between gray-edged clouds, and a breeze sent the pine boughs waving.

"It's hard to sleuth on an empty stomach." Beth deftly assembled the toasted English muffins, Canadian bacon, and poached eggs, then drizzled the hollandaise sauce over the top. With Aynslee's help, she placed the three plates on the table next to my Bible, blank paper, and Scripture magnet.

I sat down and avoided Beth's gaze. I could feel my face growing warm.

"Dear Father," Beth began. I gratefully bowed my head. "Bless this meal, and send a special blessing to Gwen, that she may discern the path You would want her to take. Amen."

"Amen." I kept my head down until I felt the hue of my face return to normal.

"This is so good," Aynslee said around a mouthful of egg. "Will you adopt me?"

"Only if you bring your dog and clean your room." Beth grinned at my daughter. My shoulders relaxed, and I smiled slightly at Beth. We finished and left a reluctant Aynslee to clean up.

I led Beth into the office and pointed to the foam-core display.

She touched the Phineas Priesthood symbol and nodded at me, then examined the drawings of the girls. "All this should be enough to convince everyone that you need to talk to Mattie and draw that composite, right?"

"It's circumstantial at this point. And I need to figure out a few more things."

"Now my turn." Beth left and returned with a canvas bag holding six books. "These were all that the library offered, but I got more off the Internet." She stacked the books next to the previous day's selections, then added a computer printout. On the top she placed the pamphlet she'd taken the day before. *The* Brüder Schweigen *Declaration of War.*

I picked up the pamphlet. "You've had a chance to look at this more?"

"Yes. The *Declaration of War* part was written by Robert Jay Mathews, killed in a shootout with the FBI in 1984. He was the leader of The Order, a white separatist movement. The back of the pamphlet is about the church and the upcoming torchlight parade."

"I see. And these . . ." I lifted each book in turn. "*The Turner Diaries, The Phineas Priesthood, Christian Identity, Aryan Nations.* Charming reading material."

Beth took the pamphlet, selected a book, opened it to a bookmarked page, then sank into the desk chair. "Listen to this. 'We must secure the existence of our people and a future for white children.'"

"What?"

"That's a quote from David Lane, a buddy of Robert Jay Mathews." She waved the pamphlet again. "In the white separatist's movement, it's called 'the Fourteen Words.'"

"He's—"

"Dead. Died in prison. But his words, all words, have power. Proverbs 12:6 says in part, 'The words of the wicked are like a murderous ambush.' What is written in these"—she touched the books she'd brought—"may be driving our killer. But before I tell you more, first tell me I'm brilliant, clever, and a permanent partner."

"You're brilliant. The rest I'll hold until you tell me what you found."

"I'm going to demonstrate how clever I am. First of all, the symbol of the Phineas Priesthood—"

"I already made that connection."

"I saw that, but there's more. You told me Mattie repeated the numbers twenty-five and six. But what she really meant was Numbers 25:6. Ta-da!"

"You've lost it."

She lifted a sheet of paper. "I downloaded this. In this chapter in Numbers, the people of Israel were having sexual relations with the Midianites, a pagan-worshipping group. God sent a plague as punishment. Though the Phineas priests *say* Numbers 25:6 as a kind of tagline, the important part to them is verses seven and eight. 'And when Phinehas, the son of Eleazar, the son of Aaron the priest, saw it, he rose up from among the congregation, and took a javelin in his hand; And he went after the man of Israel into the tent, and thrust both of them through, the man of Israel, and the woman through her belly. So the plague was stayed from the children of Israel.'"

"And—"

"I'm not done. The Phineas priests also point to Psalms 106 where Phinehas's action was 'counted to him as righteousness from generation to generation forever.' The group considers this evidence that God approves of vigilante actions to prevent the mixing of the races. This is not a good crowd to mess with. And you"—she pointed to a computer printout—"made front-page news by stopping them."

I carefully placed my pencil in the desk. "I didn't personally stop them, but go on."

Beth turned toward me and held up the pamphlet. "The killer's declared war on you." She nodded at the piece of paper found under the cat. "He believes he's on a mission from God for revenge."

"Gwen Marcey will be coming by," Dave said to the sole dispatch operator. "Buzz her in when she gets here." The officer nodded. Dave continued through the nearly deserted sheriff's department to his office. He'd barely sat behind his desk when Gwen burst through carrying a large sheet of foam core. Beth and Aynslee were right behind.

"So what's so all-fired-up important that I had to give up a perfectly good Saturday?" Dave asked.

Gwen perched the foam core against a chair. "This is."

He stood and moved closer to study the display. "Okay. What does it mean?"

Beth cleared her throat. "Let me start at the beginning. This mark, the letter *P* combined with a cross, is the symbol of the Phineas Priesthood."

Dave sat back down and crossed his arms. "I see."

"You recognize this from the piece of paper found on the dead girl in the cow pasture," Gwen said. "And on a piece of paper found under a dead cat."

"The one found on your doorstep," Dave said.

"Yes." Gwen held up a plastic bag. "The cat was mauled to death."

"Okay, and speaking of dead, did you finish that drawing?"

"It's here." Gwen pointed. "And we'll get to that. A member of the Phineas Priesthood is stalking me, and I think he's choosing victims that look like Aynslee—"

"Whoa, slow down. You're saying a priest is after you?"

"Don't picture a Jesuit in Roman collar or black cassock. These guys are part of the Christian Identity movement."

"Ah," Dave said. "More Presbyterian than Catholic."

"Very funny, Dave," Gwen said.

"I'm not following all this."

Beth shook her head. "Christian Identity covers a range of beliefs and is more along the lines of the Ku Klux Klan, Posse Comitatus, the Aryan Nations, and The Order."

Dave furrowed his brows. "Dad told me about the troubles in the nineties with the Militia of Montana. I knew we had a resurgence, with all the brochures showing up around town. And the torchlight parade's tomorrow."

"Technically, most militia groups are not part of the Christian Identity movement," Beth said. "They deal with gun control and the federal government, but the founders of the Militia of Montana also carried anti-Semitic views. I wouldn't be surprised if there's a connection."

"Of all the Christian Identity groups, the Phineas priests are unique in that they believe they were chosen to be God's executioners," Gwen said.

Dave raised his eyebrows. "Where did you get—"

Beth placed a small stack of papers on his desk. "Here's some of my research. I found the background fascinating."

"I'm sure you did," Dave said.

Beth tapped the papers. "This movement roughly originated in the British-Israel doctrines from the nineteenth century. The core foundation is that the ten lost tribes of Israel are the Anglo-Saxons."

"Not the Jews," Aynslee added.

Dave nodded.

"The concept moved from Britain to America where racial and anti-Semitic beliefs were added," Beth said.

"You won't believe this part." Aynslee leaned forward.

"At their most extreme end," Beth said, "they teach that Adam and Eve begat the white race, Eve and Satan begat the Jews, and people of color were subhuman 'mud people,' created before Adam and Eve and are without redemption. Basically, the idea is that race, not grace, defines salvation."

"I get the background and history. I'm hoping that somewhere in here you're going to tell me how all this relates to Gwen, a dead cat, and a girl killed by a wolf."

"We're getting there." Gwen waved her hand impatiently.

"What makes this group different," Beth said, "is that they have no structure, no meetings, no leadership. You don't join. You *become* a Phineas priest by your actions, which include bank robbery, bombings, murder, and arson—"

"And mauled cats and wolf attacks?" Dave grinned.

"You're interrupting." Gwen cleared her throat. "All that is directed at the government, people of color, Jews, homosexuals, and abortion clinics."

"You said they were after you. But you don't work for the government, you're white, Protestant, heterosexual, and not pregnant."

Gwen narrowed her eyes at him.

"If I may continue." Beth stood straighter. "The movement lost ground for a time, but two events happened in the 1990s that fueled their resurgence."

Gwen leaned on his desk. "The siege at Ruby Ridge in Idaho, and the standoff with the Branch Davidians at Waco, Texas—both involving the US government."

"Off the desk," Dave said.

Gwen straightened. "Louise needs to make you some anti-grumpy tea."

"I'm waiting for you to get to the point." Dave tapped a finger on his desk.

"Now we get to the good part," Beth said. "After the two events, the Christian Identity and militias increased in members. You just mentioned one example of this, the Militia of Montana."

Dave nodded.

"This little book"—she held up a tattered volume—"was one of the triggers for additional incidents."

"It's *The Turner Diaries*," Aynslee said.

"I see that," Dave said.

"But did you *read* it?" Beth asked. "It's a work of fiction about a future war between a small group of white people and the Jewish-controlled government. The book describes how a man filled a delivery truck with about five thousand pounds of ammonium-nitrate fertilizer and fuel oil, drove to a government building, and blew it up."

"Timothy McVeigh used that book as a template for the Oklahoma City bombing," Gwen whispered. "And the book was presented as evidence at McVeigh's trial."

"Yes, and the date of the bombing was April 19, the same date as the final assault at Waco."

Dave stood and looked closer at the display. "April 19. Tomorrow. The day before Hitler's birthday. And the day of the torchlight parade." He swallowed hard.

"Something big's going down, Dave," Gwen said.

"What really scares me," Beth said, "is a somewhat obscure fact. April 19 has another connotation to the Christian Identity. It's considered the martyrs' day. A sacred day connected to acts of resistance and sacrificial death." Her face flushed with emotion.

"Law enforcement has associated the actions of such people as McVeigh, the Unabomber, and Eric Rudolph—the Atlanta Olympic Park bomber—with the Phineas priests," Gwen said.

The room seemed smaller, and Dave tugged his collar open to get more air. He sat, took out a yellow legal pad, and looked at Gwen. "So how are you connected to all this?"

"I did some composites that resulted in the arrest of one of them and the death of two more," Gwen said. "Some of the material I read indicated there was a fourth member of the Spokane Phineas Priesthood cell. He's . . . targeting me."

"Do you have any idea who this Phineas priest is?" he asked.

"No. Not yet. But I intend to find out—"

"No. I want you to steer clear of this whole group." Dave put down his pen. "Go stay with Beth. At least until after the twentieth. I don't have the manpower to protect you until after this torchlight parade."

Her expression said he was wasting his breath. "Right. That's what I thought. You're not going to listen to me." He looked at the foam board again. "At least connect a Montana serial killer, a Phineas Priesthood cell, and a girl killed by a rogue wolf."

"We left out that part," Gwen said. "I don't know how he did it, but do you know what the Phineas Priesthood calls their strategy?"

"What?"

"Lone Wolf."

CHAPTER NINETEEN

"HERE." DAVE GRABBED SOME PAPERS OUT OF his in-box. "Since you're determined to work on this." He handed the papers to Gwen. "You asked about the Spokane serial killings when we were at the McCandless farm. They faxed over what they had. Please leave it to me to look into the Phineas Priesthood angle."

I took the materials from him and started for the door.

"I mean it, Gwen. You need to stay clear and stay safe," Dave called after me.

Once we reached the sidewalk outside, Beth grabbed my arm. "Are you going to do what Dave said?"

"Half of it. Stay safe."

"Are you sure—"

"Whose side are you on?"

"How can you ask me that? I'm your partner, sidekick, Friday to your Robinson Crusoe."

I strolled toward my parked car. "Okay, Friday, let's go to work."

Dave leaned back in his chair and studied the display propped against the wall. The murmuring of the dispatch operator into her headphone in the other room and the buzzing florescent light overhead provided background noise. He picked up the phone. "Yeah, FBI? I need to speak to an agent. This is Sheriff Dave Moore."

The phone clicked. "How can we help you, Sheriff?"

"I was wondering if you guys were tracking any Phineas Priesthood activities in this area or know anything about a church called, uh, just a minute . . ." Dave found the brochure. "The American Christian Covenant Church?"

"We haven't heard of any Phineas Priesthood members around here. Do you have something for us?"

"I might."

"We'll have someone contact you in the morning. On that church, I assume you're calling about their torchlight parade."

"You know about it?"

The agent chuckled. "Yeah. We've been keeping an eye on them. We have no creditable threat at this time, but if previous parades are any indication, you'll need a lot of police presence to keep the peace."

"Yeah. I already figured that out. Thanks." Dave hung up.

His gaze lingered on the Phineas Priesthood symbol. "What are you planning?"

"What are you going to do, Gwen?" Beth slipped into the passenger seat.

"Fit the last pieces of the puzzle together. I still have one more drawing I can finish." I started the car.

"The skull Winston found?" Beth asked.

"Right."

We didn't speak as we drove through wisps of fog floating near the ground, like tattered sails in the still air. The sullen clouds blocked the tops of the mountains and crowded the scenery. Headlights from the few passing cars dimly glowed like jaundiced eyes through the mist.

"This is interesting." Beth looked up from the papers in her lap.

"What is?"

"The materials Dave handed you. The police reports on the Spokane serial killings."

"Would you follow up on it?"

Beth's eyes lighted up. "Absolutely. Will we work at your studio? Do I need additional files? Are we going undercover? Do I need a gun?"

"Yes. Maybe. No. You can borrow mine if you bring your own bullets."

"Gwen!" Her face flushed. "Why do you answer me like that? I can't follow what you're saying."

"I'm teaching you how to ask questions one at a time and wait for the answer. A good interview technique. And besides, I couldn't resist."

We arrived home, unlocked the door, and moved to the studio. Stagnant air greeted us, and I cracked open a window. The room soon filled with the scent of wet grass and flowering bushes.

Aynslee paused in the doorway.

"Homework," I said.

"Oh, Mom—"

"Don't 'oh, Mom' me. I want it done. Remember, you're going to a movie with Beth this afternoon."

"We'll make it dinner and a movie," Beth said. "You'll dine at my house."

"Mom said I could spend the night."

"Yes, it's all worked out," Beth said. "What's the movie?"

"*Beverly Hills Chihuahua 2.*"

I tried not to look at my friend. Beth sniffed once, then settled at the computer.

"This is what I need you to do," I said. "We've linked the Phineas Priesthood to these murders here in Copper Creek."

"The symbol and Numbers 25:6. Right."

"Now I want you to find a connection between Spokane's Phineas Priesthood case and here."

"That missing fourth member. That makes sense."

"Also, see if there's any link with that old Spokane serial killing and the present murders here."

Beth nodded.

"But before you start your research, could you print out some digitals for me?" I pointed to the images, and Beth soon had them ready. I took the photos of the cranium and mandible and scaled them to the same size. Placing the cranium on my light table, I cut out the mandible and arranged it in the correct location, then placed a piece of velum over the top and taped everything down. Normally I would have prepared for a two-dimensional reconstruction by applying tissue depth markers—erasers from an electric erasing machine cut to precise lengths. They would then be glued to the skull, but I no longer had the skull. Jeannie had whisked it away before I'd had a chance to do anything with it. Now I'd have to rely on the metric ruler I'd placed in the photo and the measurements I'd noted.

The printer clacked into life and soon churned out a mound of papers.

"Are you printing out a manuscript?"

"You did ask for research." She collected the pile of papers, sat at my desk, and tapped them into an orderly stack. "This all was most interesting."

"Yes?"

Beth pulled her purse closer and rummaged through the depths before tugging out a lavender-and-white cube of Post-it Notes.

"Beth?"

She continued to look in her purse, placed it on the floor, then pulled out the top drawer of my desk. "Do you have a highlighter?"

"On your left."

"That's yellow. Do you have a purple or—"

"No. I'm waiting."

She ruffled through the stack, pausing to apply a lavender tab or highlight a line.

"I'm growing old here. Could you share your results in my lifetime?"

"*Hmm.* Almost done."

I gave up and went back to my sketch.

"Okay, okay, okay." She again tapped the heap of paper into order. "The only thing everything has in common is you."

"Define 'everything.'"

"First of all, there's the serial killer here in Copper Creek. You were lured to Mattie Banks and found the grave. You return and find a piece of paper with a Phineas Priesthood symbol under a dead cat. The two events *could* be unrelated, but Mattie told you the numbers and you found the symbol on the map someone took from your show. I don't know yet if the church pamphlets and the torchlight parade are part of this or not."

"Okay."

"You drew three composites on the Phineas Priesthood case in Spokane several years ago, and you tried to draw a composite on the Spokane serial killings."

"Not so surprising. I work on a lot of cases. Make that past tense." Opening the book *Forensic Guide to Facial Reconstruction*, I found the charts for an average weight, European-Caucasian female.

"There is an interesting connection I didn't expect to find." She selected a lavender tab and peered at the page. "The son of the lead detective on the Phineas Priesthood case was a victim of the Spokane serial killer."

I paused in my drawing. "That's what the clerk said on the phone, but I hadn't really thought about it." *Coincidence?* "Remind me, you said I *tried* to do a composite on the Spokane serial killings."

Beth shuffled the papers for a moment. "This report doesn't say why. Just that you were called in but no composite was drawn." She marked something with the highlighter.

The phone rang. "Hello?" I said.

"Is this Gwen Marcey, the forensic artist?" a male voice asked.

"Yes."

"Ms. Marcey, you don't know me, but I have some information you need."

"Oh? What information?"

Who is it? Beth mouthed.

I shrugged at her.

"Not over the phone." The man cleared his throat. "I need to meet with you. In person."

Yeah. Right, Mr. Serial Killer. I resisted the urge to laugh at him. "You'll need to tell me what this is in reference to."

The man didn't speak for a few moments. "Did you recently get a subpoena on a case out of Spokane? A case involving the Phineas Priesthood?"

Goose pimples prickled my neck. "Who is this?"

"My name is Scott Thomas. I was supposed to prosecute the case."

"The clerk I spoke to on the phone mentioned a prosecutor. You're the one who left town?"

"Yes."

"I did receive a subpoena."

He didn't speak for a moment. "Do you have a child? A daughter?"

I gripped the phone tighter. "Why?"

"I heard about the dump site and young girl on television, did some calling around, then drove down from Medicine Hat, Alberta, to talk to you. But not over the phone. Not to sound melodramatic, but you and your daughter are in great danger."

I leaned on the desk, my legs suddenly weak. "Why can't you tell me over the phone?"

"I need to give you something."

"Put it in the mail. Or UPS. Or FedEx."

"You wouldn't get it in time. And time is something we don't have."

"Where and when?"

"Tonight. Ten thirty. There's an all-night restaurant north of you on Highway 93. A town called Florence—"

"I know it."

"Country Inn. Make sure you aren't followed."

"How will I know you?"

"I'll know you." The line went dead.

My hand shook slightly as I hung up. "Could you keep Aynslee a bit longer tomorrow? It could be a late night, but I may get some more answers to our questions."

"Sure. And since I won't see you before church, you be careful at that service tomorrow."

"Yeah." I explained what I had planned for the following day.

"Are you taking your gun tonight?"

I made a wry face at her. "My choices are a bit limited right now. I can go into the café with a pink camouflage rifle and be laughed out of the building by the locals, or I can be Barney Fife and take my SIG Sauer with the single bullet."

Before Beth could answer, Aynslee entered with a backpack. "Mom, Beth, if we're going to eat before the movie . . . ?"

I checked my watch. "I didn't realize it was so late."

"I've put my notes on your desk," Beth said.

"Thanks, Beth." I trailed after the two and locked the door behind them. The house suddenly felt cold and empty, I retrieved an old, snaggy sweater from my bedroom.

Returning to my studio, I clicked on the radio for company, then continued to work on the facial reconstruction. Measuring down nine millimeters from the frontozygomatic suture, I placed a dot. A second dot on my paper marked the lacrimal crest. I drew a line between the two points to place the eye, then used a circle template to draw the iris.

I calculated the upper and lower lip thickness by measuring the teeth, and marked a point between the first premolar-canine junction. Sketching in the wings five millimeters outside of the nasal aperture, I roughed in her nose. Her face took shape under my rapidly moving pencil. A face I knew very well.

She looked like my daughter.

"The signature, Dave!"

Dave held the phone away from his ear to keep from going deaf.

"There's absolutely no doubt of it," Gwen said. "I know his signature."

"Whoa, hold on, Gwen. You don't need to shout. I appreciate yours and Beth's research, but you're not becoming a rookie sleuth and trying to solve this on your own. I told you I'd take care of it." He took a sip of the tea, then quickly spit it into the garbage.

"But there's another body that looks like Aynslee. I need to interview Mattie Banks. She's the key, and I'm the only one who can draw the face of this killer. I just finished sketching the woman in the grave at the McCandless farm—"

"Wait, stop right there! Who authorized you to reconstruct that face?"

"Well—"

"And why are you even thinking about Mattie Banks?"

"Because—"

"Both those cases are under Missoula's jurisdiction for now.

Under no circumstances do I want you within a country mile of Mattie or anything to do with the McCandless farm. Do I make myself clear?"

Click, then a dial tone.

Dave dry-washed his face, stood, and moved to the display. He removed the original sketch of the Jane Doe from the cow pasture, slipped it into a large envelope, and wrote Craig's name on it. Craig could work on the girl's identity. After looking up the number, he dialed Jeannie. The call went to voice mail. He left a message to call him.

Tugging out the duty roster, he checked to see who he had to work the torchlight parade. The answer was grim. He didn't have a spare officer to keep an eye on Gwen. He'd have to convince her to find a safe place to stay until Monday. Otherwise, she was on her own.

CHAPTER TWENTY

AFTER COPYING THE RECONSTRUCTION, I TUGGED
another piece of foam core from the closet, took it to my office,
and taped up the sketch. I added duplicates of the other drawings
across the top of the board, a photo of Aynslee, then sat at my
desk. I'd attached my county map to the display I'd given Dave,
but I might have a second one. Tapping a pencil against the drafting table, I searched my brain.

I'd used a county map when I did the art show.

Returning to the studio, I moved to the center of the room
and stared at the bookshelves against the wall. Below were cupboards containing art supplies.

Map. Flat. With miscellaneous papers? I opened a cupboard
and pulled out a black zippered portfolio underneath a stack of
cut mats. A map was in the second divider. I took it to the office,
opened it, and taped it to the foam core.

Someone knocked at the front door.

I jumped, knocking a tray of drawing tools off the desk and

to the floor. *Doggone it!* I'd just shattered the graphite in every pencil. Leaving the mess, I charged to the door and peeked out.

Robert.

The hot flash shot up my neck and onto my face. I leaned against the wall until it passed.

Robert knocked again, harder.

I fluffed my short hair, then yanked open the door. Robert froze, arm still raised to knock again. "Well. Hi. I wasn't sure you heard me."

He looked good. He'd had his hair styled, and his shoulders looked fuller, as if he'd been working out. His nails were professionally trimmed, and he smelled of expensive cigar.

I put my hands behind my back. "Come in."

Robert sauntered to the center of the room and slowly turned in a circle, staring as if he'd never seen the furnishings before. Aynslee'd left a half-filled glass of soda on the rustic end table. The sofa, a massive leather monstrosity Robert fell in love with years ago, showed stains where I'd dropped a glass of red wine last year. My torn gray sweatshirt draped over an antique Eastlake chair, and muddy shoes peered from under the battered cedar chest that served as a coffee table. "What do you want, Robert?" My voice sounded strained. "Are you back for the last of your stuff?"

"No, I got it all last time. Besides, the access door to the attic is broken."

I strolled to the hall and looked up at the ceiling. "Nice to tell me this now. Were you going to fix it?"

"No. It's not my problem."

"So how will I get the Christmas ornaments—"

"I'm not here about the attic or ornaments. We need to talk."

"Aren't we doing that now?"

"You know why I'm here."

"No."

He raised his eyebrows. "Don't play stupid. You're far more clever than that."

I tapped my head. "Maybe it's my chemo brain."

"Gwen—"

"You know, you wrote about it in your tell-all book. Damaged goods. Isn't that what you called me?"

"Can you just put all that behind you and move on?"

"I have moved on."

Robert ran a hand through his hair. "I didn't come here to argue."

"Good, then get to the point. I have work to do."

Robert held up a Missoula newspaper. "I saw the photo of the girl Winston found. She looks like Aynslee. A lot."

A hot flash burned across my face. I waited until I could speak in a normal voice. "She has a slight resemblance to our daughter. So?"

He ignored me and moved to the studio, stopping dead when he saw the original photograph of the girl in the cow pasture still on the light table. His face blanched. "So." He cleared his throat. "Another one."

"That's a case I'm working on and none of your business."

Robert spun on me. "None of my business? There's a serial killer murdering less than half a mile from our home, and his choice of victims looks like my daughter." His voice rose. "Where is she?"

"Who?"

"Aynslee!"

"She's safe. She's with Beth. You're the one who wanted to see me alone—"

"Don't change the subject—"

"I'm not." I placed a piece of paper over the mauled girl's face. "This woman was killed by wolves. It's a coincidence that she looks like Mattie Banks." I turned and jabbed a finger at him.

"Liar."

I couldn't meet his gaze. "Why are you calling me a liar?"

"Gwen, I was married to you for sixteen years. I listened to you when you gave your deception programs. Your pointing finger came at the wrong time, after your statement, not before, then you had a significant pause, followed by a question."

"So what?" I sounded like a truculent child.

"So, I'm not leaving Aynslee with you while you try to catch this guy."

"I have a gun, you know. I'm capable of protecting her."

Robert pivoted and raced from the room. I followed. He entered my bedroom, opened the closet, and pulled down my SIG Sauer.

"Put that back," I said.

He checked the clip. "Just as I thought. One bullet. Did you bother to buy more?"

"Bullets are expensive. Put it back."

Robert returned the pistol to the shelf, then turned to me. "I'm taking my daughter away from here."

I didn't want to be in my bedroom with Robert. Turning, I left the room and strolled to the living room. "Aynslee's been trying to call you for the past few days. You weren't home, or at least not answering your phone." I put my hands on my hips.

"See? She wants to be with me."

"Hardly. She wanted to go to some movies in Missoula. Vampire stuff. I said no."

"At least you got that right."

"Why are you suddenly so fired up to see your daughter?"

Robert ticked the reasons off on his fingers. "Number one, because she's my daughter. Number two, there's a killer loose. Number three, I have someone she needs to meet."

"I'm not going to let you take her under some stupid pretense of safety just so you can parade her in front of your adoring readers—"

"I want her to meet my fiancée."

My legs became weak and I reached back to find the sofa, then sank down. "Your fiancée?" I said faintly.

"Yes. I'm getting married."

I didn't know what to do with my hands. I finally laced my fingers together and stared at them. "Isn't this rather sudden?"

"Not at all. I've known her for several years."

I looked at him. "*Several* years? We've only been divorced for a year and a half."

Robert shrugged. "I'll pick Aynslee up tomorrow."

"You can't do that!" I jumped to my feet.

"Sure I can. Every other weekend. She can come for Sunday, at any rate."

"But it's not your weekend to have her."

"I missed a few. Remember the clause where it said I could make up weekends or days if my work took me out of town?"

"Your work?"

"Book signings, you know."

"Not really. Are you planning on spending the day with her? All day? Just the afternoon? Every minute? What are you going to do if she hates your girlfriend?"

Robert glanced away. "Fiancée."

"Whatever. Unless you are going to sit at home with her, or take her with you if you decide to socialize with your . . ." I couldn't say the word. "She needs to be with me."

A blood vessel pounded in Robert's forehead. "You're less than half a mile from where that girl was found."

"And you live in Missoula, where Mattie was abducted!"

"If I have to, I'll get a court order."

My hands ached, and I made an effort to loosen my fists. "You know I can't afford a lawyer." I took a deep breath. "The best way to keep her safe is to find the killer. That's what I'm doing—"

"See? That's what I mean. You're *looking* for this guy. You seem to think that just because no one has taken revenge on a forensic artist in the past, you're safe. But you're lying to yourself. All I have to do is tell the court about how much danger Aynslee was in just seven months ago when that madman—"

"That was an isolated incident!"

"Hardly. What about that serial killer in Spokane?"

"What are you talking about? That was years ago, and I was never in danger . . ." Something tugged at my memory. Something I needed—

"You had to leave home to work on the case. What are you going to do if you have another case where you need to be gone? Park Aynslee back in a juvie school? Kennel her like Winston?"

"Get out!" My voice shook.

"I will. But I'll be back."

CHAPTER TWENTY-ONE

MY HANDS WERE STILL SHAKING AS I WATCHED the taillights of Robert's Porsche disappear around the driveway. So, Robert was getting married.

I should have seen this coming. Robert wasn't one to go solo long, but I thought his casual affairs with beautiful women, designer clothes, and an ultramodern bachelor's pad would keep him busy.

Leaning my head against the living room window, I took a long, shuddering breath. The poignant sound of Kenny G's "Going Home" floated from the radio. *You told Beth there was no way you'd ever reconcile with Robert.*

"That's true," I whispered. "But why does it hurt so much?" Swallowing hard, I pushed away from the window. "Stop it!" I raced into the studio and snapped off the radio. I wanted to throw it on the floor and stomp it to electronic smithereens.

Robert was just trying to hurt me. Again. He used the pathetic excuse of caring for Aynslee to personally deliver the news of his pending marriage. His sudden passion to take care of his daughter, to protect her, would be short-lived. He was too much in love with his new lifestyle: a whirlwind of book signings and fancy parties . . .

And a new wife.

Where in his world would a rebellious teenager fit?

You didn't ask him for money to pay Winston's vet bill.

I'd just have to leave Winston at the vet until I found the money. At sixty-five dollars a day.

Better find some funds quickly.

I found myself in the bathroom staring at my face in the mirror. My bloodshot eyes glared under eyebrows drawn together, forming a deep furrow. My skin was pale with blotchy red patches, and my lips were thin and tight.

Splashing cold water on my face didn't seem to erase the distorted image staring back at me.

Robert's right on one count. Aynslee won't be safe until someone catches the murderer.

I applied fresh makeup, then changed into a navy blazer and slacks. I wasn't quite sure how long it would take me to drive to the restaurant to meet the former prosecuting attorney.

I decided to take both the rifle and pistol with me. Double-checking to be sure I locked all the doors, I raced through the cool evening air to my car. I'd grabbed the notes faxed to Dave about the serial killings as well as my own known/unknown list.

Concentrating on my driving, I made an effort not to think about Robert, but I could so clearly hear his voice in my mind. *"You seem to think that just because no one has taken revenge on a forensic artist in the past, you're safe."*

"Revenge usually involves a personal hurt." I answered his imagined voice. "I was just doing my job."

Dave's voice now echoed in my head. *I don't think that matters. In the killer's eyes, you've wronged him. His natural instinct is to hold on, let the hurt fester, then strike back.*

"That's not logical."

People don't have to act logically. Look at you.

"What do you mean? You're not putting me into the same category as a sociopathic serial killer, are you?" I swerved over the center line, and an approaching car blasted its horn. I jerked my car back into my own lane.

Think about it, Gwen. It's a matter of degree. If you keep holding on to anger and past hurts, you eventually may want to strike back, get even.

"I'm not like that, Dave."

That's exactly what you're like. Robert once again intruded on my thoughts.

"Shut up, Robert. You just want to stop feeling guilty for abandoning your family and getting engaged."

Don't you get it? I don't feel guilty. You think I'm a prisoner, trapped by your feelings. But you're the prisoner.

I overcorrected on a curve. My right front tire hit the gravel on the side of the road. The rear swung right. Twisting the steering wheel, I attempted to straighten the car, but I was too close to the edge of the pavement. I hit the berm and slid off the highway.

CHAPTER TWENTY-TWO

THE CAR BOUNCED ONTO A GRASSY DIVIDE. THE soft dirt slowed the momentum, and I stopped short of the railroad tracks. I sat for a moment, waiting for my heartbeat to slow and hands to stop shaking, then stepped from the car.

No traffic appeared in either direction. Good. I felt foolish for losing control of my vehicle.

I shook my head. Maybe my brain was like an Etch A Sketch. If I turned it upside down and shook it, all the bad thoughts would be erased. Instead, they crowded together and pounded away: *serial killer, Phineas Priesthood, revenge, Aynslee, fiancée, vet bills . . . forgiveness . . .*

Headlights appeared, slowed, and signaled that the driver would pull over.

Doggone it. I'd been hoping I could slink back onto the highway unnoticed. I reached back into the car and snatched up my SIG.

The car slid onto the shoulder of the road and rolled down the window. "Need help?"

"Dre?"

"Yeah. You okay, Gwen?" The deputy started to get out of his car.

"Fine. Don't bother to get out. I just . . . um, a deer . . . so . . . spun out on the gravel." I was glad he couldn't see my face. I jumped into my car and slipped my pistol under my purse. Before I could put the car into drive, Dre appeared and made the motion to roll down my window. I hesitated, hoping my color was back to normal, then did so.

"Do you need a push?" he asked. "Or a tow truck?"

"I think I can drive out." Gently applying gas, I trundled forward. Fortunately the ground was relatively flat. I waved as I hit the pavement. He'd probably be on the radio as soon as he got in his sedan, calling Dave.

I should be grateful he hadn't asked me to take a Breathalyzer.

I almost missed the restaurant. A florescent sign in the window announced the place was open, and a collection of dusty pickup trucks hugged the front. I parked, tucked the pistol into my purse, and grabbed up my papers. *I didn't check to see if I was followed.*

Quickly I locked the rifle in the trunk, then raced to the restaurant and waited just inside the door, watching the road. No car pulled into the parking lot or slowed down when passing. When I turned, the waitress was watching me with a wary look. "You okay, hon?"

"Yeah. I'm just . . . yeah."

She shrugged, picked up a coffee carafe, and waved it around. "Sit anywhere."

The décor had been quite modern in the early seventies, with an abundance of harvest-gold and burnt-orange wallpaper and upholstery. I found a booth near the rear and sat facing the door. The orange pendant light overhead cast a mini spotlight onto the table. I leaned back so I would be in relative darkness.

As the waitress moved my way with a menu, I peeked into my wallet. A lonely five-dollar bill and some loose change limited my choices of dining. I was suddenly starving.

"Coffee?" She held up the pot.

"Sure." As she poured, I quickly scanned the menu.

"What else can I get you?"

"Uh, I'm fine."

As she took the menu back from me, she gave me a look that said I was anything but.

Wrapping my fingers around the cup, I surveyed the other patrons. A weary-looking family sat by the door, and a middle-aged man in jeans and a T-shirt ate a slice of lemon meringue pie at the counter. I tried not to stare at the pie.

This was a stupid idea. The killer knew my phone number. He easily could have called me and arranged for this meeting. I took his word that he was Scott Thomas.

At least I was in a public place.

Headlights flashed outside, and I sat up straighter. Two men wearing camouflage jackets and Seahawk baseball hats entered, waved at the waitress, and took seats at a booth to my left. Without asking, the waitress brought them both a slice of apple pie and coffee.

I stuck my hand in my purse and felt for loose change on the bottom—two pennies. I emptied two creams and a sugar into my coffee cup and stirred.

The meringue-pie man scraped the last few flakes of crust off the plate, picked up his coffee cup, and walked over to my table. "Were you followed?"

I dropped the spoon. "No. I don't think so."

He sat across from me, then silently studied my face for a few moments. "When I was prosecutor in Spokane, I saw a number of your composites. You do nice work."

"Thanks. Ah, if you don't mind, would you show me some identification?"

He pulled out his billfold and handed me his driver's license. While I inspected it, he took a sip of coffee. Satisfied, I returned it.

"You've probably looked up the Phineas Priesthood case by now."

I nodded.

"They made sure we knew it was them, and not the Aryan Nations or skinheads. They left notes, shouted slogans. We caught Jerome Daly right away. He was the driver of the get-away van. He has Parkinson's disease, and he's pretty much confined to bed or a wheelchair now."

I nodded again.

"We figured we'd closed the book on the group when Evans and Weeks died, but we missed it. A single line in a police report. On the day of the shootout and fatal accident, the officer noted he saw someone running. He didn't get a good look at him, and running isn't against the law. Right after that was the shootout, then pursuit."

"So, by the time the officer returned to the house the two men were hiding in—"

"No sign of a fourth man. Weeks, Daly, and Evans weren't smart enough to have pulled off the bombings."

I leaned closer. "So you think the one that got away was the mastermind."

"Yes. And he likes killing."

CHAPTER TWENTY-THREE

SCOTT LEANED CLOSER. "WE CONTINUED TO investigate. The threats came first. Some biblical quotes. A few from Christian Identity books. Like this." He handed me a crumpled piece of paper in a plastic sleeve.

> As the kamikaze is to the Japanese / As the Shiite is to Islam / As the Zionist is to the Jew / So the Phineas priest is to Christendom. It makes little difference whether you agree or disagree with the Phineas Priesthood. It is important that you know that it exists, is active, and in the near future may become a central fact in your life.

"I ignored them. At first. The threats increased." He handed me a second sleeve.

> Soon, the fog that comes from heaven will be accompanied by the destroying wind of a righteous God.

I handed the note back to Scott, then wiped my hands on my jeans.

"Yeah, my thoughts exactly. That's why they're in plastic. Classic Phineas Priesthood materials," Scott continued. "Next came messages left on my phone warning me not to prosecute Jerome. I ignored them. I found a dead cat—"

I sloshed my coffee cup.

"I see you got that message too."

"Why a cat?" I asked as I mopped up the liquid with a napkin.

"I can't prove this, but the lady in Kellogg who first called the police had cats. She was in a hit-and-run car accident less than a week after the two men died in a shootout."

"So both a warning and a hint."

"That's what I think. Under the cat was a threat directed at my family, with the Phineas Priesthood symbol and the word *traitor*. I told the police, but they couldn't do anything." He shifted in his seat and looked around the room. "Then one day a photograph was stuffed in my mailbox. A photo of my daughter going to school with a red *X* drawn over her."

"So you moved."

"As fast as I could. Later I heard about the lead detective's son being murdered by a serial killer."

"That's what I was told."

He glanced around the diner again. "I decided I had to do something. I contacted some friends at the prosecutor's office and told them I wanted to know whenever a trial date was set."

"Because?"

"Because everyone who had been linked to this case would be in danger."

"So you're running around warning people—"

"Not people. You. You're the only one left who was directly involved with the investigation."

"Wait. Didn't you mention the police in Kellogg?"

"Officer Mike Higgins was the investigating officer. He moved to California. Then dropped out of sight. Maybe a good thing for him. He had a ride-along that day. Gal named Margie Sheehan."

"Is she . . . ?"

"Dead? Yes. Fell down a flight of stairs. Because some of the deaths seem to be accidents and each was different, no one put it all together."

"Until you did. What do you know that can help me?"

The waitress warmed up our coffee, and he waited until she'd moved on to another table. "I think the killer was the mastermind of the Phineas Priesthood cell. I think he threatened the detective and his family, but the threats were ignored, and his son was murdered. I think that's why the detective committed suicide. Guilt."

Scott's eyes were red rimmed with purplish bags under them. He hadn't shaved in a day or two, and his hair needed a trim. "He was your friend, wasn't he?"

Scott nodded and leaned back from the table. After clearing his throat, he reached into his pocket and pulled out a coin. He gazed at it for a moment, his fingers stroking the edges, before handing it to me.

I recognized it immediately. "A challenge coin."

"Yes. Originally given in World War I. Now they're awarded in law enforcement as a motivation to achieve a specific goal."

"And this particular goal was?"

"Find the remaining member and bring him to justice. There's a part of this whole thing that's never been released. After the shootout in Kellogg, we raided the house where the two men had holed up. We found evidence of a carefully crafted plot to derail a train, a train carrying chemicals, on either April 19 or 20."

"The nineteenth because it is the anniversary of Waco and Oklahoma City. If caught or killed, they would be placed on the martyr's honor roll."

"Right, and the twentieth would be Hitler's birthday."

"Do you know where this was to have happened?"

"No. Rail lines in Idaho, Washington, and Montana were marked, but no one line or shipment was identified. Needless to say, such an event could have been catastrophic if the chemical spill were to occur near a major city." He took back the coin. "We put together a task force to find the author of this plot, the man that got away. There were ten of us. We each got a coin to remind us of the stakes should this sociopath succeed."

"Were the task-force members also threatened or killed?"

"No. Just the initial investigators. He probably held them accountable for the deaths of his co-conspirators. And, since time had passed with nothing to show for it, the task force was dissolved."

The clatter of the restaurant receded. The glow of the pendent light above the table illuminated the gold finish on the coin in his hand. "My friend, the one that committed suicide . . . I was there at his funeral." He took a deep breath. "I got to thinking about the coin. I asked the widow about it. She looked me in the eye and said, 'My son is dead. My husband is dead. I gave the coin to someone who will find and punish the man responsible.'"

I leaned forward. "Do you know who she gave the coin to?"

He handed me the coin, then dropped some money on the table to pay for my coffee. "No. Just whatever you do, don't get caught between the two."

I thought about Scott's warnings all the way home, my brain bouncing over each nugget of information, trying to make sense of it. I checked the rearview mirror often for any signs I was being followed, but the highway was free of traffic.

Once home, I returned to my foam-core display in the office. The ceiling light was stark, as were the empty walls. I'd hang some paintings once the walls were painted. Picking up a black Sharpie, I drew a timeline across the bottom of the foam core. I really wanted Dave or Beth there to bounce my ideas off of, but it was after midnight, and neither would appreciate a phone call. Arranging the desk chair and folding seat in front of the display, I addressed my imaginary audience. "Serial killers don't just dive into that career path. They evolve over time. So."

I made a mark at the far left side of the line. "Let's start here. You're a Phineas priest. You have a boatload of things you hate, and you believe God has given you the Good Housekeeping Seal of Approval. You bomb the Planned Parenthood building. You even kill a few people. That probably felt really good."

"Next." I made a mark an inch from the first and wrote *Identified*. "You and your friends are wanted by police and every law-enforcement agency in the Inland Empire. They call me in to draw your buddies' composites. Your 'team' is either arrested or dies. And your grand plans for mass destruction are discovered."

I paused and listened for any questions from the empty chairs. Both imaginary friends seemed attentive to my logic.

Pulling the challenge coin from my pocket, I taped it on the board. "You also have a team of professionals looking for you. You don't dare form another Phineas Priesthood cell. You have to go it alone. Lone wolf."

I made the next mark on the timeline and scribbled *Revenge*. "Your original mission was thwarted. It's payback time." Another mark and the word *Threats*. "You decide to go after the people who are rocking your world. The ones directly involved. You threaten the prosecuting attorney, but that didn't work, did it?" I looked at the drawings of the girls, then the photo of Aynslee. "So you move on to threaten the family. The children. Something no parent can ignore. This works and Scott moves away. A continuance on the trial of your buddy, Jerome." A mark. *Success*.

The chairs remained silent. "Now on to the lead detective, the next one on your list of enemies. I bet you skipped personal threats and went straight to threats against the family. You learned your lesson. But this is a cop. And he was determined to find you." I tapped the coin.

My gaze drifted back to the line of girls. Striding to my desk, I found Beth's notes and the police reports. Spokane had faxed photos, but the fax machine turned them into abstract Rorschach tests.

I found the names of the murdered boys from the report, then went to my studio, plugged them into the computer, and printed the results.

The boys, like Mattie, Aynslee, and the young women, looked like siblings. I brought the boys' images to the office and taped them to the wall.

The victims are different, boys before, now young women, the Dave chair whispered.

"I see that. I wonder . . ." I retrieved the case information and sat. I quickly found what I was looking for. The boy was shot from some distance away. And he lived near the detective.

I pointed. "Was this first boy a mistake? Did you think it was the detective's son?"

Yes. That's what happened, the Beth chair murmured.

"But something else happened." Standing, I stepped to the timeline and wrote *First Victim.* "You liked it. You liked the fear everyone felt. But it wasn't enough. You needed to prolong that fear." Another mark. *Second Victim. Failure.* I put a star next to this, opened the closet, and retrieved the top box. Placing it on the desk next to the squirt gun, I quickly rummaged through the contents. I didn't have that many out-of-state cases and soon found the one from Spokane. A copy of my interview notes refreshed my memory. I taped the interview form to the board. "Victim two was too traumatized to give a description. He'd been driven from his home in Spokane to North Idaho and tortured. He escaped. Turned out he was a cross-country runner."

And the killer learned from this, the Dave chair said.

I nodded. "He learned he liked it even more. He liked hunting, the pursuit, but he needed more control. He's evolving as a killer. Honing his trade. So now we have victim three." I marked the timeline and wrote *Third Victim, Son.* "The intended victim, young . . . a . . ." I reread Beth's notes. "The boy's name was Hudson?"

The notes slipped from my numb fingers. I heard the killer's creepy, disguised voice from the phone call. *"I know you found my blanket . . . the Hudson's Bay blanket. The cream one with the stripes."*

194

I sank into the nearest seat, my heart thundering in my ears. "The killer made a point of telling me the name for that type of blanket."

He wants you to be afraid. Terrorized, the Dave chair said softly.

"And he's succeeding," I whispered.

CHAPTER TWENTY-FOUR

I DIDN'T FALL ASLEEP UNTIL AFTER THREE, THEN woke up at six. I gave up trying to sleep and wandered from room to room, eventually ending up in Robert's office. *No. My office. Keep saying that.* Robert. Just the thought of him made me grind my teeth. He was planning to pick up Aynslee tomorrow. No, today. I moved the case box back to the closet and sat at the desk, rubbing my fingers across the battered oak surface. I'd already tried to convince him that Aynslee was safer with me. That just left catching the killer before Robert showed up. I had maybe six hours. Eight?

Maybe on television the bad guy was identified and caught in an hour, minus commercials. In reality, I'd have to convince Dave and the Missoula police to allow me to interview Mattie for a composite. If he wasn't immediately identified, the police would have to release the sketch to the media.

That would only be the beginning.

Then hopefully someone would recognize the image and call law enforcement, then the police would have to gather enough evidence for an arrest.

Impossible.

It took years for the Green River Killer to be caught. The same for Ted Bundy. The Zodiac Killer was never identified.

Jack the Ripper probably died of old age.

The clock *tick, tick, tick*ed away the morning. I should call Beth and ask that she bring Aynslee home. I wanted to wrap her in my arms, as if that would be enough to shelter her. Picking up the handset, I dialed Beth's number. It took me a moment to realize there wasn't a dial tone.

Terrific. The worst possible time for the phones to go out.

As I debated jumping in the car and driving over to Beth's house, she drove up. I opened the kitchen door to let them both in. "I tried calling—"

"I know. Your phone is out. I called it in, but they said they couldn't come out until tomorrow, then I got worried about you. I thought we'd drop by before church."

When I stepped aside to let Beth and Aynslee enter, I noticed an envelope poking out of the mailbox in the driveway. Odd. It was Sunday. I'd brought in the mail from yesterday.

I trotted over and tugged out the envelope. Unmarked.

I quickly glanced around. No one in sight. I swiftly returned to the house.

"What?" Beth asked.

I closed the door and locked it, waited until my daughter had drifted away, then jerked my head toward the studio. Once there, I closed all the blinds.

"What?" she asked again.

"This." I held up the envelope by the edges, grabbed a pair of scissors, and cut open one end, then peeked inside.

CHAPTER TWENTY-FIVE

TILTING THE ENVELOPE, I DUMPED THE CONTENTS onto my drafting table. A familiar lock of red hair landed on the surface along with a sheet of paper.

I ran my tongue over dry lips.

"What on earth . . ." Beth's eyes were huge.

"Aynslee, come in here." I hid the hair under another piece of paper.

Aynslee sauntered into the room drinking a Mountain Dew. "Yeah?"

Beth started to say something, but closed her mouth when I glanced at her with a warning look.

"Beth said she thought you needed your hair trimmed." I strolled to her and pulled back her long hair. In the center was a missing chunk.

I cleared my throat and waited until I could speak. "*Hmm.* Well, maybe a few split ends."

"See? I told you." Beth's voice was high and squeaky, but Aynslee didn't seem to notice.

"Whatever." She took a swallow of pop. "When do we pick up Winston?"

I turned my back so Aynslee couldn't see my face. "Well, we'll pick Winston up . . . soon . . . but first we have . . . you and Beth have church. I have to run a few errands." I picked up a pencil. "Is that what you're wearing?".

"Yeah. My other pants are dirty." She left.

I sat on the wingback chair before my legs could give way beneath me. "Beth, who was near you at the movies? Did you see anyone you knew? Did anyone come up behind Aynslee?"

Beth folded into the office chair. "It was dark—"

"Think!"

"The-the theatre was crowded—"

"How about when you were seated?"

"No one . . . wait." She looked at me. "Someone, a man I think, sitting in the row behind us got up in the middle of the movie."

"Yes?"

"As he passed us, Aynslee reached for her hair."

I rubbed my sweaty hands on my jeans.

"I didn't think anything at the time." Beth swallowed. "The seats are close, and it isn't uncommon to have your coat or hair accidently caught up."

"And you didn't recognize him?"

"It was dark!" Beth grabbed a tissue and blew her nose.

Aynslee appeared at the door with two cups of hot chocolate. "I made some hot chocolate."

We took the cups. "Thank you, sweetheart." I waited impatiently for her to leave.

The elusive thought that had plagued me since seeing Robert surfaced. "I think I know who it is."

"A name?"

"No. A connection." I put down the mug of chocolate, stood, and moved to my drafting table.

Beth followed. "What's that?" She pointed to the piece of paper included with Aynslee's lock of hair.

I found a pair of tweezers and carefully unfolded the note. "Exodus 21:24–25." I shot Beth a puzzled look.

Beth returned to the computer and typed a moment. "'Eye for eye, tooth for tooth, hand for hand, foot for foot, burning for burning, wound for wound, stripe for stripe.'"

"So. It's started. No longer hints under dead cats. Direct threats." I tried to give Beth a reassuring smile, but my upper lip seemed frozen.

"What are we going to do?"

I found myself pacing around the room like a caged tiger. "I'm not moving away, nor am I going to put my daughter at risk. I need to move forward with my plan."

"Are you still going to that Nazi church?"

"Yes."

"Why?"

"I'm tired of being reactive, waiting to see what this . . . monster is planning. I'm going to be proactive. Go someplace he's likely to be. But not like this. The Lone Wolf knows what I look like." Leaving Beth in the studio, I rummaged through the closet in my bedroom. A box held all the hats and wigs people gave me when I lost my hair from chemo. I found the wig I was looking for. My own hair was short enough that I didn't need to put on a wig cap. The shoulder length, ash-brown color was wrong for my face and made me look pale and gaunt. I took off my special bra holding my breast prosthesis, then selected the dress I'd found in a secondhand shop three years ago. The dress looked cute in the store and cost three dollars, but hung on me like a sack. I returned to the studio.

Beth glanced up as I entered, then did a double take. "You look awful. Like you're living without running water."

"Dirty?"

"More like the pregnant-in-summer, barefoot-in-winter, downtrodden wife. It's perfect. I would never have known you."

"Good. I have no illusions of who I'm up against. The northwest is a breeding ground for serial killers and white separatists." I ticked off on my fingers. "Gary Ridgway, the Green River Killer, Robert Yates, Ted Bundy, the Molalla Forest Killer, Dayton Leroy Rogers, and more. On top of that, this area is like a magnet to such groups as the Phineas Priesthood, The Order, Militia of Montana, Posse Comitatus, and the Aryan Nations."

"So—"

"So the man who is after me is both a serial killer *and* a violent white separatist. He's the perfect storm."

CHAPTER TWENTY-SIX

AYNSLEE COULDN'T STOP GIGGLING AT MY appearance, and her mirth became contagious. "It's too bad I'm not still bald," I said when I could catch my breath. "I could attend church as a skinhead." That set us off again.

I knew the laughing was a tension release. I was grateful for it.

After agreeing to meet at Nora's Coffee Shop for lunch after church, I made sure Beth and Aynslee were off safely before grabbing my Bible and leaving.

I stowed my sketching supplies in the car. If needed, I could draw the faces of anyone attending services that looked suspicious.

The address on the pamphlet turned out to be a small strip mall just off the highway. I'd driven past it a number of times and never noticed the small, hand-lettered sign in the window. A used bookstore and a saddle repair shop bracketed the church. I parked around the side of the building between two oversize pickups. Waiting until a small group of people entered, I slipped in behind them. An undersized lobby held a few chatting teens, but most of the congregation proceeded forward through a double set of open doors to the sanctuary beyond. A rack of pamphlets sat on a small table to my left. I recognized the one I'd received, but decided to wait until later to grab more.

My attire drew no particular notice. Fashions included jeans, T-shirts, dresses, and a sprinkling of camo. The church bulletin, handed to me by a smiling, plump woman, looked like the bulletin from my own church.

The room had no windows, with a small, raised stage in the front. Black fabric draped from the ceiling, forming a backdrop for the stage, and a large, hand-carved cross stood behind the podium. An American flag was attached to the wall on my right. I settled in the last row of white plastic lawn chairs nearest the exit.

The room soon completely filled. I kept my head down, fiddling with my Bible and the bulletin. The worship team entered the stage; three women and a man, each carrying instruments. Four songs, slightly off-key but sung with enthusiasm, followed.

So far, the American Christian Covenant Church was disappointing. Not a single "Heil Hitler" or cross burning, and the music wasn't as good as my own church.

Every chance I got, I checked out the congregation. I didn't recognize anyone. Paying particular attention to the men, I made sure I could recognize and sketch them later if needed. Finally a distinguished-looking man with blond hair took the podium as the musicians left. "Good morning," he said.

"Good morning," we all replied.

"A few announcements before we begin. Remember tonight is the torchlight parade."

I sat up straighter and pulled a pencil out of my purse.

"We assemble at seven p.m. in front of the grocery store on Main. It should be . . ." He chuckled. ". . . an interesting night." The people around me joined in as if all sharing an inside joke.

I shifted in my chair, then quickly looked down as a hot flash shot up my face.

"I want to thank the committee who came up with this event. I see some of you here."

Some of you here? That means members of the church were missing this service. Could my Lone Wolf be absent? I risked another glance around the room.

"Turn with me in your Bibles to Numbers 25:6."

My suddenly damp fingers stuck to the thin pages.

"'And, behold,'" the pastor read, "'one of the children of Israel came and brought unto his brethren a Midianitish woman in the sight of Moses, and in the sight of all the congregation of the children of Israel, who were weeping before the door of the tabernacle of the congregation. And when Phinehas, the son of Eleazar, the son of Aaron the priest, saw it, he rose up from among the congregation, and took a javelin in his hand; and he went after the man of Israel into the tent, and thrust both of them through, the man of Israel, and the woman through her belly. So the plague was stayed from the children of Israel.'" The pastor looked up. "We've studied this passage many times."

I bet you have.

"But pay attention to the insight we have here. When Phinehas killed the man and woman, he was killing one of his own kind, a 'man of Israel.' In the past we've talked about the true, literal, chosen people of Israel: the white, Anglo-Saxon, Germanic people."

I glanced around. Heads nodded all around me.

"So what is God saying here? He's identifying race traitors. Those who destroy and betray their own race, and those who are creating mongrels." He paused and looked at the congregation. "This is war, people!" His voice rose. "War! And what do we do with traitors during war? What did Phinehas do? He killed them. This includes anyone, *anyone*, who betrays us."

I gripped my Bible so hard my fingers ached. There was the answer to the question Dave asked, *"Why me?"* The Lone Wolf decided I was a race traitor for the work I did to identify his group and foil his plan.

The pastor jabbed the air with a finger. "Death is the only way to treat race traitors. Death in such a way so as to send a message to other possible defectors. Remember the Fourteen Words, 'We must secure the existence of our people and a future for white children.'"

The whole congregation chanted the words together, as if repeating the Lord's Prayer.

Sweat dampened the back of my dress. I could barely breathe.

The pastor's voice dropped, and he said quietly, "This is survival of the fittest. We must cut the chaff from us and their seed. You have a duty, a God-given duty, to seek revenge on those who have harmed our race!" He flung his arms out to the side, perfectly matching up with the cross behind him.

I glanced at the people around me. Their faces were blotched and red, jaws clenched, hands drawn into fists.

I had to get away from this man, this room, this vitriolic speech.

Slipping my pencil back into my purse, I pulled out a tissue, placed it over my mouth, and started coughing. Swiftly I stood, made an apologetic gesture, and continued my fake coughing attack to the exit. A few heads turned, but most seemed riveted by the sermon.

No one was in the lobby, nor could I see anyone loitering in the parking lot. Before making my dash for freedom, I snatched a selection of pamphlets from the rack.

Once out of sight of the church and heading toward my rendezvous with Beth, I yanked off the wig and fluffed my hair. I didn't want anyone connecting me with the woman who had attended that church. After parking behind Nora's Café, I thought about the hatred I'd just witnessed as I finished my transformation back to my regular appearance.

I looked in the mirror to apply eye shadow, then stopped. The expressions on the faces of the congregation had looked familiar.

I'd seen it on my own face after my fight with Robert.

I dropped my hands into my lap and bowed my head. "Heavenly Father, I know everything happens for a reason. I know it was by divine appointment that I was at that church today. Please help me, guide me, and protect me through this time. In Jesus' name, amen."

Someone tapped on the car window.

I jerked up my head. Beth and Aynslee were staring at me. I got out of the car and joined them. Beth looked ready to question me on my praying, but she didn't say anything. *Good.* I wasn't ready to share my moment of self-discovery.

The after-church lunch rush was in full swing, and we quickly grabbed the last empty table.

"Well," Beth said. "How did it go?"

Before I could answer, the waitress appeared. "The usual?" she asked Beth and me. We both nodded. "How about you, hon?" she asked Aynslee.

Aynslee pointed to the menu. "Pancakes, eggs over easy—"

"Um, sweetheart—"

"I'm buying," Beth said. "So go ahead."

I gave her a grateful smile. "You are absolutely the best friend and partner."

"Do I get that badge?"

"How about a shiny belt buckle?"

"You said that before."

After Aynslee placed her order, she popped in earbuds, closed her eyes, and tapped the table lightly in tune with her phone.

"Did anyone recognize you?"

"No. I got a good look at the men. I'll sketch them this evening." I finished quietly updating Beth on my church visit, then placed the selection of pamphlets on the table.

Beth unfolded each one.

We both spotted the Phineas Priesthood symbol on the third pamphlet. Across the top was a quote. "It is our God-given duty to execute righteous judgment."

"Wow." Beth dropped it like it was on fire.

"So, this is what I think we're dealing with. I think this killer evolved to what is called a thrill-oriented serial killer," I said. "Looking at his actions in Spokane, he started by bombing and killing people, using the philosophy of the Phineas Priesthood as his reason. Then his buddies are caught or died, so again using the Christian Identity as a justification, he embarked on revenge."

"Rather a common theme, using religion as a rationalization for amoral behavior."

I nodded. "He may have used revenge as an excuse, but he found he craved the excitement of killing. When his second victim escaped, the killer chased him, but failed to catch him. That hunting of another person was immensely satisfying, a total adrenalin rush."

Beth placed her fork on the table and pushed away her salad.

"Serial killer Robert Christian Hansen," I said, "murdered between seventeen and twenty-one women in Alaska, many of them taken to a remote region, allowed to run for their lives, hunted down, and killed. I think the bodies in the grave were killed like that."

"But how?"

"He must have given them a head start, then caught up with them at the McCandless farm."

"What about the body in the cow pasture?"

"She also ran. I think they all were given a map, maybe a compass, but the Jane Doe in the pasture probably couldn't read it. She ran the wrong way, and the wolves found her instead of the killer."

"And Mattie?"

"I thought about her. She's really the key. It was raining that night."

"What?"

"Rain. That's why he didn't make Mattie run. He'd lose her in the downpour."

Beth leaned closer. "Did her juvenile arthritis have anything to do with it?"

I glanced around the restaurant. "I suspect he chose his victims based on both a resemblance to Aynslee and . . . their having 'undesirable' traits. Like Hitler killing disabled and mentally handicapped people."

Beth took a sip of water.

"The Lone Wolf's intention was to sustain his own fantasies and to exact revenge on me as a race traitor. I was *supposed* to find the girls, adding another layer to his experience. But I didn't, at least not for a time. He got tired of waiting. When he picked up Mattie, he decided it was time for me to discover his plan. He could have lost her in the deluge, so he simply took her to where he'd killed and placed the other bodies, tortured her, left the clues, then lured Winston to the site."

Beth didn't talk for a few moments. "You said this man is the perfect storm. Both a serial killer and a violent white separatist."

"Yes."

"But he waited, what was it, five years to go after you."

I leaned my elbows on the table. "He's tying up loose ends. I assume it was because the case is finally going to trial."

"But everything was so planned out. Every detail."

"Ooookay. Where are you going with this?"

"What if, once the last of the 'race traitors' are murdered, he decides to go back to his original plan?"

"Derail a train carrying deadly chemicals." I thought about the railroad tracks running alongside of the highway. I was pretty sure it went right through Missoula. I finally shook my head. "He had three other men helping him with that plan. It would be something else."

Beth pulled a purple notepad and lavender pen from her purse. "Like what?"

"Um. Well, it would probably need to be on the nineteenth or twentieth. If he thinks he might die in the attempt, it would be the nineteenth."

Beth started the list. "Hate would be involved. That seems to be a theme."

"Destruction, death, maybe a bomb and shooting. Hitler? Swastika, something that would sear into the American conscience. I don't know." I leaned back.

Beth leaned back also and stared at the ceiling. "Something maybe like Germany's *Kristallnacht*, the night of broken glass. Pre-war, maybe 1938 or '39, when civilians and the military attacked Jewish temples—"

"Yes! A Jewish target," I said.

Aynslee pulled out the earbuds. "Battery's dead. I heard all that. I know what date he's going to strike. And what time. You might have figured out where."

"What do you mean?" Beth asked.

"Your list," Aynslee said. "April 20, eleven a.m. The anniversary of the shooting at Columbine High School."

CHAPTER TWENTY-SEVEN

I STARED AT MY DAUGHTER.

"We read about it in school," she said. "The two boys that did it really got into Hitler and the Nazis. They wore swastikas and did the 'Heil Hitler' thing. They were going to blow up the school and shoot anyone who tried to escape."

"So maybe a school?" Beth said. "Rather than a Jewish target?"

"Give me a minute." I jumped up from the table and headed outside. Once there, I quickly called Dave. It went to voice mail.

I checked my watch. Dave usually didn't turn on his cell until well after church. I left a message for him to call me.

Beth and Aynslee joined me.

"We have a possible day and time, but not an exact target," I said. "Mattie is the key to finding this guy quickly. We'll go to the hospital, get that composite, and turn it over to Dave. He'll yell and squawk at me, but then we can step back and let him handle it." I forced a smile.

Aynslee smiled back. "Don't worry, I'm not afraid. You'll keep me safe."

We stopped at a grocery store on our way to the hospital and purchased a bouquet of flowers and glass vase. I parked my car in the visitors' parking lot and turned toward Beth, seated beside me. She was almost hidden by the flowers. "I know this hospital rather too well," I said.

"Because of all your surgeries and cancer treatments, I would imagine you would."

"The room used for isolation is near the nurses' station and in the old part of the hospital. That's the bad news. It's also near an elevator. That's the good news. You know the plan. Ready?"

Beth nodded. Aynslee and I slipped from the car and headed across the nearly empty lot to the back of the building. I'd condensed my composite supplies to paper, a few pencils, an eraser, a photo reference book, and a cell phone, all which fit into a small canvas bag. The hospital was a cream-colored, single-story building sprawling over a gently rolling lawn. In the rear, a sloping ramp led to a service entrance belowground with both regular and vehicle-sized doors. Dumpsters lined up on the left, and just outside the employee entrance was an overflowing container for cigarette butts. After one of my surgeries, I'd overlooked this popular spot for the smoking staff members.

The garage door was open, and Aynslee and I slipped inside. A hallway bisected the lower floor. Listening for any sound of approaching staff, I moved forward past closed doors: *Maintenance, Mechanical, Plant Operations, Housekeeping*, and finally the door I sought. *Supply.*

The room was empty and filled with rows of neatly labeled, gray metal shelves. The section on my left held blankets, gowns, towels, spreads, and other linen. Behind the door were lab coats with the hospital's name and logo embroidered on the pocket. I pulled on one, then found a small gown for Aynslee. "Put this on."

"It's, like, ugly."

"Yeah. I know. Put it on anyway." The gown covered her T-shirt and draped to her knees, with blue jeans and muddy sneakers below. I snatched a white cotton blanket, then peeked out the door.

Two orderlies sauntered toward the smoking area.

I ducked back and put my finger to my lips. Aynslee looked as if she might start giggling.

Coast clear, Aynslee and I crept down the hall. At the end, an arrow pointed left and noted *Cafeteria*. The elevator was straight ahead. I spotted a wheelchair. I'd just gotten Aynslee seated and covered her jeans and shoes with the blanket when the elevator door opened.

I gripped the armrest of the wheelchair.

"Need help?" a male voice asked.

"No, I got it." My back was toward them, blocking Aynslee from their sight. "Now, listen to me, young lady, just because you have a wheelchair, you can't just go anywhere in this hospital. Let's get you back to your room."

Aynslee had both hands over her mouth, and her eyes streamed tears from holding in her laughter. A hot flash bathed me in sweat.

"You bet," the voice said. Footsteps retreated.

"Aynslee," I whispered. "This isn't funny!"

"I can't help it, Mom." She gasped. "I gotta go to the bathroom now."

I waited for the hot flash to pass and Aynslee to get control of her mirth before entering the elevator. The timing had to be perfect.

The ride up seemed to take forever. My hands were slick on the wheelchair handles.

The door opened.

Beth stood at the end of the hall, peering at a room number. The nurses' station sat on my right, with a short hall to my left, ending with a door blocked by a young police officer engrossed in a book.

Beth dropped the vase. The piercing crash echoed down the hall. Flowers splayed across the shiny floor, and glass shards flew in all directions. "Oh no!" she shrieked.

The officer dropped the paperback, put his hand on his service revolver, and charged past us. Nurses and orderlies popped from nearby rooms.

I shoved the wheelchair out of sight behind the nurses' station, grabbed Aynslee, and flew toward the now unguarded door.

The room was dim, with the blinds half closed, but I could clearly see Mattie lying on her back, eyes open, staring at the ceiling. Cloyingly sweet-smelling flowers overwhelmed the odor of rubbing alcohol and cleaners. An IV line hooked into Mattie's wrist, and her splinted hands lay crossed over her waist.

"Hi, Mattie; it's me, Gwen."

No response. I moved closer. "Do you remember me? We met . . ." *Don't remind her of the house.* "Is there anything I can get for you? Mattie?"

The *click* of the IV pump created the only sound. I leaned over the bed so Mattie could see my face. "Mattie?" I asked quietly.

"Hi," she muttered.

"Can I get you anything? Water, a soft drink . . ."

"I'd kill for a cigarette."

"There's no smoking in here with the oxygen and all, but maybe I can get you some gum."

"Nah. That's okay."

"This is my daughter, Aynslee."

Aynslee moved closer so Mattie could see her. The two girls studied each other. "Hi," Aynslee said.

"Hi." Mattie looked like she wanted to say more but snapped her jaw shut.

A single chair sat beside her bed, and I pulled it closer. Aynslee moved to the far side of the bed and sat on the floor. I concentrated on my senses; focusing on every movement, comment, pause in speech, subtle sound. "Mattie, I'd like to draw a picture of the bad man. That's what I do, I draw faces."

Mattie's head moved just a fraction.

I unpacked my facial identification book and pad of paper. Speaking slowly and quietly, I said, "I have no idea how terrible it was for you, but maybe we can do this drawing and make sure he doesn't do this again to anyone else."

Mattie didn't move.

"You might think this will be like on TV. That I'll ask you a lot of questions, wave my pencil over a piece of paper, and, poof, I produce the spitting image of the suspect. Well, this isn't television, and I'm not a movie star."

"Okay," she whispered.

"I don't know how long I can stay, so we'll work fast. When

we're done, it won't be a portrait, only a drawing of your memory. It might eliminate some people and hopefully lead to an identification. An innocent person won't be arrested because of this sketch." I finished reciting the litany of disclaimers. It always reminded me of the flight attendants spiel just before takeoff. *Keep your seat belt low and tight across your lap.*

"Could I have a drink of water?" Mattie turned her face toward the window.

"Sure." I poured a glass and then found the control to raise the bed. I held the straw so Mattie could drink.

Mattie sipped, then cleared her throat. "Thanks."

I put down the glass and sat on the chair. "Just so I have an idea of what happened, think back to the day and tell me about it. Don't leave anything out, even if you think it's unimportant."

Mattie's eyebrows furrowed. "Why every detail?"

"You might have seen something that you think is unimportant but is very critical. You may have information stored on what we call a memory peg. For example, let's say you saw a small dog just before the incident. You watched the dog cross the parking lot and wondered if it was a stray. It passed in front of a car with an unusual bumper sticker."

"I didn't see a dog."

"Uh, right, I mean, there may be clues, such as the bumper sticker, connected to unimportant details, like the stray dog, and if the details aren't mentioned, the connecting clues might be lost."

"I told you I didn't see any dog or bumper sticker." She glanced out the window. "I had a dog once, but not anymore."

"Uh, never mind. Just tell me what you did see."

She paused, looked away, then said, "You're asking me what I did see? I didn't see his face."

My heart sank. She was lying. "You can tell me—"

"But he came here. He called me. He said you'd come."

The sketchpad dropped from my suddenly numb hands. "What?"

"He said I had to tell you something. He said . . . he said you were a traitor. And you owed him three."

"Three?"

"Lives." She looked at me and her lips trembled. "Your dog. Your daughter. And you."

CHAPTER TWENTY-EIGHT

DAVE STEPPED OUT OF CHURCH AND TURNED on his phone. Three missed calls, two from his department and one from Gwen. He hit Redial.

"Dave," Louise said. "This is Louise."

"I know your voice," Dave said dryly. He handed the car keys to his wife and waved her on.

"Oh, well, yes. I stopped by the office to drop off some rhubarb for you. I know your lovely wife makes pies—"

"You called me two times about rhubarb?"

"No. I was getting to that. Anyway, I found a man in your office."

Dave clenched the phone tighter. "Who was it?"

"I didn't recognize him, but one of the fellows said he was that artist fellow from Missoula."

"Wes Bailor? What was he doing in my office?"

"That's just what I asked him. He said he was looking for you, then he left."

"How did he get in?" Several people leaving church stopped talking and looked at him. He made an effort to lower his voice. "How could he get past the front desk?"

"I guess he told them he had a critical report on the Mattie Banks case to drop off. They buzzed him in, he gave them a big envelope, then they thought he left."

A vein pounded in Dave's forehead. "What was he looking at on my desk?"

"Oh. I didn't look. Give me a minute."

Dave paced.

"I'm back," Louise said. "Your desk was a mess—"

"Not now, Louise."

"Well, ah . . . I think he was looking at a copy of the toxicology screen on Mattie Banks."

"What does it say?"

"She had Ketamine in her system. What's Ketamine?"

"An animal tranquilizer. Where is Wes now?"

"I don't know."

"Who's on duty?"

"Uh . . . Dre—"

"Get him to start looking for Wes. I'm grabbing some lunch with my wife, dropping her off, then I'm coming to the department. Heads are going to roll on this one."

The hospital door slammed open.

Mattie jumped.

A young cop charged into the room, grabbed Gwen, wrenched her from the chair, and cuffed her. "Out!"

Gwen twisted in his grip. "But—"

"You press won't stop at anything." He dragged her from the room and firmly shut the door. They could hear his voice in the hall. "You, there. Stand here until I get back. No one goes in or out. Understand?"

Aynslee jumped to her feet. "Did that guy just arrest my mom?"

Mattie was already sitting up. "Yeah. He didn't see you down there on the other side of the bed. Hurry. We don't have much time. You have to help me."

Aynslee crossed to the door, but paused before opening it. "Like, how?"

"First we gotta get this thing out of my arm. Help me. My fingers are broken. We can escape through that window. You're small, like me, so we'll fit. And it's on the ground floor. We gotta do it now!"

"But—"

"Never mind. Forget it." Using her teeth, Mattie tore the white tape around the needle, then pulled the IV out. Blood dribbled from a tiny catheter still in her wrist. She tugged at the remaining tape holding the tube. Blood smeared on her face.

"Here, let me help." Aynslee returned to the bed and eased the catheter from her wrist. She grabbed a tissue and placed it on the IV site. "Hold this for a few minutes to stop the bleeding."

Mattie held up her splinted hand.

"Sorry." Aynslee gently pressed the tissue in place.

A cart squeaked outside the door, stopped, then voices, speaking softly.

They froze.

The cart squealed again, fainter, then gone.

Mattie stood. Her legs were rubber. She fell, slamming into the hard floor.

She gasped and curled into a ball, holding her broken hands close to her stomach. Tears leaked from her eyes.

A soft hand touched her shoulder. "You're really scared. Look, it'll be okay. Mom will be back and get us out of here."

"Didn't you hear me when I told your mom that the guy was going to kill you, your mom, and your dog?"

"I heard, but it's safer in here, with a cop at the door and all."

Gulping, Mattie used her elbows to right herself and shoved against the floor until she was sitting. "Listen to me. See those flowers? *He* brought them. He can get in here anytime he wants."

Aynslee bit her lip, then looked at the bouquet. "Okay. So. Where are your clothes?"

"Look in that closet."

Aynslee stood and disappeared around the bed. "Empty." She returned and helped Mattie stand.

"Never mind. Let's go." Leaning against Aynslee, she made it to the window. "Pull down the handle." Aynslee complied. A small pane opened inward.

Using her foot, Mattie shoved a chair to the window and stepped up on it. The world twirled for a moment, and she held on to the chair until the dizziness stopped. She stuck her foot through the opening to a brick ledge. Slowly lowering her body, she wiggled through, the latch on the top of the window gouging her back before she was free. She fell.

Pain shot up her arm and she moaned. *Get up! Get up!* She rolled over to her knees. The hospital was on her right, the windows safely above her head. The ground fell slightly in front of

221

her before ending in a short cement retaining wall. A line of trees and hillside were on her left.

She stood and peeked back into the room. Aynslee was on the far side of the bed. She snatched the flowers out of the vase, dropped them into a trash container, and grinned at Mattie.

Mattie pumped her arms.

Aynslee soon wiggled out the window and dropped to the ground. "Ouch!"

"Come on," Mattie said. "We can go hide in the forest. Live off the land. I saw a television show—"

"Do you like the woods?"

"No."

"I have a better idea," Aynslee said. "Follow me." They crept to the wall. "You'll be caught in two seconds wearing that nightgown. And I can see your naked rear."

Mattie's face grew warm.

"We can sneak into the hospital," Aynslee continued, "and find you some scrubs, then at least you'll look like a nurse or something."

"What about these?" Mattie held up her splinted fingers.

"I don't know yet. We'll think of something." They peered over the wall. "Follow me," Aynslee said. They scurried left around the wall, then to the employee entrance and plastered themselves against the wall.

Mattie licked her dry lips and nodded. Aynslee eased the door ajar. They shot to the supply room and ducked inside just in time.

Footsteps and voices echoed down the hall, getting closer.

Aynslee yanked down several sets of small scrubs from the shelf, then pulled Mattie behind a row of gray metal shelves.

Mattie sat on the floor, wrapping her arms around her legs, and found an opening between boxes of gauze where she could see the room.

The voices paused and the door creaked open.

"Did you hear what happened?" someone asked. A chunky woman entered.

"How could I miss it?" A straw-haired, middle-aged woman followed. "There's still a bunch of cops in the front parking lot. Did you see the one cop? The tall one that looked like, I don't know, a movie star? Yum. He can search my body anytime."

"Julia, you hussy! Remember, you're married."

"Yeah, but I can look, can't I? Do I have time to dash outside for a quick smoke?"

"You shouldn't smoke. Neither should I. We'll make it fast." The women left, letting the door swing shut behind them.

Aynslee and Mattie waited a moment before standing. Aynslee helped Mattie tug off the nightgown, then stuffed it behind a box marked *Admissions Kits*. The scrubs were huge. "Why'd they call these small?" Mattie asked. "They'd fit a hippo."

"They'll do," Aynslee said. "Shoes next." Both girls circled the room, but all they found were some slipper-like paper things and socks with rubber strips on the bottom.

"Let's get out of here," Mattie said. She ran for the door, but stopped. One of the women had left her purse on a box near the door. Pulse racing, Mattie prodded the purse open and dumped the contents.

"What are you doing?" Aynslee hissed.

"I'll pay her back. We need money." A red leather wallet landed on top. Mattie stuck the edge of the wallet in her mouth, shoved the purse and contents behind the box, opened the door, and jogged left. Aynslee followed. Voices echoed behind them. *Move it.* They sprinted around a corner.

More voices, this time in front, and the rasp of an approaching gurney.

Mattie felt like a rat in the bottom of a Dumpster as she frantically looked around. The door beside her was locked. Aynslee tried the next one. Locked. The sounds were getting louder.

The third door was marked *Morgue.*

Aynslee reached for the knob.

"Morgue? Isn't that dead people?" Mattie whispered.

"Yeah. But at least they won't yell for help." Aynslee opened the door and they dodged through.

Mattie leaned against the wall. She didn't want to turn around. The room smelled like a chemical plant and felt cool.

"Come on. Move away from the door." Aynslee gripped her arm and dragged her from the wall.

A quick glance assured Mattie that the two steel tables were empty of bodies. Ahead, a metal desk overflowing with papers faced the room. To their left, a narrow table held a microscope, slides, racks of tubes, and other instruments Mattie didn't recognize. They hid behind the desk until the voices passed.

Aynslee started searching, opening and closing drawers. "Mom told me these old doctors sometimes keep—ah ha!" She held up running shoes. "Give me your foot."

Mattie spit the wallet out of her mouth, sat in the chair, and held up a foot. Aynslee slipped on the shoe. "Too big." She reached for a box of tissues on the desk and stuffed them into the toe, then tried it on again. This time it fit a little better. Swiftly she stuffed the second shoe.

"What about my hands?" Mattie asked.

Aynslee slowly circled the room, arriving at an old bamboo coatrack. A red plaid jacket hung on one side, an umbrella on the other. She lifted the coat. "Drape this over your hands. You'll be a tired technician just getting off work and heading home."

Mattie nudged the stolen wallet into the pocket.

Aynslee picked up the phone on the desk, started to dial, then quickly hung up. "This goes through a switchboard or something."

"Who were you going to call?"

"My dad. We can meet him somewhere. We'll be safe with him, and he can help Mom. So can Dave. He's the sheriff."

After easing the door open, Aynslee checked the hall, then jerked her head that the coast was temporarily clear. They fled to the exit.

Mattie's heart pounded. What if the two women were still smoking outside? What if they knew she was here and were waiting for her? For both of them? What if—

Aynslee opened the door.

CHAPTER TWENTY-NINE

I TRIED TO REASON WITH THE OFFICER, EXPLAIN that I wasn't a reporter, point out that I was in law enforcement. He wasn't buying any of it. With my feet barely touching the ground, he marched me down the hall past curious doctors and nurses. I spotted Beth and managed to mouth, *Get Aynslee*, before he hustled me out to a parked patrol car and shoved me into the back. A few visitors to the hospital paused to watch the show. My face flamed with a hot flash, leaving me uncomfortably damp.

The backseat of a patrol car isn't made for human comfort. The officer left me to cool my heels for what seemed like hours. He finally returned, leaned against the side, and placed a call. I could hear his side of the phone conversation. "Yeah, hi, Jeannie. This is Ken. Say, I caught a reporter that sneaked into the room with the girl. Yeah. Yeah. I don't know." He looked at me. "Do you have ID?"

"In a canvas bag. In Mattie's room. Who—"

"Nah, no ID. Okay." He looked back at me. "What's your name?"

"Gwen Marcey."

"She says her name is Gwen Marcey." He listened for a moment. "You're kidding. Really? Not as far as I could see. Will do." He hung up and opened the door. "Jeannie said to let you go, but if you ever do that again, she'll arrest you." After unlocking the handcuffs, he paused to listen to his shoulder mic.

"Attention all units. There's a 10–80 at 1512 West Fir—"

I knew that 10-code. Explosion. And that address. The veterinary hospital. Where my dog was locked up in a cage.

Mattie let out a sigh of relief as soon as she made it outside. The sooner they got away from the hospital, the safer she'd be. While they'd been looking for the scrubs, someone had parked a white pickup truck with a cap over the bed and left the motor running. A sign lettered on the side read *Andersen Upholstery and Office Designs, Copper Creek–Missoula*.

A middle-aged man in a denim jacket and jeans came toward them from the rear of the truck. He carried several large rings with fabric samples attached. "Ah, just in time. Can you hold the door?"

She bit her lip, unable to move. Aynslee stepped aside and nodded. The man strolled past them and turned right.

It took a moment before Mattie's legs would move. She caught Aynslee's attention and nodded toward the truck. "Can you drive?"

"I'm not stealing a truck."

Mattie dashed to the rear. Two chairs and numerous bolts of fabric jumbled together in the back, almost filling the space.

"What are you doing?" Aynslee asked.

"If you don't want to steal a truck, then let's steal a ride. He left the engine running, so he'll be right back. Come on." She clambered up, shoved one chair aside, and slipped behind several colorful stacks of fabric samples. After a moment's hesitation, Aynslee followed, knocking over a chair. She reached over to straighten the chair, then ducked.

The man stood by the open tailgate.

Mattie held her breath. *Oh, please.*

He slammed the tailgate up and pulled the door down. *Clank!* The vehicle rocked slightly, and the driver's door banged shut. The engine revved as they backed from the loading dock.

The two girls huddled together, keeping their heads below the window to the cab. Aynslee pulled the plaid jacket over their legs for warmth. The day had turned cool, and the truck bed was unheated.

Mattie's hands started to hurt. She hadn't thought about that. "Aynslee," she whispered. "I gotta get some drugs." She held up her splinted hands.

Aynslee chewed on a hangnail for a moment, eyebrows furrowed. "We have to go to my house. I can call my mom and dad from there. And Mom still has some drugs from when she had cancer—"

"But the guy knows where you live! He said he was going to kill you."

"No, it's okay. He can't get in. There're bars on the windows, and we'll lock all the doors. Mom has a cool pink rifle, and a gun too."

Mattie stared at her. "I don't know."

"We won't be there long. Just until we get ahold of my mom and dad."

The throbbing pain in Mattie's hands grew by the minute. "You're sure about the drugs?"

"Yeah. Don't worry. We'll be safe."

CHAPTER THIRTY

I RACED AROUND THE PARKING LOT, NARROWLY missing being hit by a white truck, and found my car. As soon as I located a phone, I'd let Beth know what was happening. Aynslee would be safe with my friend.

Not pausing to check for oncoming traffic, I gunned toward the vet hospital. The explosion had leveled the lobby. Flames snapped out of the treatment-area window as I slammed my car to a halt behind Dave's sedan. Black smoke and the stench of burning plastic rolled over me as I raced through the parking lot. Dave had already corralled the milling neighbors into the far corner of the asphalt. "Get back!" he yelled. "There could be more explosions." The crowd shifted farther from the building.

It seemed impossible that anything could survive the inferno.

I covered my mouth to keep from crying out. My legs felt like cooked pasta, my throat squeezed tight.

A fire truck stretched across the street, and the volunteer firefighters yanked a hose toward the building. More howling emergency vehicles arrived by the minute, strobe lights glaring like a grim festival.

The rear door of the hospital flew open, belching inky smoke. A Schnauzer dodged out, followed by a lanky black Lab, a German shepherd, and finally a Bernese mountain dog, tail between its legs. The crowd surged forward to rescue the frantic canines.

I charged toward the door just as a figure materialized carrying a huge dog.

Winston.

I gasped. *Please let him be alive.*

Wes, barely visible behind the dog, staggered forward, coughing. Dave and I reached his side just as he placed the dog on the ground, then collapsed next to him.

I knelt and lifted the dog's head. *Alive!* "Wes, you're crazy, but right now you're my hero!" I gave him a quick kiss, then hugged Winston.

"Did you see anyone inside?" Dave asked.

"I couldn't see." Wes coughed. "Dark, couldn't get beyond the back section. Flames too hot . . ." He coughed again.

"Both of you are in serious trouble." Pointing a finger at Wes, Dave said, "What were you doing—"

The screech of tires made us turn around. Dr. Hawkins jumped from his truck and shot toward the burning structure. "No! Oh no! Oh—"

Dave caught him before he got closer. "Pull yourself together! Who was working here today?"

Backing away from Dave, Hawkins's brow furrowed and his hand came up as if to ward off a blow. "Are you saying . . . you can't mean someone was in there?"

"Just answer me," Dave said. "Names!"

"It's Sunday." He looked at his watch. "It's a little after three. The weekend staff shouldn't arrive for another half hour. I don't know. If there was an emergency . . . I don't know." He hunched his shoulders.

"Is there anyone I can call?" Dave asked.

"I don't know. I can't think."

"What about the owners?"

"Yeah. Partners, but they're away. Left me in charge . . ."

I approached the veterinarian and touched him on the arm. "I'm so sorry."

Wordlessly, Hawkins folded to the ground and covered his face.

A gust of heat and smoke blew in our direction. Even though the day had turned cooler, the heat was almost unbearable. I retreated to Winston's side.

Dave tugged Hawkins to his feet and shoved him from the flames. Hawkins staggered a few steps before a firefighter grabbed him and led him to the curb where he draped a blanket over his shoulders.

Two firefighters approached me. "We need to get you and your dog a safer distance away," the first one said. "Can he walk, or do we need to carry him?"

"I don't know." Winston's left leg was bent tight to his body and taped into place. "Help me get him up." I pulled on the dog's ruff while the men hoisted him.

Standing on three legs, Winston swayed before gaining balance. With my urging, he hobbled forward until we reached my car. "Now I will need your help," I said. Between the three of us, we lifted the dog to the backseat where he sprawled, panting.

Wes sat at the rear of an ambulance holding an oxygen mask over his face.

I strolled over to him. "Hey, Wes, I want to thank you again for saving Winston. What were you doing here? I understood the place was closed."

Wes glanced at the hospital. "Why was I here? Good question." He took a deep breath.

"Don't bother to answer," I said. "You're getting ready to lie to me."

Wes's eyes opened wider.

Crack! Whoosh!

I spun. A section of roof caved in, sending a heat wave outward. I stepped farther away and looked at Wes. "Well?"

Wes took another puff of oxygen. "I was following up on a lead."

"Why don't you let the police do that?"

"Hey, I saved your dog."

I didn't know whether to thank him again or hit him for being such a jerk. Instead, I spun and headed for Dave, who was bent over Dr. Hawkins.

"Dr. Hawkins." Dave touched the man on the shoulder. "Dr. Hawkins! I need to ask you something."

The vet tore his gaze from the burning practice. "I'm sorry. Yes?"

"Ketamine—"

"Did you catch who did it? Maybe they blew up the building!"

"Huh?"

Dr. Hawkins stood. "We had a break-in last month. I reported it myself. Someone took all our Ketamine. Now I'm wondering if this is revenge for calling you."

Another fire engine arrived, and we moved farther away from the inferno. "I'll look into it." He looked at me and lowered his voice. "I can't believe you ignored everything I told you and tried to interview that girl. You're suspended until further notice."

I rocked backward. "But—"

"I don't have time for this and don't want to hear any excuses." He spun away from me. "And right now I really don't want to even see you."

I looked at the fire. The killer said I owed him three lives. He'd already tried to kill my dog. Aynslee would be next.

Mattie's hands pounded with a relentless ache, keeping sleep at bay, although she was bone-tired. She crouched next to Aynslee by a rusty green Dumpster. The truck driver had stopped to eat at the Huckleberry Café. They waited until he'd gone in to eat, then jumped out of the truck.

"How far are we from your house?" Mattie asked.

"Too far to walk. We need to get a ride."

"Like hitchhiking?"

"No. We need to call someone to pick us up." She nodded at the café. "I could go in and ask to use their phone."

"Who would you call?"

"Mom or Dad. I'll try Dad first."

"What if someone else sees you in the café? What if *he* sees you?"

Aynslee frowned. "I think there's a pay phone on the other side, by the road." She looked around. "We can keep the cars between us and the café. We have to move anyway. It stinks here."

Crouching down, both girls crept around the building until

they could see the pay phone. They hid behind a cedar, the fragrant boughs providing a needed break from the stench of the Dumpsters. "Give me that purse. I need change," Aynslee said.

Mattie turned so Aynslee could fish the wallet out of her pocket, then Aynslee raced to the phone.

Mattie's hands now throbbed with every beat of her heart. She shifted from foot to foot, watching for anyone paying attention. One car left the parking lot, but the driver seemed intent on the road.

After what seemed like hours, Aynslee finally returned. "Dad wasn't home and his answering machine is full. Mom must not have her phone with her because she didn't pick up. I can't remember Beth's number, and Dave is at a fire or something and they wouldn't let me talk to him. Now what?"

Mattie looked at her splinted hands. "Now we call someone *I* know. And it's going to cost us."

CHAPTER THIRTY-ONE

"HEY, ACE, IT'S ME, MATTIE. THAT IS, CHERRY."
Aynslee held the phone to Mattie's ear and stood so her body
blocked Mattie from the road.

Mattie still felt naked and exposed.

"Whatda you want? I heard you were dead."

"I'm not. I need a fix. Something strong 'cause I'm in a lot
of pain."

"Yeah, right. You owe me for the last one."

"I paid you." Voices and the slam of the restaurant door made
her duck. "I've got money," she whispered. "I need some percs or
kickers."

Silence for a moment. "Thought you were getting off all
that. Whatever. I can meet you—"

"No! You have to come here. And you have to drive me and
a friend someplace." She told him her location and where she
wanted to go. He hung up after a few parting cuss words.

Mattie moved aside so Aynslee could hang up the phone. "Is
he coming?" Aynslee asked.

"Yeah. He's already south of town. He'll be here in about twenty minutes." The smell from the restaurant made her stomach growl, then made her want to puke.

"Let's move away from the road." Aynslee pointed. "We could hide behind those trees."

"Good idea."

"How are your hands?" Aynslee asked as they trotted toward the trees.

"Bad, but I'm tough," Mattie said through clenched teeth. They ducked behind the nearest pine. She felt like a rat, slinking around. The forest behind her muttered like an old drunk talking to his paper bag of booze. She nudged the collar up on the stolen coat. She'd never liked the woods. Too many animals.

A van pulled in and parked near where they were hiding. A family piled out. "Loser." Mattie whispered.

"Why?"

"He's driving a minivan. Loser car."

"Loser car," Aynslee repeated. "Cool."

The father lifted a small blonde girl from the rear seat, gave her a hug, and gently placed her down. "You're the birthday girl, princess, so order anything you want." He took her hand and led her toward the front.

The lights blurred together. Her broken fingers hurt less than the empty hole in her chest. Why couldn't someone say that to her? Just once. She rocked back and forth slowly.

Aynslee gave her a quick hug. "He'll be here soon. I'm sorry you hurt."

Hot tears briefly warmed Mattie's face, then chilled to icy lines on her cheeks. "S'okay. No one's ever said 'I'm sorry' to me before."

A second car parked, but no one emerged.

Mattie caught her breath. *Ace?*

The headlights flashed once.

Her heart pounded faster, making the pain retreat slightly. She jerked her head at Aynslee, checked the parking lot, then hurried to the passenger door. It opened, and she slid onto the warm seat. Her teeth started chattering, and she hunched forward. Aynslee hopped into the backseat.

The car reeked of cigarette smoke, dirty clothes, and body odor. Discarded fast-food containers littered the floorboards. The ashtray overflowed with cigarette butts.

"Give me the money or I'm dumping you right now." Ace had a cigarette dangling from his lip and spoke around the smoke. He stuck out a dirty hand.

She awkwardly removed the wallet from her pocket, but before she could open it, he snatched it from her and lifted the bills. Swiftly counting the money, he grunted, then pulled out a plastic sandwich bag full of pills and tossed it into her lap.

Using both hands, she lifted the baggie to her mouth to open it.

He grabbed the bag and dumped out a small green tablet. "Open."

She opened her mouth, and he tossed in the pill.

"Swallow it whole. Don't chew it." He folded the baggie and stuffed it back into his pocket.

She tried to gather enough spit, but the painkiller was like swallowing a boulder. Slowly, ever so slowly, the throbbing ache retreated.

"I kind of like this rescue stuff." He leaned back and cracked his knuckles, then tossed his cigarette out the window. "Yeah.

How about you giving me a thank-you gift? Maybe both of you." He reached over and squeezed her leg.

A wave of disgust flooded her. "Don't. Touch. Me!" Her voice was guttural with loathing.

He snatched his hand away like he'd placed it on hot coals. "Fine with me. Just don't come whimpering to me again. Ever. Don't need no gimp to work for me. Plenty of fresh meat out there." Putting the car into gear, he spun his wheels on the gravel, fishtailed once he hit pavement, and raced down the street.

She closed her eyes, not wanting to see the blur of trees or flashing white lines. She wanted to pray, but didn't know how. Or to whom.

When they reached town, he slowed.

"Aynslee, we'd better duck out of sight." Mattie slumped in her seat until only her eyes were above the bottom of the window. Gaudy-colored lights from the downtown businesses danced like a stripper light show on the dashboard. He cranked up the radio, blasting her with heavy metal, and stepped on the gas. The lights disappeared.

"Turn up there," Aynslee directed. "Now stay on this road for about six miles."

No one spoke as the asphalt gave way to a graveled county road.

Finally, Aynslee leaned forward and pointed. "Stop there."

He didn't even bother to look at either of them, just slammed the brakes so hard Mattie flew forward. "It's your funeral. Go turn a few tricks out here."

They both jumped out.

He revved the engine. Aynslee pulled her aside as he reversed direction and spun his wheels, flinging gravel at them.

Dodging the small rocks, Mattie shot a few more cuss words at him, then stuck out her tongue. Aynslee stared at her.

"What?" Mattie asked.

"My mom would wash my mouth out with soap if I talked like that."

"Well." Mattie shrugged. "I don't have a mom. And he deserved it. He's a soggy wooker."

Aynslee giggled. "What's a soggy wooker?"

Mattie thought for a moment. "I'm not sure. I just like the sound of it."

"Oh. Mom would call him a scumbag. But I like soggy wooker." She pointed left. "We're almost there."

The dirt road stretched in both directions. The trees reached for Mattie on the right, and the splash of a creek reminded her that she still needed to pee. *There's nothing out there in the dark. Just deer and stuff like that. Bambi.*

They started walking.

It took almost an hour for me to extract my car from the maze of trucks, people, and emergency vehicles. The car reeked of smoke and dog. Winston panted on the backseat, nervous, ropy drool hanging from his mouth. I'd get him water as soon as I got home.

Beth was going to be steamed at my leaving her at the hospital. Maybe I could do a portrait of her as a thank-you. Or better yet, paint Norman, her husband. I'd better start thinking of paying jobs as well. I was once again officially unemployed.

Beth must have been watching for me. She sprinted out of the hospital lobby and yanked open the car door. "Aynslee's gone!"

I gripped the wheel tighter. "What?"

"Aynslee. And Mattie."

"How—"

"Open window."

"Get in."

Beth jumped into the car. "I tried to tell him—"

I slammed the car into gear. "I'm dropping you off at your house."

"What's going on? Where have you been?" She looked in the backseat. "Why does your dog smell like smoke?"

"Someone blew up the animal hospital," I said.

"Oh no, were any dogs hurt?"

"I don't think so."

Her eyes grew shiny from unshed tears.

"This is twice that the Phineas Priesthood murderer has tried to kill Winston. Once when he called Dave and said my dog attacked Mattie, then today. I need you to take my dog. Norm can look after him—"

"Norm?"

"Tell him I'll clean his fish for a month. I need *you* to call Dave. He's not exactly talking to me at the moment. Tell him about the girls, then tell him Mattie said the killer was after Winston, Aynslee, and me."

She gasped.

"Tell him about our ideas on tomorrow and possible Columbine-type action. It's a long shot, but worth mentioning. I'm going home in case Aynslee's heading there. If she's not there yet, I'll leave her a note and tell her to stay put and not answer the door for anyone, then I'm going to look for her."

"Aren't the police looking—"

"If she's with Mattie, which I believe she is, she'll be hiding from everybody. But she knows my car."

"Where's your cell phone?"

"At the hospital with my drawing supplies. If Aynslee calls you, tell her to stay put and call Dave to pick her up. I'll check in with you."

"What about calling Robert?"

I pulled up in front of Beth's house and looked at her. "I . . . I think you'd better call him too."

CHAPTER THIRTY-TWO

DAVE GULPED THE SCALDING COFFEE, CUPPING his hands around the plastic cup to garner its warmth. The stench from the burned-out building made his nose twitch. The firefighters seemed to be winning the battle, with just a few areas still burning steadily.

He hoped all the animals inside were freed by Wes. *Wes.* He'd need to talk to the man about why he'd been snooping in Dave's office. And how he got into the animal hospital. There was also Gwen's idea that Wes was responsible for chucking his cell phone into the bushes at the McCandless farm. He looked around. The man was missing.

Dave's right hand burned. Hot coffee coursed through his fingers from his squashed cup. Relaxing his grip, he let the cup drop. It hit on the ground and skidded ahead as the wind lifted it. He chased the cup, snatched it up, and stuffed it in his pocket, then pulled out a handkerchief and wiped his fingers.

He checked his watch, then tugged out a small notebook.

Dre should be out looking for Wes, but that could keep until after the torchlight parade. He'd have to call in a reserve deputy to guard the charred animal hospital until the state guys could check it out. Maybe ATF should be called because of the explosion. He started writing. He had the sketch on the girl in the cow pasture. He could pull a deputy following up on the wolf attacks to work on the girl's identity tomorrow.

He finished writing and put the notebook away. Spotting Ron on the street directing traffic, Dave jogged over. "I'll have someone relieve you as soon as possible. Head over to the torchlight parade route. The FBI said there was no credible threat from that church, but we can't be too careful. I suspect our problems might come from the people protesting the parade."

"Okay. Did you hear the news? That girl that Missoula was supposed to be guarding got away."

"What do you mean, 'got away'?"

"I guess she ran away."

"This whole afternoon has turned into one big goat rodeo." Dave crossed to his car, got in, and called dispatch. "Where's Dre?"

"He's 10–7."

"Call me when he's back in service."

"Ten-four. I have a note here for you from a reporter—"

"I don't have time for the press right now."

"This one was returning your call. She said she did see a man reach into your car at the McCandless place and grab something out, then toss it. She was going to say something to you, but forgot."

"Did she say who it was?"

"Just that he wore blue rubber gloves."

Wes. "Can you patch me through to Detective Jeannie Thompson, Missoula PD?"

After a few moments, Jeannie answered. "Yeah, Dave, what can I do for you?"

"I heard about the girl. What can you tell me?"

"Apparently Gwen Marcey broke into Mattie's room—"

"I know." Dave gripped the mic tighter. "She's been suspended for it."

"My officer caught her trying to draw a composite. He arrested her, thinking she was the press. I had him let her go. Anyway, Mattie was left alone for less than an hour. The nurse checking on her discovered she was missing. The window was open. An aide reported a stolen wallet a short time later, so we checked the supply closet where she'd left her purse. We found what looks like Mattie's hospital gown. That makes me think she grabbed some scrubs. Beats the heck out of me how she could have done that with two broken hands."

"Are you sure she ran away? Could someone have taken her?" Dave asked.

"The deputy guarding her put an orderly by the door while he took Gwen away. No one went in or out. The window she crawled through was tiny."

"Okay." He thought for a moment. "Was there any money in the wallet?"

"Less than a hundred dollars."

"Mattie's pain medication should be wearing off. She'll be looking for a fix. Do you have her known associates? Her supplier?"

"I'll call the narcs. We're talking to the hospital people who left around the same time. Of course we put out an Amber Alert.

And we've checked Search and Rescue to see if they could put some dogs on the ground, just in case she made it to the woods."

"It sounds like you have things covered on Mattie. I'm also looking for your Wes Bailor."

Jeannie didn't respond immediately. "*My* Wes Bailor? What's he done now?"

"So you're not happy with him either." Dave started the car and turned up the heat. "I have a confirmation that he was the one to throw my cell into the bushes at the McCandless place. And my secretary saw him going through my case files."

"So, in addition to conducting his own investigation, he's tampering with a crime scene." Jeannie cleared her throat. "He's turned into a real loose cannon. We're going to fire him . . . as soon as we find him."

"Start by looking where he shouldn't be."

Mattie stared at the neat log home surrounded by a well-tended lawn. Daffodils poked up through colorful river rocks next to the house, and a row of flowering shrubs lined the driveway. "Are you rich or something?"

Aynslee stopped. "Hardly. I've been asking for an iPhone for months. And my laptop is at least two years old. And you wouldn't believe my TV . . ."

Mattie glanced at her. Aynslee had a hand over her mouth and was studying Mattie's stolen, oversize shoes.

Mattie cleared her throat. "Ah, what if the house is locked?"

"Mom keeps a spare key under a fake rubber dog poop in the yard."

"You're kidding!"

"Nope. It's right over . . ." Aynslee dropped the rubber poo. "Great. She forgot to put it back." She tried the door. Locked tight.

Mattie glanced around. "Maybe we could hide until someone comes home?" The distant throbbing in her hands grew. The pill was wearing off. If they couldn't get into the house, she'd have to try to call Ace again. But how? They were in the middle of nowhere without a phone. Mattie hugged herself and tried not to think about it.

A lone howl wavered on the slight breeze before a second howl joined in.

Mattie spun around. "W-what's that?"

"Coyotes. Don't worry, they're only dangerous to cats and small dogs." She thought for a moment. "We can't wait. It's almost dark. And getting colder by the minute." She glanced at Mattie. "Are you afraid of spiders?"

CHAPTER THIRTY-THREE

MATTIE FOLLOWED AYNSLEE TO THE SIDE OF THE log house. Aynslee parted the shrubs and pointed at a window-like shape near the ground.

A small sigh escaped Mattie's lips. It was an access door to the space under the house or maybe a basement. The door hinged on one side and was held shut by a sliding lever on the other.

Aynslee knelt and tugged at the lever, then reached for one of the smooth river stones edging the bushes.

"What if we can't get in?" Mattie's voice sounded high-pitched even to her.

"We'll get in." Aynslee hit at the latch, breaking the bolt. "Yesss!" She pulled the hatch open, then looked up at Mattie. "Are you *sure* you're not afraid of spiders? Mom's terrified . . . and . . . I hate them too."

"I don't much mind spiders. Now snakes, that's different."

Both girls stared at the inky opening.

"Tell you what," Aynslee said. "Why don't I go in there, unlock the kitchen door, and let you in."

Mattie shivered, the afternoon chill and pain in her hands growing by the minute. "We made it this far together. I'll go with you. Help me down."

Aynslee held Mattie's elbow as she eased to her knees, then to her stomach.

"You're going to have to crawl in first," Mattie said. "I don't know which way to go."

Aynslee took a deep breath and crawled forward, disappearing under the house.

Mattie used her elbows to pull her body forward. Blackness engulfed her, and she waited until her eyes adjusted to the dark. Soon she could see Aynslee's prone shape ahead of her. Heavy beams crisscrossed overhead, providing ample places for spiderwebs to create dense, lacy curtains. The only sounds were the tiny skittering of disturbed mice. "Which way?"

"Give me a minute," Aynslee answered in a raggedy voice. She sneezed, then crawled forward.

Mattie followed, elbows pushing the cold dirt aside. One of the oversize shoes slipped off her foot, and she used her toes to propel forward.

Up ahead a faint light marked out a square.

"Soggy wookers," Aynslee said as she pushed through the spiderwebs and stopped.

Mattie caught up with her.

Three feet above their heads, edges outlined by the light passing through the cracks, was a trapdoor.

"Please, oh please, don't let it be locked." Aynslee rolled to her side, pulled her knees to her chest, then rocked up until she was kneeling. She crouched and stood, keeping her head bent so the weight of the door was across her shoulders. It moved.

"Yes!" She slowly stood. The weight moved down her back, then crashed open with a bang.

Mattie let out a deep breath she didn't know she'd been holding.

Lightly hopping through the opening, Aynslee quickly reappeared and reached down.

Mattie wasted no time in scuttling out of the crawl space. She was in a small pantry with the door open to an old-fashioned kitchen. A low humming sound came from an ancient refrigerator. Like vomit, a memory came into her mind.

She let out a slight grunt.

Aynslee frowned at her. "What's wrong?" She helped Mattie to her feet.

"Thanks. Your kitchen kinda reminds me of someplace." She sat in a nearby chair.

"Really?" Aynslee sat beside her. "Where?"

"A bad place." Mattie placed her now filthy, splinted hands on the table in front of her. "I've been in foster homes since I was eight." She'd learned at an early age to recognize the look in the eyes of men who wanted her to call them "dad." The crazies. That's what she'd thought of them. Groping hands with sweaty bodies.

So how did the man fool her when he'd picked her up? The question tumbled in her mind like clothes in a dryer. She'd never made that mistake before. Never.

"Helloooo?" Aynslee gave her a funny look. "So where did you live before you were eight?"

"With my grandma."

"That's cool."

"I guess. She was real religious, then she died."

"I'm sorry." Aynslee crossed to the fridge. "Do you want something to eat?"

"What time is it?"

"About four something, but I'm always hungry."

"Okay, yeah. But what about those drugs?"

Aynslee left the room, returning a few moments later with a handful of amber bottles. "I'm not sure which ones are for pain and which ones are for puking. Mom had plenty of both." She placed the bottles on the table and returned to the fridge. "Um . . . I can make us a . . . jelly and, ah . . . jelly sandwich."

"Jelly's good." Mattie swiftly went through the bottles before selecting one. "Would you open this?"

Aynslee brought her a glass of water, then opened the bottle. "How many?"

"Uh, maybe two, no, three."

Biting her lip, Aynslee complied. "Are you sure? That's a lot. Mom only took one at a time."

"I'm used to drugs." She opened her mouth.

Aynslee popped three pills in, then held the water so she could wash them down. "I'm going to try and get ahold of Dad or Mom." She picked up the phone, listened, and returned it to the cradle. "The phone's dead."

Mattie glanced quickly around the room.

"Don't worry, we're safe. When Mom tries the phone and it doesn't work, she'll come or send someone." Aynslee brought her a sandwich on a chipped plate, placed it in front of her, and sat.

Mattie looked at the snowy-white bread, then at the dingy bandages covering her fingers.

Wordlessly, Aynslee picked up the sandwich and offered it to her. They quickly consumed the simple meal. "Do you want to see the rest of the house? Mom's set up a, like, investigation room. And she has an art studio."

"Your mom has an art studio too? Yeah." She followed Aynslee down a central hallway, through a living room, into a large, converted porch. A drafting table and small set of drawers on wheels sat in the corner. Mattie crossed to the table. Pencils, erasers, and a host of other art tools rested in a tray attached to the side. The wide window ledge held an assortment of sketch-pads and drawing papers, and half-finished paintings filled a deep bin against the wall. *This is what heaven would look like.* "Maybe she'll teach me to paint."

"Sure. Now come and see the investigation room."

Mattie reluctantly followed Aynslee into a rather cluttered office.

A large whiteboard sat on an easel with taped drawings, writing, and arrows. One of the drawings was Mattie. A photo-graph of Aynslee was next to it.

Mattie moistened her suddenly dry lips. "What is this?"

Aynslee slowly approached the display. "Mom's been work-ing on it. It looks like her form of link analysis."

"What's that?"

"A way to connect parts of crimes."

"Is that why a drawing of me is on it? She's trying to find the crazy who did this?" She held up her splinted hands.

Aynslee studied the board. "Yeah. According to this, the killer started a couple of years ago. You weren't the first, but you were one of the only ones to live—" She looked quickly at Mattie. "Sorry." She rubbed her arms as if cold.

Mattie leaned against the wall to steady herself. "You said your mom has a gun?"

"Yeah. A pistol and a rifle. Follow me." The girls entered the living room, and Aynslee opened the rifle display case.

"I've never seen a pink gun," Mattie said.

"It's pink camo. Mom says pink is a killer color." Aynslee lifted the rifle from the case, clicked something, and pulled on a lever.

Mattie took a step back. "Do . . . do you know what you're doing?"

"Sure. Dave, the sheriff, made me take a bunch of NRA safety courses." She put the rifle back into the case. "Now for the pistol." The girls trouped into Gwen's bedroom. "She keeps it on the top shelf in the closet." Aynslee grabbed a chair from the corner of the room, stood on it, and reached to the back of a shelf. "Ta-da!" She held up a gun.

"What's that?"

"A 9mm SIG Sauer," Aynslee said proudly. "Cool, huh?"

"Is it loaded?" Mattie asked, then yawned.

"Of course." Aynslee opened the clip. "One bullet, at any rate."

Mattie tried but couldn't hold back another jaw-cracking yawn. "*Ahem* . . . could we put that gun someplace easy to reach? Just in case?"

They returned to the living room where Aynslee placed the pistol next to the rifle. "There. Now we just have to wait."

Mattie could barely keep her eyes open. "Do you have someplace I can crash?"

"You can sleep in my bed. Come on."

Mattie followed the other girl down a hall and into a cluttered bedroom.

Aynslee swept the collection of stuffed animals, pillows, and clothes onto the floor, then helped her take off the remaining shoe. She frowned at Mattie's feet. "I was going to say the sheets aren't all that clean, but never mind."

Mattie sat on the bed, then rolled onto her side.

"Hear that?" Aynslee said. "I told you we just had to wait for a bit. I hear a car outside. I'll be right back."

Mattie was asleep as soon as her head hit the pillow.

CHAPTER THIRTY-FOUR

DAVE CHECKED HIS WATCH FOR THE THIRD TIME. Five thirty. His cell phone rang. "Dave Moore."

"Dispatch said to call you," Dre said.

"Where have you been? This place is a madhouse."

"Hey, I stopped for lunch. Got the be-on-the-lookout on Wes. Been on patrol ever since. Cell's worthless most of the places I've gone."

Dave dry-scrubbed his face. "So what do you have? And please make it good news for a change."

"No sign of Wes. I swung by Gwen's place about two twenty. All's quiet. Swung by the animal hospital. Ron's watching it for now but said a reserve deputy should be arriving shortly."

"I got ahold of the ATF at the Missoula satellite office. They're sending some agents first thing in the morning. FBI will be here as well. Missoula's working the Mattie angle, all my reserve staff— Hello? Hello?" Dave thumped the cell on his desk. Maybe dispatch could get Dre back on the line.

The phone rang. "Yeah, Dre—"

"It's Beth. Gwen told me to call you." She explained about a possible terrorist attack the following day.

Dave scribbled notes. "You have no idea where this might happen?"

"No. Just the time."

"I'll see what I can do. Maybe the FBI will have some ideas."

"Good. Aynslee is with Mattie—"

"Where's Gwen now?"

"She's on her way home. If Aynslee isn't there, she's going to go looking for her."

Dave gripped the phone tighter. "Winston?"

"The dog's here. What do you want me to do?"

"Stay put." Dave thought for a moment. "The girls have a three-hour head start. If they were heading to Gwen's place, they'd be there by now and Gwen will let us know when she gets home."

"But her phone is out."

"She'll manage somehow. I don't have a single available officer to put on this thing because of that stupid parade. Gwen's on her own for a bit."

I pulled up next to the house and parked. Stepping from my car, I stopped.

The front door stood open.

My stomach twisted. I crept to the entrance, then paused and listened for voices.

The house was deathly silent.

I slipped inside. My rifle from the gun-display cabinet was missing. I turned left and entered my studio. Empty. I spun and raced to the kitchen. Two dirty plates lay on the table along with a number of amber prescription bottles. I picked up one bottle, then another. All were in my name. "Aynslee? Mattie?" The backdoor was still locked. I ran to my bedroom, opened the closet, and reached for my SIG Sauer.

Gone.

Frantically, I checked the bedside table, then my dresser. "Mattie? Aynslee?" My voice echoed in the empty house. I sprinted to the living room, this time looking in the drawer under the gun display. A full box of .22 bullets sat untouched. Pivoting, I charged to Aynslee's room, abruptly halting at the door. The floor was covered with Aynslee's stuffed animals, clothes, and pillows. Bedding tangled in a heap at the foot of the bed.

A smear of blood stained the sheet.

The room seemed to spin, then blackness.

CHAPTER THIRTY-FIVE

MY HEAD RESTED ON A STUFFED BEAR. UNDER Aynslee's bed were a pair of jeans and a sock. The chill from the hard floor seeped into my side. I pushed up and got to my knees, then waited until the room stopped swirling. Vomit burned the back of my throat.

I stood and aimed toward the kitchen, reeling from side to side, holding on to the wall for support. Once there, I snatched up the phone and dialed. Nothing happened. *Of course, you idiot, the phone's dead.*

Remain calm. I moved back to the studio, looking for any clues to the girls' location. Methodically I advanced through the living room, my bedroom, then Aynslee's room. It didn't look as if Aynslee had changed her clothes, but it was hard to tell with the clutter. I forced myself to look at the bed again. A considerable amount of dirt clung to the fabric.

Aynslee didn't have a key.

The thought pounded into my brain. How did they get into the house? I sprinted to the kitchen, unlocked the door, and checked under the plastic dog poop. No key. Bars covered all the windows. Circling around toward my car, I checked the access to the crawl space. It was unlatched. Returning inside, I looked in the pantry.

The trapdoor was in place, but dirt rimmed the edge.

I forced my brain to think logically. The girls got in through the crawl space. They ate. Mattie must have helped herself to my drugs. Probably Mattie, still very weak and sleepy from the meds, lay down to take a nap.

Someone came to the door. What ruse had he used to get Aynslee to open it? A promise to call me? A message? And it had to be someone Aynslee knew or would trust.

I started down the hallway toward the front of the house but paused in front of the office. A slight odor I couldn't immediately identify came from behind the closed door.

Reaching for the knob, I froze. I *did* know that smell. Copper, sulfur, and singed hair.

CHAPTER THIRTY-SIX

THE BOTTOM OF A LEATHER SHOE PEEKED OUT from behind the desk.

My feet cemented to the floor, my breath came in harsh gasps. *No, please! Please, no!*

I forced myself to look at the shoe. Big. Man-sized. Not Aynslee. Or Mattie.

Moving closer, the shoe was attached to a leg, the leg to a body slumped against the wall.

Wes Bailor.

Blackness edged my vision.

A deceptively small hole in the center of his forehead leaked a rivulet of blood down his face and a deep gouge crossed his cheek. The dark-green plaid wallpaper behind him had a pink-and-burgundy spatter with a trail, ending at his still form. My SIG Sauer lay on the floor next to the door. I reached for it, then stopped. It only had one bullet in it, which was now in Wes's brain, so the gun was useless as a weapon. And this was a homicide scene.

I moved to the body, leaned down, and touched his neck for a pulse, but it was obvious he was dead. "You poor, stupid fool," I whispered. "Thought you could solve this case on your own. Superman." My voice shook, and I clamped my teeth shut.

Did *he* have a gun?

I swiftly checked his pockets, finding only his wallet. Inside the wallet was a challenge coin. I lurched to my feet. The challenge coin Scott gave me was still taped to the foam board. Wes had been the friend looking for the Lone Wolf. And now he was dead.

So where was his car?

And where were the girls?

If the killer went after Wes, and the girls heard the gunfire, then maybe they were hiding. "Girls? Mattie? Aynslee? You can come out." I tried to make my voice calm, but the words wavered. "It's okay. I'm home. I'm here now."

They couldn't be in the attic. Robert said the access door was broken.

Could they have hidden in the crawl space?

I raced from the room to the kitchen and opened the pantry door. The trapdoor opened easily. "Aynslee? Mattie? If you're hiding down there, you can come out. It's safe. I'm home." A long-legged spider hunkered down on its web and glared at me. I jumped away, dropping the trapdoor with a crash.

There's no way the girls would hide down there.

Dashing to the outside door, I yanked it open. "Mattie! Aynslee! Where are you?" Only the *shhhhh* of the pine's sighing in the evening breeze answered. I ran left, toward the garage. Wes's Forest Service pickup was parked on the far side, out of casual sight.

Why would he park there?

He didn't. I could hear the killer's voice on the phone whispering in my brain. *I hid his truck so your house would look normal. I have the girls.*

I clapped my hands over my mouth to keep back the scream. My thoughts jammed together. *Call Dave. No. Phones don't work. Cell? At hospital. Get help. Takes too long. How long has he had them? Find them.*

Spinning, I flew to the house, ending up in the studio. The county map was still taped to the foam core. "You're a thrill seeker," I whispered. "You want them to run. Where do you start?"

Wrong. Start where the bodies were found.

I found the tiny, black square of my house, then the crumbling McCandless farmhouse. Leaving my finger to mark the McCandless place, I traced the route Beth and I drove the day before, where we'd found the girl in the cow pasture. The two points were opposite each other, only separated by a long ridge. "He wanted the women to end up at the McCandless place. He gave them a map and compass, probably told them to run downhill and north. But the girl in the cow pasture couldn't read a compass. She ran south."

I stared at the map. "You don't want your victims to make that mistake again. So you'd start at a lower point on the hillside. It's natural to run downhill, especially if you live in the mountains."

I tapped the map. "This ridge is the key. There has to be a road he could access. Didn't the farmer say they'd logged here?"

Dave's voice answered. Something he'd asked Dre. *"See what you can find out about any logging or Forest Service roads north of here."* I could get ahold of Dre. Find out what he'd discovered.

But what if Dre was the killer? He was a lateral transfer from Spokane. Worked around woodpiles so could conceivably smell of wood chips. Saw Aynslee . . .

Stop it. Find them.

A drop of water struck Mattie's face. She shifted, trying to find space in the crowded compartment.

Aynslee, curled up next to her, sniffed. "Wha . . . what should we do?"

"I don't know. My head's all screwed up." She drifted in a river of blackness until Aynslee poked her. Hard. "Ouch."

"You gotta stay awake," Aynslee said. "We need a plan." The truck rocked and bounced around them, knocking them from side to side. "Where do you think he's taking us?"

"Back to that . . . place." Mattie tried hard not to cry.

"No. We've been driving too long. And we're going uphill."

Mattie tugged at her hands, but the zip ties held tight. Matching ties held her ankles together. "We're gonna die."

"No, we're not." Aynslee shoved against her.

"Stop it."

"I'm rolling over. Maybe I can reach your hands."

Between the bandages and pain medication, Mattie couldn't tell what Aynslee was doing.

"I can't . . . I can't get the zip tie off you without something sharp. Do you have a knife or X-ACTO?"

"What's an X-ACTO?" Mattie asked.

"Never mind. Okay. Let me think." Aynslee was silent for a few moments. "Okay. There are two of us and one of him—"

"Why'd you let them in?"

"I didn't have a lot of choice. That artist guy asked me about Winston. That was my code word with Mom. I didn't know there was someone else with him. Not at first. The other guy was hiding. He must have been waiting for someone to come. Or maybe he followed the artist guy."

"You shouldn't have opened the door."

"I had the rifle—"

"But he took it away." Mattie shivered.

"I didn't think he was a bad man."

"You *knew* him?"

"Yeah."

CHAPTER THIRTY-SEVEN

"I THINK HE KILLED THE ARTIST," MATTIE SAID.

"He couldn't have." Aynslee's voice wavered.

"Yeah. Put it together. He hit the artist guy in the face, then held a gun on him and made him put zip ties on us."

"He looked like he hated the artist."

"He did. After he left us on the sofa, he took the artist into that room. You heard the gun. And the guy didn't come out."

Aynslee sniffed. "Maybe . . . Mattie, listen. We can't do anything about that. Mom will come for us. But we gotta stick together. We gotta fight him. We have to run—"

"But we're tied up!" Mattie struggled, kicking the side of the compartment. Something crackled. The tarp, the one that had covered her before, was at her feet. She smelled mold and sweat.

"Shhh. Don't let him hear you." Aynslee moved so she was close to Mattie's ear. "Here's my plan, but first we need to pray."

The back of Mattie's throat burned. "Like for angels to help us?"

"I'm going straight to the top."

Hot tears cooled on Mattie's face. "I . . . I don't know how to pray."

"Don't worry. I'll do it. Um, God, please save us. We don't want to die . . ." Mattie heard her swallow hard. "And zap this guy or whatever You do so he can't do this again."

"I agree. Um, vote yes . . ."

"Just say amen."

"Amen."

Distant thunder echoed as I jumped into my car and checked the time. Six thirty. I had an hour—maybe hour and a half—to find the road, and the girls, before dark.

At the end of the driveway, I turned left. I'd searched on Google Earth and found the satellite image of my place. A ribbon of tan showed at the ridge's crest south of me, hinting of an old road, but I couldn't find where it started. I knew a small road circled behind the McCandless place. It was well below the top of the ridge, but conceivably could be used. And it was close.

Dirt flew from my racing tires as I shot down the county road. I passed the McCandless turnoff and slowed down, watching on my right for a break in the trees. I finally spotted it about a half mile farther down.

A gray metal gate chained shut blocked the access.

Gripping the steering wheel tighter, I spun around. The car bucked and skidded on the loose gravel before straightening. I stepped on the gas and doubled back, checking my odometer as

I passed my home so I'd have some idea of where I was. I just hoped, and prayed, that I could find the turnoff.

Before it was too late.

The truck stopped moving.

Mattie froze and drew short puffs of air, concentrating on sounds.

"Remember," Aynslee's voice whispered in her ear. "Mom and Beth talked about it. Mom called him a thrill seeker. He'll want us to run. No matter what he says, run downhill. That's where we'll find roads and people. He'll untie our ankles. That's when we'll make our move."

A cool wind pushed through the seams of their tiny cubicle.

Mattie shivered. Even with Aynslee's body next to her, neither one wore thick enough clothing, and they were cold.

Mattie tried to make her brain work. The drugs numbed her hands but also muddied her thinking. "But if all he's going to do is make us run—"

"We have to make sure he doesn't hurt us first."

The top of their compartment opened.

Mattie blinked. Somehow she'd expected it to be nighttime.

The killer's face appeared above them. "Hello, girls. Are you ready for some fun?"

The county road dead-ended at Copper Creek Lake, and no one lived east between my place and the lake. Numerous wooden bridges spanned the winding Copper Creek, and distances were often measured by how many bridges were crossed. Given the steepness of the ridge, I figured at least two bridges before a road could be a reasonable grade for a logging truck to use.

The mountain crowded the road, offering a sheer, rocky wall. Another bridge.

The sun just tinted the tops of the trees as it settled for the night. "Come on. Come on. I have to find it. Lord, I have to find that road."

Yet another bridge.

He reached in and grabbed Mattie by her arms and slung her to the ground in a heap.

She struggled to stand.

He slapped her face.

Tears filled her eyes and she slumped to her side.

Aynslee slammed to the ground next to her. She opened her mouth and seemed to gasp for air.

"I've been looking forward to this for a long, long time," the man said.

"You . . . you won't . . . get away with this," Aynslee said, still trying to breathe. "The police are everywhere."

The killer cocked his head to one side. "Is that what you think?"

"They'll be here any minute." Mattie couldn't see his reaction from the angle she was lying.

"I wouldn't count on it. There's a little matter of a torchlight parade by a bunch of neo-Nazi wannabes. Every law enforcement officer in the county will be tied up with that. One of my little diversionary tactics. I have all the time in the world with you two."

"Then are you going to go out and shoot up that school tomorrow?" Aynslee asked.

The man gave a sharp intake of breath. "Well now, aren't you the clever one. But my plans are much bigger—"

"The University of Montana?" Aynslee asked. "Or the Jewish—" A slap. Aynslee grunted.

Mattie felt something sharp on her ankles, a tug, and her legs were suddenly freed. Blood rushed to her feet, and she winced at the sharp, prickly feeling. He shoved her to her stomach and, with another pull, freed her hands. She rolled to her side. Something dropped over her head.

Mattie yelped and swatted at it, pulling it from her face.

A coat.

"You'll need that," he said. "It'll be dark soon. There's a map and compass in the pocket."

He bent over Aynslee and cut the zip ties on her ankles. "You are far too clever. You, I'm going to—"

She kicked him.

He stumbled backward.

"Run," Aynslee screamed.

Mattie got to her knees.

He stepped back to Aynslee and wrapped his hand in her long, red hair.

"Run," she screamed again.

He smashed her face into the earth.

Mattie was on her feet. She ducked her head and ran. Her head slammed into his side, sending both of them tumbling. Sparks flickered behind Mattie's eyes. She grunted in pain.

He recovered first. A vein throbbed in his temple as he glared at her, then looked around as if seeking something.

She spotted the gun first. It was lying next to the truck.

He reached for it.

Aynslee, arms still tied behind her, crashed into his back, sending him forward. His head connected with the bumper. Mattie stood, lifted the coat, hooked her arm under Aynslee's, and yanked her upright. Steaming blood gushed from her nostrils.

"Grab his pistol," Aynslee whispered.

Mattie used the coat as a basket and scooped up the gun. As one, they turned and ran.

CHAPTER THIRTY-EIGHT

MY EYES BLURRED, AND I ANGRILY SWIPED AT them. *Not now.* I rolled the windows down, ignoring the chilly air, and slowed my car. The road had to be around here somewhere. The sun set and the forest crowded the road, sucking out the last of the light.

I almost missed it.

Coming around a curve, the road widened slightly. I stopped and stared. In the gathering dusk, a few tiny pines were growing crooked on the side of the road. *Or a truck drove over them.* I backed up and turned left, wincing at the sounds coming from under my car as I crushed the small trees under my wheels.

Noting the odometer reading, I knew I'd need to go about five miles west to put me above my place on the ridge. But since I was also climbing uphill, I'd need to increase that number. I wanted, needed to drive faster, but the track was more an impression than a passageway. The seconds ticked away in my mind. I jammed down the thoughts of what he might do to my daughter. I found myself chanting, "Lord, protect her. Save her."

I thought I heard something. I stopped the car and shut off the engine.

"Ruff . . . ruf . . . aaaaeeeeeeeeee."

Coyotes. I started the car and pushed forward. The lane cleared somewhat and climbed toward the top of the ridge. I was now running parallel to the county road far below to my left. This had to be the road suggested by Google Earth.

I had to turn on my headlights to see the bent grass in front of me. The temperature dropped still lower. I turned up the heat to offset the open window.

A mile, two miles, three. The road grew steeper, switched back, and widened. I'd reached a landing, a place where loggers assembled the cut trees waiting to be picked up by the trucks that would haul them. The mountainside had been thinned in the past year, and the remaining seed trees were widely spaced. The ground was rocky and the road split, with no indication as to which direction I should take. I got out of the car and inspected the ground with the illumination from my headlights.

Faint tire marks and a dislodged rock indicated he'd taken the upper road. I got back into my car and shifted into low. The way was steep, and the rocks gave way to dirt and mud, with a raw, bulldozer cut on my right and a sheer drop on my left, bare of trees, indicating a skid trail. Twice my tires spun in the thick muck before finding purchase. I'd only gone a short distance when I spotted the downed tree across the road. Scraped bark on the top showed where tires passed over it.

My little Audi didn't have the clearance of a truck. If I got high centered, my car would be stuck. I pulled the emergency brake and stopped.

Mattie hauled Aynslee as fast as they dared down the steep slope. With her arms tied behind her back, Aynslee stumbled over hidden roots and downed branches. Pausing under a pine to catch their breath, Mattie draped the coat over Aynslee's shoulders.

"You put it on," Aynslee said. "You're shaking in the cold."

"So are you."

"Then we'll share it. Next time we stop, you put it on."

They ran. Both of them fell and rolled over a thick bramble of snowberries. The coat flew off Aynslee's shoulders. The pistol, now tucked under Mattie's arm, dropped.

"Ouch." Aynslee sobbed.

"Are you okay?"

"No. My foot's tangled up."

"Maybe we can hide here?" Mattie looked around.

"No. We have to keep running."

"But I dropped the gun."

"Leave it. The important thing is *he* doesn't have it."

Mattie's hands, still wrapped in their filthy, tattered bandages, were starting to ache as the drugs wore off. She used her feet to feel Aynslee's legs and trace back to the tangle of brush enclosing her ankle. "I'm going to stomp this branch down. See if you can free your foot." She stepped on the limb, then pushed her weight against it. The *snap* seemed deafening.

"Shh," Aynslee whispered. "I'm free. Where's the coat?"

"Ah . . . here it is."

"Your turn. Put it on."

"I can't. My hands." Mattie could just make out Aynslee in the darkness.

The other girl rolled to her knees. "I see it. I'm going to grab

273

it with my teeth, then stand. You should be able to slip it on if I hold it, right?"

Mattie nodded, unable to answer past the lump in her throat. The coat was oversized and slipped easily over her hands. She looped her arm through Aynslee's, and they continued their headlong race through the trees.

Something howled behind them.

Mattie screamed.

I got out of my car.

Excited howls echoed from the road above me. Not coyotes.

My blood ran cold.

A distant scream. I plunged off the muddy track and raced downhill.

Dave's ear hurt from all the phone calls he'd made. Now he'd have to pray that nothing else went wrong. The torchlight parade officially started at seven thirty with a speech in the grocery-store parking lot. The parade application said the church group would walk down the main street of town. Missoula had loaned him three officers in riot gear, and Dave had assigned them to pace with the marchers.

Both sides of the street held protesters carrying signs. His own men covered the six-block route the best they could, but it was a circus.

Dave glanced at his cell for the hundredth time. He still hadn't heard from Gwen.

Gwen's and Beth's words kept rewinding in his mind. The

Phineas Priesthood liked to use bombings, and the vet hospital *had* been bombed. But why? It wasn't connected to the government. Could it be a cover-up for the missing Ketamine? Or was it to kill Gwen's dog? If an entire animal hospital were leveled just to kill an innocent dog, then Gwen was facing a level of destruction, hatred, and revenge beyond imagination.

What about Beth's suggestion of a terrorist attack tomorrow at eleven? He'd called that one in to the FBI. They said they'd look into it.

A scuffle broke out ahead of him and he raced forward. "Okay, now, break it up. Come on, fellows." The pushing stopped, but the jeers and chanting didn't.

The marchers formed a raggedy group behind three men carrying a banner stating *White Man Awake*. Behind the banner was a pickup truck with the name of the church, followed by the rest of the participants. Four men lit torches and positioned themselves at the front and rear of the marchers. At some unseen signal, all the church members lifted small American flags and started forward. The yelling from the sidelines increased.

His deputy, Craig Harnisch, suddenly appeared beside him. His face was pale and eyes bloodshot.

"Don't you have the flu?" Dave asked.

"I'm better. Thought you could use a hand."

Debating only briefly on sending the man home, Dave pulled out his car keys. "I shouldn't be long."

CHAPTER THIRTY-NINE

I REACHED A ROW OF TREES AND STOPPED TO catch my breath and get my bearings. The moon was out, but passing clouds allowed it to cast only intermittent light. The girls would be west, and going by the scream, almost parallel to me. Aynslee would know to run downhill. If he'd given her a map and compass like he did the girl in the cow pasture, she'd be able to locate the McCandless farm. If I ran diagonal, I could hopefully intercept them. I had to find them before he did.

Another howl, higher up on the ridge.

I leaped ahead.

Mattie's hands throbbed. Branches slapped her face. Aynslee, bent forward to protect herself from the reaching limbs, panted beside her. "Where are we?"

"I'm . . . not . . . sure." Aynslee slowed, then stopped, breathing hard, and looked around her.

"What's that howling?"

"Coyotes."

Mattie knew she was lying. Whatever they were, they were big. And following them.

It was dark by the time Dave pulled up next to Gwen's house. No lights shown from any of the windows. He parked, pulled out a flashlight, and got out of the car. Gwen's vehicle was missing, so she must be out looking for the girls. He checked the front door, then the door to the kitchen. Everything locked. He turned to leave.

A Forest Service truck sat next to the garage. Dave strolled to the pickup and flashed his light into the cab, illuminating a forensic art kit. Wes Bailor.

Dave gazed back toward the house. Gwen really disliked Wes, but her car was missing, and so were both of them.

Did they join forces to find Aynslee and Mattie? He trotted to his car and got in.

Wes was at the vet hospital when it was bombed, had been in his office reading reports, showed up at *both* the McCandless place and the cow pasture.

Dave started the engine and turned the sedan around. Was Wes on some misguided scheme to catch the killer? With Gwen's help?

Or was *he* the killer?

Headlights poked through the trees and a car pulled up next to him. A gray, 911 Turbo Porsche. Robert.

Dave rolled down his window. Robert did the same. "I suppose Gwen called you to keep me from picking up Aynslee," Robert snapped. "But it's within my legal rights—"

"That's not why I'm here. You didn't get a call from Beth or Gwen?"

"No. I turned off the phone. I knew they'd try and talk me out—"

"Robert, Aynslee's missing."

"What do you mean, 'missing'? Has Gwen concocted some harebrained plan to—"

"Listen to me! This isn't about Gwen. Your daughter ran away with a young girl named Mattie. Gwen's out trying to find them." *And so is the killer.* Dave shoved the thought down.

Blood drained from Robert's face. "Aynslee's running around with a druggie prostitute?"

Dave clenched his teeth, wanting to throttle the man. "The important thing is finding the girls. Why don't you wait here—"

"Forget it, Dave. There's no way I'm going to sit around here waiting for something to happen."

"What are you going to do?"

"If Aynslee's with that . . . other girl, she might be hitch-hiking to the vampire movie in Missoula. She's pulled stunts like that before."

"Yeah, but not for a long time—"

Robert slammed his car into gear, shot forward, spun around, and charged past Dave.

Dave followed. *I just hope Robert doesn't find Gwen in his search for his daughter.* He looked mad enough to murder her.

Mattie and Aynslee cleared the trees. Ahead was a field of thigh-length grasses barely visible in the patchy moonlight. "Listen," Aynslee said. "What's that sound?"

"Wind?"

"No. Water. Running, a stream. Streams lead to people."

They sprinted toward the creek.

Behind them, something crashed through the trees.

With renewed speed, they fled down the sloping field. The gurgling water seemed to be directly ahead.

The burbling sound grew louder. The girls dashed toward it. The clouds parted, offering wan illumination. The crashing behind them was replaced by the thudding of footsteps.

"The stream . . ." Aynslee panted. "Must run . . . through those woods."

A blacker row of pines edged the field, and Mattie hurtled toward them.

The footsteps grew nearer.

The moon disappeared, then appeared, casting cerulean-blue light on the landscape. Something slate gray flashed to Mattie's left in her peripheral vision. She turned her head.

The trees parted and an ashen monster reared from the earth.

She threw up her arms and dove to the ground, taking Aynslee with her. "Mmmmmmm . . ." She couldn't make her mouth work.

The monster remained motionless.

She strained her eyes. The moon dipped behind a small cloud, then appeared. Not a monster. *A gray house.* The *house*.

Aynslee rolled to her feet. "Come on. I know where we are."

Mattie couldn't hear the runner. That meant he was in the tall grasses. She leaped to her feet. "We gotta hide. He's getting closer."

Aynslee jerked her head slightly to the right. "Home. There."

Mattie ran, pulling on Aynslee's arm. Two black sentinels

rose on either side of her. She slowed. They meant something. She should know what they were, but her brain wouldn't work. She plunged between them.

The barbed-wire fence caught her in the chest. Aynslee fell against her. The coat took the brunt of the rusted barbs, snagging on the material.

Thump . . . thump . . . thump . . . The runner picked up speed.

Mattie rolled, but the wire tangled more into her clothing.

The creature howled in the distance.

Hands grabbed Mattie's arm.

She screamed and lunged backward. The wire pulled from the post with a piercing screech.

Aynslee was saying something, but Mattie couldn't figure out what. Stumbling, she drove forward. Now her legs were encased with wire, barbs ripping into her flesh.

"Mattie! Stop, Mattie! Mattie!" The voice wasn't Aynslee's.

"Mattie, hold still," Gwen said.

Mattie stopped twisting. "You?"

I tugged and pulled on the wire to free Mattie. "Aynslee, help me."

"I can't, Mom."

I looked up. Aynslee's arms were behind her back.

He tied up my little girl. I fought the urge to reach for her. "What did he use?"

"Zip ties."

I'd have to get a knife to set her free.

Another howl, now from a different direction. There were at least two of them.

Redoubling my efforts, I lifted the wire from around one of

Mattie's legs. "Bend your left knee. That's it. A bit more. Okay, hold still and we'll get your other leg." I made my voice as soothing as possible, but my heart raced.

The wire was still snagged in Mattie's coat. I wrenched it off her and jerked it away from the barbs. A chunk of material ripped free, and I fell with the momentum, landing on my side.

The sharp rock dug into me.

My rib popped. I couldn't catch my breath and pain coursed through my side.

A howl, followed by a bark.

No time for pain. *The wolves are moving in.*

I grunted as I pushed off the ground. *Don't let the girls know you're hurt.*

Another howl, much closer. My stomach clenched as I thought of what Dr. Hawkins said. *Wolves don't care if the animals are dead before they start eating . . . signs of a prolonged struggle . . .*

The bones I'd found in the grave. Chewed.

No. Can't be.

Wolves don't usually hunt people down and attack them.

But dogs would.

Trained dogs. Schooled to track. Track a specific scent. All the missing pets; injured livestock. Not wolves, dogs. Practicing. I brought the coat to my nose.

"Come on, Mom!"

He must have given Mattie this coat. I prepared to throw it away.

Bad idea. The odor probably transferred to both girls. The dogs would find the coat, then keep looking. *Plan; get a plan. Come on, brain. House. No. Something with the creek.* My gaze jumped to the marshy area downstream. It might work.

A howl became a yelp of eagerness. They'd found the trail.

Lifting first Mattie, then Aynslee to their feet, I winced with agony. "Follow me." Holding on to the coat, we fled to the stream, still high from the rain. I held my side and tried to take shallow breaths.

I plunged into the water. The raw cold made me gasp.

The girls stopped at the creek bank.

"Get in the creek," I said.

"No, Mom. It's cold."

"He gave you this coat, right?" I held it up. I could barely see Aynslee's head nod. "The dogs are tracking you. You're covered in scent. You have to get in the water." I didn't wait to see if they stepped in. Opening the coat so it would float, I slipped it into the current. It drifted downstream.

Splash. A gasp from Aynslee. I turned and grabbed my daughter to keep her from falling. Mattie was still on the bank. "Mattie," I whispered, "sweetheart, get in the water. I'll catch you." I held out my hand.

She didn't move.

The eager yelping grew closer.

Still clutching Aynslee with one arm to keep her upright in the swift current, I took a step closer to the reluctant girl. "The dogs are killers."

"I can't swim."

"You don't have to. The water's not that deep." I scanned the dimly lit hillside for the dogs.

"Come on, Mattie." Aynslee's voice shook from cold.

Suddenly Mattie launched herself into my arms. I caught her with one arm, but the force of her body knocked me backward. I fell.

CHAPTER FORTY

THE WATER INSTANTLY COVERED ME LIKE AN ARCTIC baptism, dragging me downstream. I lost my grip on both girls.

Iciness pierced into my body. I opened my mouth to scream and water filled it. My broken rib shrieked in protest. Bucking against the slimy rocks, I tried to stand. I slipped and tumbled. I tried to get a grip on tree roots flashing by. Slipped again. The stream was shallower here and my head stayed free. Coughing, I shoved to my feet, clutching my side. I looked frantically for the girls.

The baying grew fainter, then abruptly intensified as the dogs crested the hill.

I spotted Mattie clinging to an overhanging root. Slogging through the water, I lifted her to her feet and pushed her against the bank. I could barely feel my hands.

Aynslee's hands are tied behind her back.

Spinning, I looked for any signs of her. My arms were contracted, grasping my violently shaking body. I sucked in air, trying hard not to move my rib cage.

Something light-colored floated ahead of me. The water shoved against my legs, forcing them ahead. Each step was a trap of slick rocks and shifting pebbles. Just a bit farther.

I reached out and used both hands to lift her body, ignoring the renewed jabs of pain. *Please, God, don't let her be dead.* She was curled inward, knees next to her head. As soon as her face cleared the water, she gasped for air.

Crying, I hugged her to me.

"I knew you'd find me," she said through chattering teeth.

Making sure her feet were planted under her, I turned to Mattie, now upstream from me. My ears ached and teeth rattled. I clamped my jaw tight. *Move! Move!*

Mattie was limp, barely conscious. I lifted her in my arms. Hot tears streamed down my face. The cold sapped my strength, and I staggered under her limp weight. The swift current tumbled the rocks under my feet.

Reaching Aynslee, I jerked my head to have her follow me. Water alone wouldn't be enough to keep the killer dogs off our scent.

We stumbled forward. Rocks gave way to mud. The push of the stream lessened, then stopped. The next step brought shin-high mud that hungrily sucked first one shoe, then the other, from my feet. *No time to find them.* Aynslee stopped. Leaning forward, I gently lowered Mattie's legs and tugged at the giant, four-foot leaves.

Skunk cabbage.

I returned to Aynslee, trailing Mattie's legs, and rubbed the reeking smell from the plant over my daughter's shivering body, then Mattie, then me.

A single bark, very close.

I slowly lowered myself behind the plant, cradling Mattie, and let the thick mud slide up my legs until it covered my thighs. Resting Mattie across my lap, I bit my lip as the fearsome cold bit into my leg. Aynslee crouched next to me, shaking violently.

Two immense dogs materialized, panting; their breath steaming in the night air.

My heart pounded in my ears. *Go away.*

The moon turned their coats into silver blue, making them look like wolves. *No. Wrong head. Mastiff crossed with bloodhound? From the size, maybe some Great Dane as well.*

They loped forward, eagerly whining. They seemed to gallop in slow motion, hanging suspended in air for a moment before their feet connected with the earth.

I breathed through my mouth as quietly as possible.

One jerked to a halt near the old house and sniffed the air. The moonlight caught its yellow eyes. Its curled ears twitched toward us. I stopped breathing altogether. Aynslee buried her head in my shoulder.

Mattie moved in my lap. *Don't say anything.*

They deliberately turned their head from side to side, as if scanning the woods, then cautiously entered the farmhouse.

My thigh and calf muscles threatened to cramp. I shifted positions.

One dog, then the second, appeared in the doorway. They sniffed the air again, then spun left and galloped downstream.

I waited a few moments in case they returned, then tried to stand, but the ooze and Mattie's weight held me down.

Please, Lord, don't let me evade the dogs only to die in the mud.

Gathering all my strength, I pushed against the clutching muck. My legs came loose, sending me backward into the stream. I slipped, dropped Mattie, and grabbed an overhanging branch. The jolt of pain from my rib rocked me to my core.

Mattie let out a cry.

I snatched her out of the water, then listened for the return of the dogs.

Hearing nothing over the sound of the stream, I covered the short distance to the bank and placed the frozen girl on the dry earth. She curled into a fetal position.

Aynslee still knelt in the mire. I bent down behind her, wrapped my arms around her chest, and pulled. I ignored the jabs in my ribs.

Her legs slowly emerged until she was upright, but she couldn't stand. Only meaningless sounds came from her mouth. "Naanaanaaas."

I lifted her up. Her bound hands made it hard to grip her body. I slogged forward toward a bank that seemed to have receded away from me. *I'll never get out of this glacial water.* Forcing one bare foot, then the next, I inched to the edge of the stream. *Shallow breaths.*

Placing my daughter clear of the water, I crawled up beside her.

I assessed my position. Home was less than a mile away, but I was barefoot, couldn't feel my feet, and had at least one broken rib. The girls were barely conscious and probably in the first stages of hypothermia. No one knew where we were except the killer and two vicious dogs. Dogs that would soon figure out they were following the wrong scent.

CHAPTER FORTY-ONE

"MATTIE." I SHOOK THE GIRL. "MATTIE! WAKE UP. You have to help me." I could tell she was aware of me more by feel than sight. "Mattie, I'm going to help you stand—"

"Noooonoooonooo." She weakly pushed my hand away.

"Listen to me, Mattie." I shook her again. "I'm going to carry you, but you must stand."

My shaking was getting through to her. Again she pushed me away, but harder. "Soggy wooker," she muttered.

"That's right, Mattie, I'm a soggy wooker, but I need you to stand." I crawled upright, not sure that I could even get up. Using a tree trunk, I pulled myself to a standing position. "Okay, here we go. On the count of three, I'm going to pull you up, just for a moment. I have to get you across my shoulders. Do you understand me?"

"Soggy..." Mattie seemed to drift for a moment, then slowly raised one arm. Wet, filthy bandages barely held the splint to her broken hand.

I ground my teeth together.

Tugging her up, I swiftly draped her across my shoulders in a fireman's carry. I tried to keep an "umph" from escaping as the weight and pain hit me. My frozen legs shook under the additional burden. "Aynslee, you'll have to walk. I'll help you."

"I can't, Mom," she said through chattering teeth.

"Yes, you can. You're brave and resourceful, and you want to help me get Mattie home."

Aynslee rolled to her knees. I clutched Mattie's arm and leg with my right hand so I wouldn't drop her, bent down, and grabbed Aynslee's arm, hoping I wouldn't collapse next to her. She sobbed as I hauled her to her feet. "Come on, sweetheart, you can do it," I whispered.

Once upright, I looped my left arm around Aynslee's right to help her. Barefoot, we staggered ahead into the forest. The pinecones and deadfall sliced my feet; tree branches yanked my hair, slapped my face, grabbed at Mattie's limp body. Every gasp of air caused stabbing pain from my cracked rib.

The moonlight disappeared behind a cloud, pitching us into darkness. Aynslee moaned next to me. I slowed, then stopped. What if I got turned around? Was the house behind me? Reaching forward as far as my bent arm would allow, I touched a tree trunk. *What now?* I bit my lip, forcing silence. *The dogs.* They were behind us, moving downstream, southwest. If I could hear—

An excited yip. Behind and to my left. Home was straight ahead. I touched the tree again, then edged around it. *Straight ahead. Three steps.* Branches cracked against my face. *Slow.* This was too slow. I quickened my pace.

The downed log caught me just below the knee. I landed heavily, rolling Mattie off my shoulders. Aynslee tumbled beside me. My head spun and I fought to stay conscious, my breath wheezing.

"I can't go on," Aynslee cried.

Excited barks erupted in the distance behind us. Had they found the coat? Would tearing it up keep them busy? What if he'd sprayed the inside of the coat? The scent would transfer easier. Had the water been enough to wash it off the girls? Were the dogs looking for them now?

I untangled my feet. *Snarls.* Not behind me, now to the left. Which way should I go? The stream ran perpendicular to the road, so if the dogs followed the coat, I should be . . . where? *Work it out; work it out. Start over. If the sound . . .* The moon cleared the cloud and briefly lit the woods. I searched for the game trail I'd followed before. There, on my right, the path marked by darker earth.

Pulling Aynslee to her feet, I propped her against the tree. Mattie lay on her back, breathing shallowly. I rolled her to her stomach, then squatting by her head, I hooked my elbows under her armpits. Lifting her to her feet, I braced my leg between hers and draped her arm over my shoulder. Squatting, I shifted her weight over my shoulder and adjusted it.

Now all I had to do was stand. My legs trembled and ribs screamed in protest. Bit by agonizing bit, I stood.

Home wasn't far. Less than a mile. We'd already covered part of it. We could do this! I tugged Aynslee more upright, then I listened for sounds of pursuit.

Frantic baying behind me. They *had* found the coat.

We lurched onward down the trail. My wet, muddy clothing held the chill of the stream, and my hands shook like quaking aspen in a strong wind.

My foot exploded in excruciating agony.

I cried out in spite of my best efforts and groped my leg. The stick was embedded in the arch of my foot. Holding my breath, I jerked it out, then clamped my teeth over the scream.

"Mom?" Aynslee whispered.

"No time, go." We pushed on. Good foot, bad foot, good foot. "'Run with endurance,'" I panted. "'The race . . . the race set before you.'" Good foot, bad foot. *Endure.* The words pounded in my head in rhythm with my hammering heart.

The trees thinned and a glint shown ahead.

"Our yard." Aynslee gasped.

We tottered faster. I didn't care about the pain. We cleared the woods. Closer, closer.

Behind us came a crash, followed by an excited, *"Woof!"*

We reached the back door. Locked. I'd made sure the house was secure before I left to find the girls. The house keys were in my car, parked at the top of the ridge. I stepped toward the hidden key.

"There's no key, Mom."

That's right. The yaps became excited howls.

I turned. *Options? Options? Run to Wes's pickup? What if it was locked as well? Garage? Couldn't make secure.* Frantically, I stumbled to the side of the house. *One chance: the crawl space.*

Filled with spiders.

CHAPTER FORTY-TWO

THE MOON OFFERED JUST ENOUGH LIGHT TO distinguish vague shapes and outlines. My breath misted in front of my mouth as I released Aynslee, then slipped Mattie from my shoulders and eased her to the ground. I knelt beside her. My cooling sweat joined with my heat-leaching clothing. Hand shaking, I reached for the latch. I could barely feel my fingers.

The latch clattered loose when I touched it. Pulling the door open, the gaping black hole faced me. *You have no options.*

I listened for the dogs, but heard nothing above the light breeze swishing through the pines. *Why have the dogs stopped baying?*

As if reading my mind, both dogs let out an eerie cry that reverberated off the mountains.

They were close.

They could get to the house before I dragged both girls to safety. But which girl should I pull in first? Mattie could hardly move. Aynslee was my only child.

I froze, my mind blank.

"Mom?"

Another howl. Closer still.

Jerking to action, I edged to my feet. "Aynslee, I'll help you lie down, then I'm going to pull Mattie inside." I tried to keep my voice from shaking. "I'll drag her to the trapdoor. You have to follow the best you can. As soon as she's inside, I'll help you. Do you understand?"

She answered with a soft sob.

Wrapping my arm around Mattie, I propelled myself through the opening. The darkness enveloped me. Ahead, a square of pale earth outlined the pantry hatch above. *It's not that far.*

Lying on my side, I hitched forward, dragging Mattie slowly through the talcum-fine dust. A gossamer web draped my face. Delicate legs skittered across my mouth.

I clamped my lips tight, desperately battling the desire to open my mouth and scream. Black widow spiders loved dark places. *Oh, dear Lord! Endurance. With endurance.* Creeping faster, something snaked up my pants. Reaching back, I swatted hard, smashing it against my leg.

A large timber blocked my view of the light. The floor joists seem to crush downward, snagging my shirt. *Trapped!* I scrabbled to my left. *There!* The trapdoor beckoned. I clawed forward. Mattie struggled against me, slowing me down further. "Mattie, it's me. Be still." The girl stopped resisting. More webs draped around the insulated pipes. A strange moaning accompanied my movements. *Endure. Endure.*

Reaching the square of light, I let go of the girl and crouched, then slowly straightened my legs, bringing my shoulders to the hatch. I pushed, trembling at the weight. The trapdoor raised, allowing more light below. I pushed harder, willing the door to open.

An excited howl seemed just outside.

Adrenaline fueled my efforts. I shoved one final time. The door flew back and landed with a crash. I reached down and dragged Mattie to a sitting position, then lifted her. She muttered a protest against me as I thrust her through the opening.

Shoving her away from the open hatch, I turned back toward my daughter. Still outside. With the dogs.

CHAPTER FORTY-THREE

THE CRAWL SPACE WAS A BLACK HOLE. GAUZY spiderwebs waved with the airflow around me.

A hot flash shot up my neck and onto my face, leaving me breathless for a moment. I closed my eyes and dropped to my knees. For a moment I couldn't see anything. Orienting myself to the outside opening, I slithered forward, searching for the beam that I'd earlier crawled around.

The beam was straight ahead.

So was a scratching noise.

Clambering faster, I reached the beam, then snaked around it. I collided with Aynslee. She'd somehow pushed herself almost halfway to the trapdoor.

Both of us gasped, but there was no time to lose. I could hear the dogs panting and sniffing nearby. They'd find the opening at any moment.

I grabbed Aynslee's arm and tugged her backward. It had to have hurt her terribly with both hands tied behind her back, but she didn't say a word. She weighed more than Mattie, but she used her legs to push.

We made it to the opening.

Crouching beside her, I grabbed her under the armpits and, ignoring the scorpion-like stab from my rib, I stood and thrust her through.

The river rock next to the house crunched under the dog's paws. A screech, and one dog yelped with excitement. They'd found the door to the crawl space.

I clawed for something to grab. *Doorjamb.*

Muffled scrabbling behind me.

Heave forward. I flung myself on the kitchen floor, rolling as I scraped the web from my face.

The dogs bayed in response.

With dirt-blackened hands, I slammed the trapdoor shut and thrust the latch, my hands fumbling before slamming it home.

Thud! Something—I hoped it was a dog's head—crashed against the floor.

Aynslee whimpered.

"'S okay, sweetheart." I pushed my body next to the wall and used my legs to inch the small chest freezer over the trapdoor.

The thumps became fainter as I jammed the freezer into place. I leaned against the wall for a moment. *Safe. They can't get in.* Pain from my rib and foot throbbed with the beat of my heart.

The dogs barked frantically under my feet.

Both girls still lay on the kitchen floor where I'd shoved them. I crossed to the wall and turned off the kitchen light.

"Mom?" Aynslee's voice was high and shrill.

"It's okay. I just don't want to be silhouetted against the curtains." Waiting a moment for my eyes to adjust, I opened the kitchen junk drawer and rummaged around until I felt a pair of scissors. Turning, I carefully moved to my daughter, then knelt beside her. "I'm going to cut the zip ties off your wrists. It won't feel good for a few minutes, but that will pass."

She let out a moan of pain as I snipped the hard plastic.

The dogs banged the floorboards under our feet.

Mattie mumbled and tossed from side to side on the floor, her breathing shallow.

I touched her skin. Icy cold.

Leaving both girls briefly, I hobbled to the bathroom. The nightlight barely illuminated the small room. I turned on the hot water in the bathtub, shut the door, and returned to the kitchen.

The dogs growled and scratched below me.

Lifting Mattie, I dragged her to the steam-filled room where I lay her on a bath mat. Aynslee was already trying to stand, and I helped her up. I could see her face faintly. Her nose was swollen and turning purple, as were her eyes. I touched her face. "Oh, sweetheart—"

She grinned. "You should see the other guy."

Supporting her under the arms, she soon joined Mattie in the steamy bathroom. "Mom, I think I know his target. Not the University. The Jewish Community Center in Missoula. Tomorrow. Eleven a.m."

Crash!

I jumped and covered my mouth. Someone, or something, shattered a window somewhere in the house.

Don't worry. You're safe. A person, or a big dog, wouldn't be able to fit through the security bars I'd had installed six months ago. I hoped.

Crash!

Another window. Leaving the girls to breathe the warm steam, I crept down the dark hall. The dogs followed my footsteps, thumping the floor hard enough to make the wood vibrate. I opened the door to Aynslee's room. A rock lay on the right, and a chill breeze tossed the drapes. Glass shards would be on the floor, and I was still barefoot.

I reached over, grabbed the blankets off her bed, and raced back to the bathroom.

Bam! Aynslee screamed. The rock smashed the tiny window over the toilet. I turned off the shower and wrapped both girls in the blankets.

Another window shattered. It sounded like the noise came from my studio.

A piercing whistle came from outside.

The dogs grew silent.

I hobbled to my room, carefully avoiding the glass on the floor, and crept to the unbroken window. Ever so slowly, I caught one side and drew open the curtain. The moon, finally freed of clouds, cast a steady gleam on a pickup with a veterinary mobile unit mounted in the truck bed.

The killer.

Dr. Hawkins.

I sucked in a quick breath. My fingers clenched the curtains.

The two dogs sat on either side of him, watching the house. "Hello, Gwen. I'm surprised at your resourcefulness." His attention was to my left. He hadn't seen the curtain move.

"You figured out the coat held the scent. Too bad you didn't get it all off of you. A dog's nose can pick up even the faintest of odors."

My teeth were locked together. His plan was now so clear. Dr. Hawkins had been the one to spread the rumor about the wolves. He'd been the only one to have seen them.

Hawkins leaned against his truck.

"I know you can hear me," he said.

Don't talk to him. Let him wonder what's going on.

"Do you think you're safe in there?" He rubbed his arm. "Behind all those barred windows and doors? You don't even have a gun." He lifted my rifle and pivoted it so I could clearly see the stock. "Not that a pink rifle is much of a gun."

I made an effort to relax my fingers. Dave would get here soon. Or Dre.

"They'll never catch me, you know, Gwen. I'm now just poor Dr. Hawkins, moving on because the animal hospital burned down."

His excuse for leaving town: starting over with another practice. I didn't want to listen to him gloat. Gliding away from the window, I stopped dead.

Hawkins blew up the practice. He'd set bombs in Spokane. What if he were throwing rocks through my windows not to cause destruction, but to make sure a bomb could fit inside?

CHAPTER FORTY-FOUR

I TRIED TO SHOVE DOWN THE PANIC. NO. HE wouldn't throw in a bomb. Not right away. That was too . . . impersonal.

But Dr. Hawkins wasn't going to hang around for hours. According to Aynslee, his big plans involved the Jewish Community Center. Eleven o'clock tomorrow.

If Columbine was his template, he would set up several bombs inside to kill and drive people from the building, then shoot them as they emerged.

But he said he would be able to move on, bragged that no one would catch him.

I rubbed my hands up and down my arms to warm up. Whatever his plans were, people would die. Dave knew the time, but no one knew his target. Hawkins could simply leave his dogs outside my home and go on the bombing and shooting rampage.

The dogs would attack anyone showing up to check on me. Dave would be armed, but what about Beth? Even Robert.

It was up to me.

But I needed time. *Get him to talk.* "Why me?"

His body pivoted in my direction. "It's very simple, Gwen. You have betrayed your race."

I was right. The thought brought me no comfort.

"We are at war. Don't you get it? Your skin color is your uniform, but you joined the enemy. Because of you, two warriors died, and a third one will be standing trial."

"I was just doing my job." I moved to the hallway and looked up at the attic access door. Even if I could reach it, I wouldn't be able to get the girls up there.

"You made a choice." His voice carried clearly through all the broken windows. "The wrong choice, and like Phinehas, I am here to carry out God's righteous commandments."

Moving to the studio, I opened the cupboard under the sink. With the plywood cover, it would take only seconds for the dogs to get through.

"The Fourteen Words, Gwen. That's all you had to know. 'We must secure the existence of our people and a future for white children.' Now you must suffer the consequences. You and your seed. Your friends, dog, everything needs to be destroyed."

I crossed to the broken window and peered out. The dogs were motionless, but Hawkins paced, hefting a rock.

"Do you really believe that?"

All three turned in my direction.

I thought about our conversations. His Nazi-like thinking had been apparent all along. He had complimented Winston on his pure breeding. And at the cow pasture, he'd spoken of survival of the fittest. I'd paid no attention at the time, thinking he was referring to animals.

I was so stupid not to put it together when I went to his church.

"Your dogs—"

"Beautiful, aren't they?" The moon glinted off Hawkins's teeth. "They're highly trained and love to hunt."

Turning, I raced through the house, testing each door. None of them would latch, let alone had locks. I raised my voice. "But your dogs aren't purebred. I thought—"

"Oh, but they are. Fila Brasileiro. I imported them."

I reached for the door to the office. My hand froze inches from the knob. I really didn't want to go in there. There was something deeply creepy about entering a dark room with a corpse still slumped against the wall.

Buck up, babe. You've seen dead people before.

Yeah, but not all that many of people I knew.

"They're known for their tracking ability, used to guard and track slaves."

Sucking up a deep breath, I turned the knob and entered. Hawkins had chucked a rock through the window, and the blinds clattered like a death rattle.

The gun was where I left it. I picked it up and stuck it into the waistband of my jeans, then returned to Aynslee's bedroom.

"They're also known for aggression. They're banned in some countries." The dogs whined with eagerness. "Once I send them to attack, they won't stop. Trained that way. No Stop command. Thought you'd like to know that." I could hear the smile in his voice.

I yanked out her bureau drawers, scattering the contents. *Must make it work. There. Grab it.* I assembled what I needed.

I quickly limped to the bathroom. Both girls were huddled together under the blanket.

"Mattie, Aynslee, stay in this room. No matter what happens—" I grabbed a towel, then wedged it between the door and jamb and yanked the knob hard. The door caught, but one blow from those huge dogs would open it.

Bam! Hawkins was using my rifle to shoot the front door open.

I turned and stumbled toward the kitchen. *Please, Lord, give me a few more seconds.*

I grabbed what I needed, placed them on the table, then raced down the hall to the living room.

Bam! Wood splintered and the door shook. I ducked, then moved to the center of the room.

Bam! The door flew open.

I moved forward until I was silhouetted in the opening.

Hawkins looked startled, then he raised the rifle.

"Coward." I spit on the ground.

He lowered the gun, grinned, and pointed. "Fass."

Both dogs launched at me.

I turned and ran.

CHAPTER FORTY-FIVE

I RACED THROUGH THE HOUSE. *FASTER . . .
go faster!*

The dogs bayed behind me, gaining ground. Nails churned on the plank flooring, seeking purchase.

I snatched the cans of vegetables from the table and threw them at the canines.

Startled, the dogs skidded to a stop.

Ripping open the kitchen door, I leapt through and sought Hawkins. He stood on the side of the house, near his parked truck.

Excited yelping seemed right on my heels.

I charged at him as fast as I could.

Hawkins stepped backward as if startled, then started to laugh.

Closer. Closer. One chance. I pulled the gun from my waistband.

"No bullets, Gwen."

I moved faster.

Wham. The kitchen door smashed open as the dogs crashed into it.

Straightening my arm, I took careful aim.

River rocks clanked against each other as the dogs plowed through them. I could almost feel the dogs' breath on my churning legs.

"Stupid woman—"

I shot him.

CHAPTER FORTY-SIX

THE SPRAY FROM THE SQUIRT GUN HIT HAWKINS in the face. The odor of lilac perfume permeated the air.

Hawkins screamed and clawed at his eyes. "What have you *done?*"

I kept running, not stopping until I'd reached the bumper of Hawkins's pickup. Spinning, I crouched and waited.

The dogs skidded to a stop and sniffed the air. Slowly turning their heads, they stared first at me, then at Hawkins. They smelled the air again.

"No. No. Get her. Attack! Fass, fass!" Hawkins, blinded, pointed as if to guide the dogs to me, but he'd become disoriented. His perfume-covered hand shot toward the dogs.

The dogs launched at the extended arm. Hawkins shrieked once before the roar of the canines took over.

I hurtled toward the truck door. I wanted to put my hands over my ears to cover the sounds. Crunching. Tearing.

With trembling hands, I grabbed the door handle and pulled.

Locked.

I heard a growl behind me.

My legs almost buckled. Slowly I turned.

The moon cast everything in a cold, blue light. My breath steamed around my face.

Both canines were glaring at me, hackles up, lips pulled over blood-blackened teeth. Hawkins wasn't moving.

One dog stepped forward, toenails grating on the gravel.

I turned and sprinted. Like a dream, my legs seemed like they were plowing through molasses. *Faster, run faster.* The panting of the dogs grew louder, nails on gravel, sharper, my breath, harsher.

Then silence. Only the sound of my breathing.

My goal was just ahead. I wouldn't make it. *Please, God, save the girls.*

I passed the lilac bush and dove into the forsythia, the branches smacking me in the face. I turned.

The dogs reached the lilac bush and stopped, the smell confusing them. The scent would only slow them for a few seconds. Hopefully long enough. I took aim and pulled the trigger. A spray of perfume struck the nearest dog.

The second dog lunged for his throat.

CHAPTER FORTY-SEVEN

MY FEET SEEMED ROOTED TO THE GROUND.
I wouldn't, couldn't move.

The dogs were evenly matched. They fought with a terrifying fury.

I wanted to look away, but I had to watch. If the dogs stopped fighting, they could reach me in just a few moves. What if one dog survived? Would he still be on a killing mission?

They were trained not to stop.

It felt like I stood there for hours, but it was probably only a few minutes before one dog lay motionless. The winner stood over him, watching for movement, before lifting his head.

I snapped a branch of the forsythia I hadn't realized I'd been clutching.

The dog's head pivoted in my direction.

Adrenaline shot through my system. I moved backward, away from the dog, one foot, then another.

The canine matched me, step for step, moving forward.

My back collided with something hard. Hawkins's truck. I couldn't retreat any farther.

Moonlight glinted off the dog's yellow eyes. His lips pulled up, revealing bloody teeth.

"Why won't you die?" I whispered as I raised the squirt gun.

The dog crouched, ready to spring.

Pumping the trigger, I aimed at the dog's eyes. Several blasts of perfume hit their mark.

The canine let out a roar, shook his head, then pawed at his eyes.

Quickly, find it. My only chance to keep the girls safe. Dropping to my knees, I looked under the truck. Not there. I stood, frantically seeking my rifle. I tried to blot out the snarling.

Look at Hawkins. He held it last.

The dog was near the prone body. Too near.

I threw the squirt gun to my left. It smacked the gravel, then skidded a few feet.

The dog pivoted toward the sound.

Racing over, I spotted an edge of the pink stock. I dropped next to Hawkins and thrust my hands under him. The rifle was slippery, but I gripped it and tugged hard.

The dog spun toward me, still digging at his eyes.

I turned and leaped toward the truck, grabbed the exterior mirror, and shoved up from the hood. The sharp bark behind me propelled me to the roof of the truck. My legs wouldn't hold me, and I sat on the cold metal.

The canine's vision had cleared. He raised his head, eyes locked on mine and muscles bunched.

I lifted my rifle and took aim. "Pink is a killer color," I whispered.

He jumped.

I pulled the trigger.

CHAPTER FORTY-EIGHT

FOUR MONTHS LATER

THE AUGUST SUN BAKED THROUGH THE STUDIO windows, casting a gamboge-yellow glow on the walls. I held up the watercolor painting and pointed. "Do you see this edge of color?"

Mattie nodded. "So how do I keep that from happening?"

"You need to keep two edges in mind while painting wet-on-wet watercolors." I placed a blank sheet of Arches watercolor paper on the table in front of us. "The edge you're actually painting and the edge where the pigment may end up. Take your stroke of water farther than you think the paint may bleed. Like this."

A rap on the studio door frame interrupted the lesson.

"Have you been outside today?" Dave asked, entering. "The smoke from the forest fires is killing my eyes."

"How close are they now?" Mattie asked, eyebrows furrowing.

"Don't worry, they're coming from central Idaho. Hundreds

of miles away." Dave wandered over to our painting. "Really nice work, Mattie."

She grinned at him.

I touched Mattie's shining hair. It was hard to picture the girl I'd found in the old house as this tanned and healthy teenager. Mattie wore white jean shorts under a bright-pink T-shirt. Her only piece of jewelry was a tiny silver dove hanging from a delicate chain. She smiled shyly at Dave and pointed to the necklace. "Thanks for the gift."

"Important occasion; appropriate gift," Dave said.

"Do you want to see my room?" Mattie asked.

"Sure."

I followed both of them to the old office. The soft-pink walls gleamed with new paint, and fluffy matching curtains hung from the windows. A wind chime of doves gently twirled over the desk.

Dave admired the décor. "Very nice."

"Mattie," Aynslee called from the kitchen, "pizza's hot."

Mattie raced from the room.

Dave waited until she was out of earshot. "Have you heard anything more?"

"The Public Health and Human Resources found some of her family, an aunt, and she is the most anxious to take her." I swallowed the lump in my throat. "They're finishing the screening and background check and will let me know. They've approved both Robert and me as foster parents—"

Dave looked at me quickly.

"Not together, Dave. It just means Mattie can visit either home."

"Well then." Dave moved toward the kitchen. "Are you ready?"

"I think so." I followed.

"When does he arrive?"

I glanced at my watch. "Anytime now. Want some iced tea?"

"Sure." Dave stopped. "By the way, how are you feeling?"

I couldn't help my snort of laughter. I really would start wearing that sign *I feel fine*. I touched my side. "All of us are healing well. Mattie had some testing on her last visit to the orthopedic specialist. He said that the damage to her fingers from her untreated juvenile arthritis, plus Hawkins's attack, will limit her hand functions, but you can see from her art that she can still use them."

Mattie and Aynslee were sitting at the kitchen table eating lunch. "Dave," Mattie said, speaking around a large chunk of pizza, "have a cookie." She pointed at a plate piled with oatmeal cookies on the counter.

"Yum." Dave selected one and took a bite.

"I made 'em myself." Mattie beamed. "Gwen's teaching me to cook."

Aynslee put her hand over her mouth and rolled her eyes.

Dave's face paled and he quickly strolled outside.

"Did I say something wrong?" Mattie asked, frowning.

"Oh, no. Dave just needed . . . to check out the sign. Out front." I poured Dave an iced tea and followed him outside. I found him near the lilac bushes, spitting cookie into the grass. "Want this?" I handed him the iced tea.

He took a long, grateful swallow. "I see she's learned your cooking ability."

"Don't be mean, Dave. Sugar and salt look alike, and her reading skills are marginal."

Dave took another long swig, then nodded at the bushes. "Something I wanted to ask you. How did you know the dogs were trained to chase lilac scent?"

I shrugged. "I didn't, not for sure. I prayed I was right. Hawkins had one victim escape, the boy in Spokane that I tried to do a composite with. Hawkins didn't want to lose another, so he bought those two dogs to track down his victims should they get away from him."

"And I suppose dogs can be trained to any scent."

"He was very clever in his choice of tracking odor. He needed something that wouldn't be noticed during training. All the slaughtered animals we thought wolves chewed up were killed in the spring, when lilacs bloom. I remembered smelling lilac when I found Mattie in the house."

"The beefalo calf was killed near a lilac bush."

"Right. I guessed it might be the tracking scent when I smelled lilac on the coat he gave Mattie."

"He probably gave the girl in the cow pasture a coat as well," Dave said.

"Aynslee later told me she threw away the bouquet of lilacs in Mattie's hospital room when Mattie told her it was from *him*."

I stared at my dirty sneaker for a moment. "He took a big risk, using perfume like that. The flowering bushes and women's perfumes—"

"Hawkins liked to give away clues, thought he was so clever that way. He started his killing spree in Spokane. Spokane's nickname is the Lilac City."

A small shiver went through me. "I didn't know that. He did use a Hudson's Bay blanket, and if you think about it, he came right out and said it was a single wolf doing the killing. In the cow pasture, he said 'single wolf.' Lone wolf. Him."

Dave took another sip of his iced tea. "Speaking of wolves and dogs . . ."

As if on cue, Winston sauntered across the yard, a large bone in his mouth.

I glanced at Dave.

His eyes opened wide. "Is that human—"

"Cow. From the grocery store." I grinned. "Got ya on that one!"

Dave watched my dog flop in the shade of a pine tree. "I don't see how a sociopath like him could have finished his veterinary degree and been such a successful businessman."

"Beth and I talked about it. She looked it up—"

"Of course."

"She said in our society, many of the traits of sociopaths are now considered positive business practices. For example, manipulation and no concern for others. His bio said he donated time to help others who couldn't afford a vet. That didn't sound like a sociopath, until I realized that's how he found his victims."

"Speaking of victims," Dave said. "The two bodies in the grave have been identified, although not yet released. Your sketches helped on the one woman."

"Did the other woman—"

"Yes, she looked like Aynslee. Like Mattie, both were high-risk victims, and both had medical conditions: one woman had scoliosis, the other a club foot."

I sighed. "Just like Hitler, killing or sterilizing people he felt were inferior. The deformity of Hawkins's spirit was far greater that the deformities of his victims."

Dave nodded thoughtfully, then said, "Both the FBI and the Jewish Community Center are keeping quiet about Hawkins's plan."

"Makes sense. It didn't happen, and he's dead. Don't need to encourage any copycats."

"Right. But I was asked to give you this." He held up a challenge coin. "And this." He handed me an envelope with some cash in it. "It's not much, but it might buy you a new dress and dinner on the town."

Before I could formulate an answer, Beth pulled into the driveway and parked next to us. She stepped from the car, looking fresh and summery with white slacks and a sleeveless peach blouse. I waved at her and smoothed my paint-smeared T-shirt.

"Are you ready?" She frowned at my attire.

"As I'll ever be. Thanks for the moral support."

The three of us strolled back into the house.

"I have another woman who wants to join your women's Bible study," Beth said. "But the pastor wants to talk to you about the title of your new series."

"I thought it quite clever," I said. "'The Bible Is Full of Lies.'"

"Yes. Um, I know you're referring to signs of deception described in the Scriptures and comparing it to law enforcement books, but the title might be a bit misleading."

"Oh. Okay. I'll give him a call."

The girls were still at the table. ". . . so I said he was a soggy wooker," Mattie was saying.

"What's a soggy wooker?" Beth asked.

"I just liked the way it sounded, but Aynslee looked it up." Mattie grinned.

"It comes from the *Star Wars* movies," Aynslee said. "From the Wookies, which are hairy. A soggy wooker is the hair caught in a sink drain. Icky."

"I see." Beth rolled her lips to keep from smiling.

"*I* looked that up." Mattie proudly pointed at the Scripture verse Beth had given me, now back on the refrigerator. "Colossians 3:13. I memorized it. 'Bear with each other and forgive one another if any of you has a grievance against someone. Forgive as the Lord forgave you.'" She lifted her bent and twisted fingers and studied them. "I'm working on it," she whispered.

My eyes blurred and I turned toward the sink, but not before I noticed Beth pulling out a hankie.

The crunch of gravel announced another vehicle pulling up next to the house. The slam of car doors, followed by footsteps, made all of us turn to the kitchen door.

Robert.

"I see everyone's here," he said through the screen. "May I come in?"

"Dad!" Aynslee raced to let him in, then threw herself into his arms.

"Hi, angel." Robert spun her around, then keeping his arm around her, he nodded to Beth and Dave. "I see there's a Sold sign out front," he said to me.

"Yes." I tugged again at my T-shirt. Why hadn't I changed into something nicer? "I couldn't live here anymore with all that happened. The new house will be done soon. And . . . thank you for taking the girls for the next couple of months."

"My pleasure." Robert gave Aynslee another hug. Mattie slipped closer, and Robert casually slipped his arm around her shoulder. The girl beamed.

"How are you going to fit both of us and our luggage into your Porsche?" Aynslee crossed to the window and peered out. "Wait a minute. Did you buy a van?" She glanced at Mattie, and both girls burst into giggles.

"Loser car," Mattie managed to get out.

"Well then . . ." I cleared my throat. "Girls, you'd better go get your suitcases."

Aynslee dashed from the room, still laughing. Mattie lingered by the fridge.

I grinned at Robert. "You traded in your Porsche—"

"Yes, well, my life is changing. Ah . . ." Robert moved to the door. "There's someone I'd like you to meet." He opened the door, and a strikingly beautiful woman stepped through. "Gwen, I'd like you to meet my fiancée, Caroline."

The room became deathly silent. Everyone stared at me.

I wiped my sweaty hand on my jeans, then looked at the refrigerator. Beth's magnetic sign hung at a slight angle.

Mattie grinned at me.

I handed Mattie the envelope of cash, turned to the woman, smiled, and held out my hand. "So very nice to meet you, Caroline."

AUTHOR NOTE

I'D ORIGINALLY WRITTEN THIS BOOK ABOUT A serial killer based on my work on the Robert Lee Yates case in Spokane, Washington. At the suggestion of my editor at Thomas Nelson, I added the Christian Identity layer. They liked the religious angle to the forensics, and for me, it was really a no-brainer which group to write about. Richard Butler's Aryan Nations compound was about forty minutes from my home. I was one of the courtroom artists when the Southern Poverty Law Center, with attorney Morris Dees, brought a civil suit against the Church of Jesus Christ, Aryan Nations. I'd have to add that this group shot my dad, then the director of the North Idaho Regional Crime Lab, and wounded him. The Phineas Priesthood group, also part of the Christian Identity movement, had a cell in Spokane in the mid-1990s. Working with the FBI, ATF, city and county of Spokane, I drew sixteen composite sketches to help identify them. In an unusual turn of events, I got to see them in person when a television news station hired me as a courtroom artist. For a complete bibliography of books I referenced while writing this, check out my web page: WWW.CARRIESTUARTPARKS.COM

READING GROUP GUIDE

1. The story covers a particular belief system, Christian Identity, and one of the offshoots of this, the Phineas Priesthood. Had you heard of this before? If so, where?

2. How does the Phineas Priesthood justify their beliefs? Are they unique in this?

3. In chapter 3, we start to meet Gwen's former husband, Robert, and by chapter 16, Beth is urging Gwen to forgive him, which is the theme of the book. Does she forgive him? How do you know? Does she need to forgive anyone else? Have you had to forgive someone who has hurt you badly?

4. Revenge is the opposite of forgiveness. Who else is seeking revenge?

5. In chapter 17, Gwen empties the contents of Robert's desk: a lined notepad, an empty tissue box, a broken stapler, a crumpled piece of paper with a list of every terrible thing

he'd ever said or done to her, a writer's magazine featuring Robert on the cover, and a squirt gun. Could these items represent her life? What six items could represent yours?

6. Robert's office goes through three changes in the book. What are the three changes, and how do they parallel Gwen's changes?

7. Gwen loses her job by exceeding her role as forensic artist. What were her stakes? Would you have done the same given her circumstances?

8. The color pink to Gwen represents overcoming adversity. What adversity did she overcome? What would represent overcoming adversity in your life?

9. Aynslee is self-centered at the start of the story. Does she change? What makes her change?

10. Beth is a friend, sidekick, and wise mentor to Gwen. Do you have someone like her in your life?

ACKNOWLEDGMENTS

ONCE AGAIN I'D LIKE TO THANK THE WHOLE world, but I've learned a certain amount of restraint over the years. I must always start with the Perettis. Frank and Barb, you both believed in me from the start. To my husband, Rick, I love you for all your help. No, I really don't care to hear about the Sharks' chance for the Stanley Cup. Again. A grateful and appreciative thank-you to my agent, Terry Burns of Hartline Literary Agency. A big thank-you to Amanda Bostic, Editorial Director, and Natalie Hanemann for your spot-on editing, and to Jodi Hughes for your polishing of the manuscript. Thank you, Kerri Potts, Senior Marketing Associate, for your work on getting this in front of the readers.

I wish to send out a great big hug and thanks to the folks who helped with this story, some of you without even knowing how much you helped. Dave and Andrea Kramer, Aynslee Stuart, and the rest of my great family. Scott, you made it. Thanks to all my forensic students and friends in law enforcement for providing suggestions from your vast pool of knowledge, with a special thanks to Detective Dave Prichard, CCA, Las Vegas Metro Police Sex Crimes Division; Sylvia Stone, Montana State Crime Lab, Missoula; Debs Laird, West Monroe Police Department, Louisiana; Heath Migliore, CFA. Hugs and thanks to very much alive Detective Margie Sheehan, CFA, Special Victims Detail, Orange County Sheriff's Office, California; and Mike Higgins, CFA, Orange County Sheriff's Academy.

The hospital thanks go to Shoshone Medical Center, Kellogg, Idaho, and Nancy Rahn Peacock, Gary Moore, and Jerry Brantz.

Thank you, my dear friends Kerry Kern Woods, Michelle Garlock, and everyone else who provided much needed insight as beta readers. A special thanks to Kelly Mortimer for all her help.

Thank you to Rogie and Papa, as well as all my beloved Great Pyrenees over the years for providing the template for Winston.

Mom and Dad, you were such inspirations. I miss you every day.

Finally, and most importantly, thank you to my Lord and Savior, Jesus Christ. To You goes all glory, and honor, and praise.

CARRIE STUART PARKS

PHIL. 4:8–9

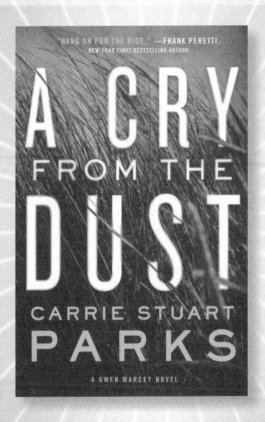

ABOUT THE AUTHOR

ANDREA KRAMER, KRAMER
PHOTOGRAPHY

CARRIE STUART PARKS IS AN award-winning fine artist and internationally known forensic artist. She teaches forensic art courses to law enforcement professionals and is the author/illustrator of numerous books on drawing. Carrie began to write fiction while battling breast cancer and was mentored by *New York Times* bestselling author Frank Peretti. Now in remission, she continues to encourage other women struggling with cancer.

VISIT HER WEBSITE AT WWW.CARRIESTUARTPARKS.COM
FACEBOOK: CARRIESTUARTPARKSAUTHOR
TWITTER: @CARRIEPARKS

327